Crooked Grow the Trees

Carmel Hanes

This book is a work of fiction. Names, characters, places, and events (complete or partial) are the product of the author's imagination or are used fictitiously. Any resemblance to actual events, locales, or persons is coincidental.

ISBN-13: 978-1975628505
ISBN-10: 1975628500

Dedication

This book is dedicated to all the people shaped and impacted by difficult life events and circumstances. You have taught me about resilience, survival, and the determination to grow in the scantest of life soils. My intersection with each of you planted seeds that grew into this word-plant. It is also dedicated to all those who have been injured by others who lost their way.

It is my hope that those of you reading find a place within its pages to temporarily belong, for we are more alike than different.

Acknowledgements

I would like to thank my team of outsourced editors for their assistance proofreading drafts for errors and providing me with valuable feedback on the content of my story, as well as advice and support in tackling the daunting job of getting it published. Your unique perspectives allowed me to experience a variety of reactions, which influenced the development of the story, improving it from its original form.

My profound gratitude to Scott Lubbock, Maggie Billings, Jan Houghton, Curt Hanes, Shirley Billings, Lee English, Julie Reimer, Barbara Moody, and Merryellen Price. Your contributions to this process ranged from nuts and bolts advice on punctuation and publishing resources, to word choice and sentence structure, to emotional reactions regarding the story content and characters, all of which helped mold the final draft. I am grateful for each of you believing in me, in my story, and in the possibility there was a receptive market for it. I give special thanks to my husband, Curt Hanes, for his steadfast understanding as I became unavailable for extended periods of time to work on this project.

I would also like to thank Timothy Ethell for the cover art. His artistic vision captured the mood and content of the story, inviting the reader inside. Timothy was born in 1996 and graduated in 2014 from the Masters School of Art in Clackamas, Oregon. In exploring the world around him, Tim strives to preserve the oddities and beauty he finds there through art; he uses watercolors, acrylic painting, pen and ink, graphite and colored pencils.

Crooked Grow the Trees

Prologue

Chameleon: a reptile with the ability to change skin color, to show aggression, to court females, to become less visible to a predator, or to adjust to environmental factors such as heat and cold; a behavior allowing for survival, hiding from predators, and safety. While not a behavior usually associated with people, for we cannot easily change color when it suits us, it does describe the way in which we try to blend into our surroundings, our various relationships, our roles with different people and the expectations they may hold for us. At times a good thing, allowing for peaceful co-existence and the achievement of common goals, at other times a damaging thing as we try to blend into surroundings that eat away at our edges and reshape us into something we were not meant to be. Pretending things we don't feel or hiding that which we do. Biting our tongues until the hemorrhage from doing so bleeds us into an unrecognizable puddle or doing things to please others while bottling up our own desires and needs until they become a darkened spot through which we can no longer see. Burying what is painful, turning away, covering up. Believing we know ourselves and each other as we are fooled by the surface camouflage. Chameleon…a changing of the outside meant to protect us, and create belonging, but which often leads to distance, damage, distress, dying by degrees, the vibrant colors ebbing into black. The world is rife with chameleons, shaped and stained by life, hiding in plain sight. We may live with them, work with them, live next to them, or be them; intersecting with each other on twisted branches.

FACELESS

July 10th 2017
1:30 pm

The cadence of drums beats against eardrums…..boom-boom, boom-boom…..a steady, rhythmic backdrop to the buzz of distant voices and laughter. Crouching, far enough away from the stage that most of the music evaporates on the airwaves before reaching this vantage point, the bass of the drum-beat surviving the travel…sturdier, heavier, denser, making itself known even when more fragile melodies lose altitude and skid into silence. Watching. Hidden in a tangle of vines beneath a canopy of oak trees, most of the park is visible due to the downward slope of the ground; it has become a place of refuge and relative peace, a place to think, to forget, to fortify. Most days the upper end of the park would be empty, offering solitude and respite from constant vigilance. Today, however, it is teeming with people who have come to enjoy the festival. Most of the booths and people are centered at the opposite end of the park, where the terrain is more welcoming to group activities, with flatter ground, fewer trees, more grass. People relax on blankets and in low-backed chairs to watch the band play. Animated screams coil around voices that rise and fall as people seem determined to outshout the music and each other; it floods over the still figure, head hooded to dampen the sounds. Knees drawn up and encircled by arms, unable to leave for there is no longer anywhere to go, he tries to endure the assault on his system and psyche, trying to think and not think; to control the self-loathing he comes here to ease.

The vortex of self-hate felt as an energy whirling wildly around the spinal column, exerting a pull on outer skin, threatening to implode from the force. On his darkest days, fear of suddenly caving inward, skin wrapping around a shrunken core like shrink-wrap crinkling around a tree branch. Wrinkled, lifeless, all essential parts evaporated. Or instead, imagining the inner turmoil touching down on some life event and in the moment of contact spewing pent-up energy outward, sending shards of bone and pulpy organs into the air.

How does one get so full of hate? Asking this daily for years…pondering while sequestered in the vine-covered hole, wondering while wandering the streets squirming with people, examining it while lying in bed with the lights out and the curtains drawn, cocooned in crushing darkness. Endless theories. Watching children build with Legos and blocks—elaborate creations that begin with a single block, then another block, and another, until they have created an intricate car, army base, space ship or robot. Feeling like a Lego creation, built by others' hands—a badly built ensemble from damaged parts, parts jammed together even when the pieces didn't fit. And now the creation exists like a reversed magnet destined to emanate a field that repels everyone. Even when closeness is sought, always the impenetrable distance like a physical barrier that skids one sideways as approach is made. Lego creations can be taken apart, rebuilt, reshaped, and recreated, but not people. People may become stuck, stuck as molded, even if loathing what they have become.

Absorbing the laughter of distant children, feeling the distance, the isolation, and the brokenness of life close in, squeezing until it is hard to breathe. He imagines looking at those smiling faces through the scope of the weapon; the crosshairs centering on white teeth, the freckle on the bridge of a nose, or green ring circling the eye's black pupil. Picturing the moment of impact, the head snapping backwards and falling out of sight, the person awkwardly splayed on the ground, while panicked others run from harm's way. The barrel suddenly turning, taking aim at his own sweat-drenched forehead. What would he feel? Satisfaction? Relief?

Revenge? Where is revenge sought? Who is to blame? Who deserves the hate? Squeezing eyes more tightly, groaning to block out the memories that wash over. He feels the vortex take over, a swirling, buffeting confusion, a blur of images and words and feelings that spin into a suffocating darkness, nothingness, a black hole of relief where the sensations stop and the mind relaxes. From the outside, looking asleep, but being far from asleep…instead, in a state of dissociated, paralyzed rage.

WITHIN THE WALLS

Sophia's stomach contracted as the guttural roar echoed in the corridor; the barren tunnel offering no shield from the force of the sound splattering against concrete like rotten fruit, staining the grim walls with the screamer's hatred. Sophia cautiously approached the open doorway. A female guard dressed in a brown and beige uniform reminiscent of honey bees sat languidly in a yellow plastic chair making notations on the clipboard in her lap. The relaxed posture of the "bee", the term used by youth for staff, contrasted sharply with the energy exploding around her, as though she were the sole surviving house in a tornado's aftermath. Sophia nodded silently to her and shifted her focus to the client strapped to the restraint bed, an inadequate mattress atop an unforgiving concrete slab. Immobilized by leather cords, the boy pulled viciously against the ties, emitting another blood-curdling scream. Sophia shuddered as it washed over her, animalistic and overflowing, like a sneaker wave. Her entire body tensed and weakened in response as she locked eyes with Quinn. A momentary hesitation and silence, followed by, "Do you want to talk?" from Sophia.

Quinn reeled his head futilely beneath the strap, a despairing bellow dismissing the offer. Sophia sighed with resignation but not surprise. Once Quinn reached this point he could not be approached until he'd expended his considerable energy fighting back the only way he knew how. Giving a half-hearted smile to the guard and asking to be informed when Quinn was out of restraint, Sophia withdrew from the room. Her skin tingled as if the walls emitted a charge from broken spirits and dismembered dreams still fighting to be recognized. Feeling heavier than when she had entered, she let herself out the multiple locked doors of the seclusion unit, heading to her next client. Wrapping her coat more tightly against the cold, her shoes percussing the sidewalk, she considered what might have led to this crisis.

Remanded to the Dalton Center fourteen months ago after being considered too dangerous for his previous treatment facility, Quinn's was a disheartening story of neglect and abuse by parents, mistreatment in the foster care system, and eventual law violations resulting in commitment to residential treatment. Quinn assaulted adults he did not trust and avoided forming close friendships with peers. He learned to take what he wanted and fight back when someone got in his way. He said what he thought without regard to others or social expectations, which Sophia found amusing and often considered quite on point. She could appreciate the honesty in it, even if it stung. Quinn was a voracious reader, devouring any kind of book he could get his hands on. Since he was often being punished for his behavior and placed in isolation, reading was the one thing he could do to calm down and break the cycle of assault. Sophia guessed Quinn had been denied a book, exploded and now was in restraints. The staff of Dalton was inconsistent in its response to the youth, leading to frequent discord among adults and confused escalation in the residents.

"Do you really think I'm going to give a book to some dirt bag that just deliberately peed all over the floor in there? Or crapped on his dinner tray and tried to dump it on me as I did rounds? You don't have to come

clean this stuff up…WE do! We aren't going to let them say anything they want or do anything they want. Someone's got to teach them respect!"

"But if he had a book to focus on, maybe he wouldn't spend so much time thinking about all the ways people have mistreated him. Maybe it would help him calm down when he's agitated, and then he wouldn't do such awful things. We have to EARN their respect by treating THEM with a little of it!"

As she ruminated on the conflicting beliefs entangling the adults in a wrestling match for control and adding to distrust in the boys, Sophia entered a nearby building where she was scheduled to meet a new admission. Needing to ground herself despite the chilled stomp just taken between buildings, she took several deep breaths before continuing on to the office she was going to borrow for the meeting; the events here still triggered her, even after years of enduring them. The interview room, like most on campus, was decorated in sterile efficiency; sharp corners and edges, empty of color and character, the place did not beckon or encourage you to sink in for an extended stay. Upon entering, she scanned the desktops, ensuring no confidential papers were visible. Taking a seat, fully aware of a still trotting heart, she tried to recall the information she had read in Derrick's file as she waited for security to deliver him and her pulse to slow, full of questions about where he'd been and what fate awaited him here. Hope and apprehension tangled like discarded cords during these initial encounters with newcomers, as she looked for information to inform her work with them; their stories so often reminding her of her own.

Derrick entered the room cautiously, visually taking in each wall before sliding into the uncomfortable chair opposite Sophia. He positioned himself to watch the open door, a habit shown by many here. Most were vigilant about monitoring their surroundings, a skill honed in dangerous streets and sometimes even more dangerous homes. One never knew when the unexpected would come rushing at you, knocking you on your ass or worse; important to keep your eyes open and your feet and fists at the ready. He adjusted the handcuffs shackled by chain to his waist, allowing him to sit more comfortably.

"Good morning, Derrick," Sophia greeted. "I'm Sophia Connelly. I will be working with you while you're here. I understand you just arrived yesterday." She paused, allowing him time to process and to see if he would respond. He did not, eyeing her suspiciously, his expression daring her to say more.

"I know this is a tough place to be," she began. "I hope as you get to know me and feel more comfortable, you will be able to tell me what your goals are because my goal is usually to help you achieve your own goals. And most people tell me that goal is to get the heck out of here, so we work on whatever helps them do that." She waited, again, to see if he had any response. Sophia knew to be patient when talking with these kids. They wouldn't be rushed. You couldn't hurry the process no matter how pressing things might seem, and you couldn't fool them; they had finely honed radar for bullshit.

Derrick's white-blond hair was cut long on top, flopping down his forehead as though fatigued, partly obscuring one eye. "Yeah, I want out of this place," he offered hesitantly, briefly glancing out the only window in the room. Outside the rain had begun to fall and the wind blew in staccato gusts, an undulating whistle through a cracked seal. The oppressive space was not the most pleasant place to have an initial conversation, or any conversation for that matter.

"Where did you come from?" she asked, even though she knew the answer from the file.

"Alder Grove," he replied after a brief hesitation. Alder Grove was a small rural town in the southeast corner of the state, with a reputation for rampant drug use; a place where marginal families hid from community watchdogs like police and social services. It was not uncommon to find several families or multiple generations of one family sharing a home, struggling to survive on welfare or disability benefits, or selling drugs. The community was often in the news in less than flattering ways.

"Did you grow up there?" she asked.

"Yeah," Derrick made eye contact with her for the first time. Aware of the town's reputation, he watched Sophia for a reaction to the information, waiting for her to say or do something to show her disdain. Having perfected her poker face, Sophia simply asked, "Do you have family there now?"

Derrick paused briefly and then sarcastically replied, "Some, if you want to call them family. I haven't been living with them for a while." Derrick went on to explain his mother had moved to another state with a boyfriend, leaving Derrick to live with various friends, his girlfriend, and a brother, depending on who was willing to share space and who he was getting along with. His story indicated he had been looking after himself for quite a while.

"So what got you here?" Sophia asked.

Again, the hesitation as Derrick sized her up. Sophia was in her late forties with auburn hair just beginning to have streaks of grey. She was tall at 5' 9" and in relatively good physical shape due to her dedication to exercise and healthy diet. She was not required to dress as the unit staff did, instead wearing casual slacks and blouses that were comfortable and conservative to fit the setting. She did not wear jewelry, other than earrings too small to be wrenched by angry hands. Sophia tried to look approachable to increase rapport, and would have worn jeans had they been allowed in the facility.

"I stole some beer," Derrick finally offered.

Sophia considered this silently. It would not be common for someone to end up in such a secure facility for the theft of beer or any other petty theft. Sure there was more to this story, she asked, "I can see how stealing might result in local detention. What got you here?"

"I stole some beer and when the police caught up with me I kicked their ass," came the somewhat belligerent response. *Okay, there WAS more to it*, Sophia thought. She was always amused at the way the stories would come out, reminding her of comic strips that showed kids taking a circuitous route to get somewhere rather than the direct one. While getting there eventually, it might take three times as long and a lot more ground was covered in the process. It was the same indirect route taken during initial interviews to discover what had happened and what relevance it had in the sequence of events that led to the current situation. Sometimes it was deliberate avoidance, and sometimes the clients really did not realize what had contributed to the outcomes they faced.

"Can you tell me what happened when the police caught up with you?" Sophia prodded.

Derrick fingered the cuffs around his wrists and looked out the window again at the pelting rain. While there was a hard edge to his tone and the set of his jaw, Sophia also noticed a pained expression in his eyes, a haunted overlay of despair and frustration. Derrick looked back toward Sophia. Regarding each other, he felt something he rarely felt with anyone. He could see the lack of judgment in her expression, and something else he wasn't sure how to understand. An openness? An objective compassion? He sighed and quietly began to speak. "I'd had a fight with my brother so I left. I know it was stupid, but I went to the little store on the corner and stole some beer. I wanted to get drunk because I was mad. I drank a couple of them, and then the cops showed up, so I ran. But they tackled me, and when they pinned me down I don't know what happened, I just blew up and started kicking their ass. I couldn't stop." Derrick's fingers had tightened around his wrist as he spoke, his skin trying to shed the scrape of asphalt and crushing weight from his body's memory.

Sophia studied him. His entire frame had become tense, but he still carried the expression of one who is baffled by what they have done, not someone who is proud of it.

"It sounds like what happened with the police was the issue more than the beer. Has that kind of thing happened before, where you just lose it and come out fighting?" Sophia knew she was walking into a potential minefield, asking this so soon after meeting Derrick. But there was something about his expression that made her think he really DID want to understand what had happened and hadn't been able to get there on his own. Trusting her instincts, she decided to push a little.

Derrick rubbed his hands across his thighs nervously, making Sophia wonder if his hands were sweating. "It's happened a few times," he responded. He looked at her quizzically. "It happened the last time I was locked up. Some kid was talking shit and came too close to me, and I went off on him. We both ended up in MSU."

Monitored Seclusion Unit (MSU) was the term for the most locked down units in the detention system, a system of single cells that kept individuals isolated from each other. Fed through a small hatch, they were monitored every ten minutes through the unbreakable glass windows on the upper half of the door. Each room had a toilet so the only time those assigned to MSU were allowed out of the cell was for showers, an hour of recreation by themselves in the yard, and meetings with administration, mental health therapists, or probation officers. It was used primarily as a consequence for aggression or when there was risk of self-harm, but could also be used if one of the boys was causing disruption of any kind.

"Can you tell me what the situation was when the fight happened?" Sophia asked.

"We'd been out at rec, and I had been playing basketball. There was a lot of arguing during the game, and I was pissed about that. I was hot too because it must have been 100 degrees out there. We come in and I go to the corner to cool off and that jerk comes in running his mouth about the game still. I told him to just shut the hell up, and he comes over to where I'm standing. I just lost it and punched him in the face. He wouldn't shut the hell up."

Sophia clarified, "So you were hot and mad from the game, and this guy is in your face still going on about it?"

Derrick nodded silently, waiting as Sophia retrieved a piece of paper and pencil from her day planner. "Let me explain something about your nervous system, Derrick". Sophia drew a sketchy picture of a person, detailing parts of the brain. She explained how bodies were constantly receiving input, affecting the nervous system in either calming or agitating ways. They created a list of things that bothered Derrick: heat, noise, having people too close, bright sun, repetitive sounds that he couldn't control (like pencil tapping), bad smells, and being touched by someone he didn't trust. Then they identified what helped him feel calmer: walking, music, being outside, being in the woods alone, having his back against a wall, and writing. Sophia explained not everyone is bothered by the same things, and people have different levels of tolerance when something does bother them. When multiple agitating things are happening at once, we can become unable to handle it and want to get away or become aggressive. Sophia asked Derrick if what she had explained made sense.

Derrick almost bounced in his seat as he answered excitedly, "It makes more sense than you realize!" Offering additional information, he shared that he had been uncomfortable due to the heat and conflict in the game, came into the unit hearing staff loudly barking directions, and instinctively looked for a quiet corner to feel less stressed. When the other boy approached, continuing the game conflict, Derrick found himself in a corner with a wall on one side and half dozen loud peers on the other and nowhere to go. Derrick was unable to handle it, and having no way to calm down he went into fight mode. Ironically, once placed in an isolation cell, Derrick escaped from the things agitating him and could then gain control.

Sophia regarded Derrick with admiration; here was a boy who was clearly bright and insightful. Not only had he understood the concepts discussed, he could apply them to his experiences in a meaningful way. It was as though the information provided him a compass and map, allowing escape from a spiraled wilderness. If he could continue to use them, they would help him leave the facility and live differently. Sophia loved these moments, which were infrequent. It was more common to see obstacles within the person (or the environments around them) trap the boys into wandering in circles, unable to recognize they had been this way before. Sophia felt more at ease with the young people she worked with than most adults she knew; having overcome difficulties of her own, she related to their brokenness and she worked tirelessly to provide some kind of compass or map to each one. She was not so naive as to think finding a new path would be easy, but Derrick's quick understanding gave her hope that he might get there eventually.

After discussing details of the fight a bit more, Sophia excused herself to go see additional clients, encouraged by the beginning conversation and the look of gratitude and understanding Derrick gave her as he followed staff to his cell. It had been a great beginning, and with that there was plenty of room to delve into past experiences determining the set point driving his stress reactions.

River

Sophia leaned back in the kayak and let the current push her along the river. Today, her day off, had dawned uncharacteristically clear and temperate for winter, thanks to an unseasonable jet stream from the southwest, and Sophia made her way to the water, determined to squeeze the most from the gift. A screeching hawk circled overhead, airborne gymnast in search of prey, the pungent odor of moss and mud riding a mild breeze. Watching shrubs and trees as she passed, she noticed root systems exposed by the ebb and flow of water surging against the bank, devouring the surrounding soil. The roots clutched the earth like a piggy-backing octopus tenaciously refusing to be thrown off. She wondered how long it would be before they came crashing down; what final current would tip the balance between grip and pull, toppling them into the river? Sophia's thoughts drifted to the kids she worked with and how the trees' tenuous grasp mirrored them; their life experiences having eroded precarious grips on who they were and what was possible, most of them existing at the mercy of the next surge or a simple weakening in the ability to hang on. The trees also gave Sophia hope. Who knows how long they had stood, or how much longer they might last, just like the resilience in her kids despite overwhelming circumstances? The human spirit could be resolute, and it often did not take much to make it so. Just one person to show love, to encourage, to hold them accountable, and to set an example could lead them to believe in their ability to overcome. Like the tree, having one persistently attached taproot might balance the weakness in the others and keep it upright. She wondered if either Quinn or Derrick had a human taproot in their past, or would find one in their future? Could she help them see or develop one?

Using her paddle, Sophia shifted her course to stay near the edge of the bank as the current carried her along. Being outdoors was her respite from the pressure of trying to find ways to help her clients change course, but it was always difficult to get them out of her head. She carried things with her regardless of where she was, which was quite exhausting. Jokingly, she had told her friend that no matter how fast she ran, she could never get away from herself. It would be funny if it weren't so true. Rarely being fully comfortable around people she often found she couldn't relate to what they cared about or what they did or said. Collecting few friends as a child, she had even fewer as an adult. The few she had, she was content to see occasionally. Sophia was comfortable being alone with her thoughts and rarely felt bored, entertained by a rich inner life. Listening to others prattle on about things she disagreed with, or was not interested in, led her to discretely slip away. Troubled youth were the exception, as Sophia found them complex and challenging, giving her many opportunities for new learning. She often thought she would like to be inside their heads, as long as she could find her way out again! A high school psychology class ignited her fascination with what made people who they were; questions were endless and answers hard to find. A misfit even then, she found few peers who shared her quest to understand the mysteries of mind and behavior. Lack of interest in sports, dances, or partying meant Sophia frequently gravitated to the solitude of her room with a good book.

An extreme introvert, Sophia had come to accept and even appreciate her comfort in being alone, requiring it, even, in order to recharge her energy. She could spot another introvert from a mile away. They arrived first at meetings; picking the seat they found most comfortable, reading material or knitting in hand to avoid the necessity of "chatting". Sophia would rather stuff hot coals up her nose than engage in social chit-chat. Not only did she not know what to say, but she often couldn't see the value of what did get said. Days filled with people and listening to kids often left Sophia exhausted, her head swirling with information that she continued to ruminate on. It was hard to turn off a head that was constantly reliving events, conversations, and feelings in order to wring every last drop of meaning and understanding from them. She could spend hours on one conversation, re-writing it, giving it new parts and endings, experimenting with how it might play out in her imaginary scenarios. Although sometimes interesting, it was also a curse, something that could have a life of its own and kept her mind captive when all she longed for was peaceful quiet. At those times she wished outer distraction could do for her what it seemed to do for others.

Surrounded by people who wore certainty like a scarf, wrapped around their sometimes unexamined beliefs, Sophia struggled with finding certainty about anything, particularly when it came to the boys she worked with. While others viewed situations, people, or issues as two or three dimensional, Sophia saw decagons, with multiple sides, influences, and possibilities. While useful in her work, it often led to conflict in her personal life; others thought she lacked conviction or did not appreciate when she played devil's advocate. She had learned the cloak of conviction was a garment others did not want rearranged or ripped off.

Just ahead, the bridge spanning the river signaled the end of her float. Paddling across the current, she slipped her kayak to the edge. Stepping out into ankle-deep water, she pulled the boat onto shore, threw the paddle inside, lifted and carried it through the park. Mothers and children scattered the park, enjoying the respite from cold and rain. Sophia smiled as she watched a golden retriever refuse to release a ball to the young boy asking for it. Just as she was silently putting her money on the retriever, the dog dropped it and sashayed backwards anticipating the next throw; a timeless dance capturing the nature of trust between two beings. The trust one would throw and one would chase, one would go away but always come back, and one would stay and wait until the other returned.

Back at her car, she loaded the kayak onto the roof and tied it down, grateful to the friend who had taken her to the drop-off point. Sophia made a mental note to take Julie out to dinner as a gesture of appreciation. She may not have a lot of friends, but they were quality friends, and she was grateful for each of them. As she opened the car door, Sophia heard footsteps and glanced up to see a person dressed completely in black passing behind her. Although the temperature was pleasant, and the sun out, there was nothing exposed that would reveal the gender of the figure, unlike others in the park. Heavy boots, denim pants, and hooded sweatshirt pulled over the head covered any hint of skin or identity. Watching the figure recede, Sophia wondered why anyone would rebuff this beautiful day's invitation to shed layers, preferring instead the sweaty rasp of cloth and leather, as though trying to hide in plain sight. There was something vaguely familiar about the figure, until she realized this was how all the kids seemed to dress these days; probably no one she knew. Shaking her head, she climbed into her car to head home, hoping the sun would not be as scarce in coming days.

ALONE TOGETHER

Entering the unit, Sophia paused, trying to spot Aiden among the twenty-some youth spread among the chairs and couches. The air was stale and bitter from a blend of state detergent, rumpled beds, close-quartered bodies and unbrushed teeth. It was impossible to inhale without worrying about how many microbes were infiltrating her trachea. Sophia was always on guard against organisms possibly floating around, scouting for a landing site, and in these perpetually locked quarters, there were times she quit breathing for a moment, willing an errant germ to another host.

Spotting Aiden, she crossed the room to get his attention. Aiden was quite thin and slightly shorter than Sophia. His close cropped hair jutted like freshly mowed grass, and he wore wire-rimmed glasses that frequently required a push up the bridge of his nose due to his obsession they sit in precisely one spot. Aiden had many obsessions consistent with his diagnosis of autism spectrum, which is what brought him to Sophia's attention. Aiden was exceptionally bright, verbal, and brimming with facts, but his social understanding was abysmal, and he often irritated those around him by offering information from his vast mental storage, usually unsolicited, and as a result, under-appreciated or downright resented.

"Hey Aiden," greeted Sophia. Sitting in the corner of the room by himself, Aiden looked up from the paper he was poised to write on.

"Hello Miss Sophia," Aiden replied, smiling. He enjoyed seeing Sophia. She understood him, and she let him talk without interrupting him, while few others did.

"Can I borrow you a minute?" she asked.

"Sure! Just let me finish this first."

Sophia knew better than to insist he come right away. He not only needed time to transition between activities, but he also needed to reach a place he considered "finished" before moving on to something else. Looking around the room as she waited, Sophia saw the groupings of youth she had come to expect. Despite the fact they all entered the facility for similar reasons, they always developed a pecking order. There were those considered cool alphas and those considered weak punks who were despised and mistreated, a separation into "us" and "them" that baffled her.

Near the windows, a cluster of six loudly discussed which rap artist was the most talented. One broke into a demonstration rap to prove his point. "You can't beat THAT bro!" he challenged as he rested his case with a wave of his hands and a defiant nod of his head.

The outcry was immediate as another stepped up to disagree. It was amazing how long this kind debate could go on, as much a pissing contest as a real exchange of opinion. Who could get the loudest, demand the most attention, and intimidate others into silence or giving up in frustration? It wasn't about agreement so much as winning the match, so much energy for so little purpose. The need to win was fierce in this place. Existing in a small environment, with so little to do and so little control, everything happening carried more importance to the one it happened to, as though trapped within a telephoto lens, losing the surrounding perspective. Here, the theft of socks injured as much as if legs had been broken. The loss of a phone call slapped like a broken relationship. Either might unleash a torrent of profane complaints or violent outbursts. Replacing the telephoto lens with a wide angle was the key to developing more patience in handling the stress they experienced; easy to recognize the need, but harder to change lenses, especially in a place where pleasure from greeting the morning waned before one rose from bed.

Four others lounged on the couch, absorbed in a ball game. Laughter occasionally erupted, as did moments of anger. "Move your ass!" or "Shut up," broke through the drone of the announcer's play-by-play. There were several foursomes engaged in card games and a few youth sitting alone. Those sitting alone resided at the bottom of the residential pecking order, the unwanted gum on the bottom of one's shoe. Socially less skilled, often more emotionally fragile, and almost without fail carrying a diagnosis or two, they drew ridicule, practical jokes, and their belongings were often violated. Aiden always sat alone.

"Okay, I'm ready now," Aiden announced cheerfully. He popped up from his seat, gathering up his notebook, magazine and pencil. Sophia followed Aiden as they crossed the crowded room, adhering to the facility rule that adults walk behind youth in order to keep them in view. While Sophia had never felt threatened by any of the boys, she did try to follow the protocols.

Nearing the office available for use, they passed two Hispanic youth who glared at Aiden as he approached, arms crossed over bulky chests. The taller of the two muttered to Sophia, "Might wanna teach Whitey to stop working with the feds or he ain't gonna like what happens," as he nodded in Aiden's direction.

"Not appropriate," barked Scott, the nearby staff who had overheard.

Sophia looked at Scott quizzically. "Working with the feds?" she whispered as she edged closer while still keeping an eye on Aiden.

"Means he thinks he can run his mouth and staff will rescue him before the people he pisses off can do anything to him," Scott explained. "He tends to set people off easily."

"Ah. Thanks." Sophia followed Aiden, who had either not heard the comment or was ignoring it. They entered the claustrophobic office and sat next to a desk cluttered with papers, a dirty coffee cup, used napkin, and someone's leather jacket. There was barely room for all their limbs as they contorted like gumbys, Sophia flinching from punctures in her personal space bubble, wondering what kind of perverse person designed such spaces.

"How do you think your week has gone, Aiden?" Sophia began.

"Pretty well," he responded. "Except we had a substitute this week in English, and she didn't know what she was talking about so I had to enlighten her."

Inwardly amused, Sophia tried not to show it. "What was she confused about?" she asked diplomatically.

"She was telling us we were supposed to do the vocabulary sheets first, do a rough draft of our compare and contrast paper next, and then do the spelling practice page. Everyone knows we do the spelling practice first, the vocabulary sheets second and then work on the papers, but no one would tell her, so I did! I told her I didn't want her to be stuck on stupid." Indignation colored his tone. Stuck on stupid was the expression indicating one was in the proverbial dark or uninformed. Unfortunately, it was not a phrase known by outsiders, such as substitutes, and therefore could sound rude and disrespectful.

"And how did it go when you gave her that information?"

"Well, the lady's got air in her tights!" Aiden fired back. "She not only didn't care but she got pissed and sent me to the office. What did she get her degree in? Master's degree in Know-It-All? Ph.D. in My-Excrement-Don't-Stink? Guess I should have LET her stay stuck on stupid!"

Well-meaning but socially clueless, Aiden had provided factual information to someone appearing to need it, and was stunned to find his efforts were not only unappreciated, but gave offense. Sophia could almost hear Aiden's thoughts lock up at the perplexing reaction of the substitute, becoming even more insistent, as though perseverance would be the battering ram to penetrate the obviously challenged brain of a substitute.

Keeping her tone neutral, Sophia offered, "It sounds like you were trying to be helpful but your attempt to be helpful didn't produce the results you were after?"

"Hell no!" Aiden responded. "I hate substitutes. They always think they know everything but they know nothing. And when you try to tell them, they just get mad and put you on blast. These imbeciles I live with are the same way. They're always talking crap and they're always WRONG about things. So I correct them, set them straight, and all they do is get pissed and start giving ME crap." His body slammed backwards against the chair in frustration.

"Aiden, why do you think people talk to each other?" Sophia asked.

Aiden looked quizzically at Sophia, wondering if she'd lost her mind. He'd always thought her intelligent, but this question gave him doubt. Sliding his glasses up his nose he replied, "To provide information."

"Is that all?" Sophia probed.

"What other reason is there?" he countered. "It's how we inform people. We tell them what we know so they can be more educated. It's just too bad some people are so freaking uneducated and determined to remain that way, because all they want me to do is shut up!"

Aiden left little doubt he was completely sincere in his limited view of the purpose and nature of communication, which was why he experienced a less than welcoming reception from others. While Aiden believed he was offering them educational golden nuggets, they often felt he had wiped a booger on their sleeve.

"You are right, Aiden. We do talk to each other to give information. But an even more important reason is to build connection or relationship. People talk to each other to find out about who the other person is and what they might have in common. We talk to each other to share who we are and to see if we can appreciate qualities the other person has, to feel closer to them through that knowledge." Sophia struggled to find words that would help Aiden understand what was so obvious to her.

Aiden stared at Sophia and then exclaimed, "Why didn't anyone ever TELL me that before?"

Aiden, despite his genius level intellectual abilities had never been able to put together the social equation of two plus two. He could memorize the periodic table, define college level words and explain concepts learned in physics, but could not understand the most basic of social behaviors without being directly taught them.

Why indeed did no one ever tell you that before? Because no one thought they had to? Because others in the interactions assumed you were being deliberately irritating with your "sharing of information" instead of being confused about social protocol? Because you come across so blasted intelligent that no one would have considered the vast difference between memorized facts and navigating social interactions?

It was easy to imagine Aiden being ostracized due to his well-intentioned blunders, or that others believed him to be "working with the feds" when staff had to rescue him from the quagmires he created.

"I don't know why, Aiden. But it's important to know people talk to one other to find out about each other. The information shared is secondary. And sometimes people don't like to have their information disputed, and disputing it hurts the relationship."

"Hold on. I need to record that," Aiden pulled out a small red notebook he kept in his pocket. He rifled through the pages before scribbling something onto an exposed page. Aiden kept voluminous notes and lists, on many things. Even though his memory was superior to most, he was nagged by anxiety he might forget something crucial. His need to keep and review his notes had caused problems with both staff and peers at Dalton. Peers assumed he was writing things about them, and staff became frustrated when Aiden was dealing with his notebook instead of doing as expected. Looking at the previous page, Aiden shared, "I now have 251 ways it would piss me off to die."

Sophia smiled, unable to stop herself. As long as she'd known him, Aiden had been generating possible ways one could die. Some were obvious, but others were things that would never occur to the average person. Again, it was one of those things that set him apart. Aiden noticed things others didn't; made connections about things others wouldn't, and was able to see possibilities in the most unlikely places.

"Number two hundred and fifty-one is that it would piss me off to die because some drunk driver drove into the honey-bucket I was using!" Aiden smirked at Sophia. "You know…those crappers they leave for road construction guys? I've seen them and wondered about using them before."

Sophia nodded in agreement. "Yes, that would be an unpleasant way to go all right." Shifting gears to steer Aiden towards the topic she needed to discuss with him, she said, "So Aiden, I hear you went to MSU last night. Can we talk about what happened?" It had not surprised her that Aiden's assessment of his week had not included this event. While he did not deliberately withhold information, he did consider some things over and done with and didn't always want to revisit them.

Aiden looked towards the outer unit with disgust. "That moron over there sent me for no reason," he nodded toward a new staff member in the day room, "The one with poodle hair and a rectangle face."

"What was happening before she made that decision?" Sophia knew better than to challenge his answer head-on, instead she would cut away at the perspectives offered a snip at a time until the issue was eventually exposed; a social autopsy with a little incision here, pull back the reasoning there, and pretty soon, the interaction that started the whole thing would be exposed like a misguided tumor. Only then could it be removed and things stitched back together in a way she hoped would lead to different outcomes in the future.

Aiden inhaled, puffing his cheeks, and then exhaled loudly. Sophia held her breath until she felt the warmth of his exhalation (with all possible accompanying germs) pass by. *As much as I like you, Aiden, I don't want your breath, she thought ruefully.*

"I was brushing my teeth like they told me to. That Nazi over there decided I had brushed long enough and told me I needed to finish and leave the bathroom, but I wasn't done so I kept brushing."

"Do you know how long you had been brushing?" Sophia asked.

"I know exactly how long I was brushing. I read an article three years, two months and seven days ago about how dentists recommend you brush your teeth. You are supposed to spend thirty seconds on each quadrant. I was on the third quadrant when she told me I had to stop. I couldn't stop until I completed the fourth quadrant. I needed forty more seconds to finish the third and then do the fourth quadrant so I took them!" was Aiden's retort. "Maybe I should send her a bill for the teeth that fall out twenty years from now! I've been keeping track of my compliance with that rule, and I wasn't going to let her ruin my record."

Sophia had no doubt Aiden knew exactly how many seconds he had spent on the quadrants, and that he would need to finish them all before being able to move on. She was equally certain staff would have given consequences to punish what looked like deliberate defiance from Aiden. These misunderstandings played out repeatedly between staff and youth. Interpretations were made based on little information and false assumptions, leading to escalations and consequences. She spent much of her time trying to bridge those gaps by helping staff understand youth needs and challenges, and helping her clients communicate better with staff and accept situations they had no control over.

Sophia spent the rest of the session with Aiden trying to help him understand why the adult had reacted as she had, and they made a plan to explain to staff about his need to follow the brushing rules created by dentists to completion. When they were finished, Sophia escorted Aiden back to his seat and left him recording the most important points of their conversation in his notebook. Making a mental note to double the mouthwash in her nightly gargle, she left the stuffy unit and headed to her car, breathing in the rain-washed air, finding no matter how deeply she did, the cleansing never quite reached the inner chamber, strewn with dust.

Traffic and buildings visually clicked by, like upright railroad ties, passing unnoticed as Sophia drove, reflecting on the conversation with Aiden, realizing how difficult relationships actually were—to understand, form, or explain; remembering some of her own, and thinking it was like a sandbox. You bring your toys, they bring theirs. Sometimes you share toys, sometimes you hoard them. Sometimes you have a lot of toys, sometimes only one. Sometimes you sit in a corner by yourself and build your own sand castle. Sometimes you create something together and then one of you destroys it, or maybe you even destroy it together. Sometimes sand is thrown and it misses, and sometimes it lands right in your eyes, blinding you for a time. Sometimes you skin your knee when you fall into it. Sometimes you cut yourself on something sharp hidden from view. Sometimes you find treasure when you dig. Sometimes you find turds buried there. And all kinds of playmates come to the sandbox during a lifetime. Some come and go and others stay. You never knew for sure what you might find when you decided to step in.

Sophia valued the few relationships she formed and held on to them with both hands. She dug deep in the sand looking for the treasure of lasting bonds and meaningful connections; living the paradox of being wired for social connection yet afraid of the intimacy that might ultimately hurt. Sophia was not afraid to be vulnerable but needed to feel her name was safe in others' mouths. She needed to trust that her friends understood and accepted her. Sophia had found both treasures and turds over the years. Her late husband, Zach, had been one of her treasures.

Sophia met Zach near the end of graduate school. Fellow students regarded her as an enigma, as she was not one to speak in class unless she felt others were entirely missing the point. Sophia didn't hang around after class to socialize or participate in any of the study groups that others seemed to seek, but she did study in the library to access the vast stores of research. It was there Zach approached her, after months of surreptitious glances from across the room. She was aware of him but kept her mind on her purpose until he stopped at her table one day. After several minutes of banter about the rigors of graduate school, he asked if she would be interested in having a coffee break one day. She accepted, and a year of getting to know each other led to a simple ceremony in a friend's back yard. Sophia's reluctance to be the center of attention ensured there would be few people in attendance and fuss would be kept to a minimum.

Those who knew her were surprised Sophia married at all; she had a fiercely independent streak and had always believed no man would be able to handle it. She'd never subscribed to the idea that marriage was a necessary or even preferred state of being and had rarely dated.

Zach not only accepted her independence, he appreciated and encouraged it. And even more importantly, he understood her more than she thought humanly possible. He understood that despite the outer presentation of a porcupine, appearing unapproachable, reserved, and occasionally prickly, she was a sea anemone on the inside, sensitive, easily hurt, ready to curl up inside herself in response to trouble or insult when her good intentions went awry. Zach saw through the outer crust to the person who longed to feel connected and accepted, but frequently didn't. He provided balance to her tendency to overthink things, gave a different perspective when she circled endlessly in a mental cul-de-sac, held her when she felt stung by someone or something, and cajoled her into easing up when she felt wound so tight she threatened to spoing apart. She missed him profoundly and was certain she would never marry again, for she knew she could never trust anyone as much as she had him.

It was difficult getting used to being alone after the accident. Even though she had previously been quite good at being alone, and even enjoyed it, it didn't feel the same when she knew he would never again massage her feet as they watched television curled up on the couch; would never again stroke the side of her face, asking how she'd slept, when the sun crept around closed blinds; would never again deliver the paper with a cup of coffee and a kiss on the forehead.

Being alone when you know someone will return to fill the silence with stories of their day was a very different kind of alone than knowing if you died in your sleep, days or weeks may pass before anyone missed you and came looking. Sophia had accepted aloneness before Zach without even noticing;

now, a seismic shift had taken place internally, permanently recalibrating how it felt, bringing with it the realization being alone was mental and spiritual, not physical, and that those who walked among crowds without a sense of belonging were those most alone. Without Zach, the aloneness she felt was persistent and profound; it swallowed up her contentment, her sense of purpose.

A double-edged sword, the new apartment bore little resemblance to the house she and Zach had shared. While it provided fewer reminders of her loss, it also lacked the familiarity of the house she'd been forced to sell. In the early days Sophia could barely function, consumed with anger that a patch of ice had taken Zach from her. Sophia believed that if you treat others well, do what is morally right, act with integrity, good things would happen, and it was excruciating to her when random bad luck disputed that. Tornadoes, car accidents, sudden rare diseases…they all jerked her backwards psychologically like a dog reaching the end of its leash, creating a sudden lack of oxygen to her reasoning. Rationally, she knew that chance operated in the world, and anyone could be the unwitting victim of a capricious aligning of circumstances. But on an emotional level, she wanted answers, damn it! She wanted to know why this person and not that one, why now and not ten years from now, why this event and not that one? She wanted order and logic, and for things to make sense and be predictable, and when they weren't, it threatened her sense of balance and peace. Icy roads, ineffective braking, sudden swerving—planets lining up just right to take Zach from her life, leaving her with questions, a sense of unrest, and another reminder that nothing in life is certain or predictable; leaving her with an aloneness akin to the swallowing of sound when snow blankets fall.

Dashing past knobby trees looking like arthritic hands reaching for help, raindrops pinging off her head, she wished that her apartment was closer to the parking lot. Once inside, she kicked off her shoes, hung the dripping coat on a corner rack, and dropped her purse on the kitchen table. Checking the phone for messages, she found none. Relieved she wouldn't have to return any calls, she changed into sweats and poured herself a glass of white wine. Looking through the mail, she found only ads, invitations to apply for credit cards, and catalogs from companies she would never use, and tossed it all into the recycle bin.

She shuffled to the living room, curling up in the black suede recliner, shades blocking the outside world, as she closed up like a pearl within an oyster. She turned on the news, running her fingers along the wine glass stem as she listened, not really focusing enough to process. The next few hours were the most difficult, hours that screamed Zach's absence. While the pain of his absence no longer throbbed loudly or continuously, it still pulsed periodically at unexpected times; catching the scent of his favorite meal of barbecued steak, or seeing the neighbor's cat, sure it would have stopped Zach in his tracks, for he never passed an animal without attempting a conversation. A comment or mannerism from a show would remind her of Zach or might be something he would have chuckled at. Initially avoiding their favorite shows, she now chose to watch them to feel his presence again.

The scream of siren jolted Sophia awake. Disoriented, it took her a moment to realize it was from the television, a police chase on a weekly drama. Realizing she had fallen asleep in her chair, she placed the empty wine glass in the sink, and began her nightly process of getting ready for bed. Zach had gently teased her about the number of things she did before going to bed. Now there was no one to notice or care. "*How sad is that?*" she thought as she turned out the light, a tear wetting her ear as she drifted back to sleep.

POWDER KEGS

Sophia stepped out of her office when she heard loud voices in the hallway.

"I din' do SHI'!" exclaimed D'Vrae, a tall, slender black kid Sophia had known for two years.

Jerry, the staff member escorting D'Vrae, was a soft-spoken bald man in his late fifties. "I didn't say you did, D'Vrae. We just need to take a quick break to sort this out. Chill, my man."

Jerry had worked at Dalton for fifteen years. He did so because he wanted to, not because he had to. His history was a difficult one, with missteps and misdeeds including illegal activities and jail. He eventually turned a corner away from that lifestyle into one that was hell-bent on helping others find a similar escape from the revolving door of recidivism. Jerry's hairless head, barbed wire neck tattoo, and earlobe enlarged from a rubber ring insert could be daunting upon first meeting him, but the hesitation Sophia initially felt quickly gave way to trust and admiration when she saw his rapport with the residents. He quickly gained their respect due to a "been there, done that" presentation. Jerry could not be bull-dozed or manipulated, but he could be a powerful ally when they sought his help to solve some problem or injustice. Jerry was not always well-liked by his fellow staff members because he did not always assume the worst about the residents and would give their versions a fair listen. Sophia liked that about him. She consulted Jerry frequently when needing insight into other adults in the facility, as he had keen powers of observation and had been there many years while others came and went.

"Sophia, I think D'Vrae could use a little time. Do you have a minute?" Jerry asked with a wry smile, slight scar snaking from the corner crease.

"I do. Come on in and have a seat D'Vrae," Sophia offered. "I'm going to ask Jerry something and I'll be right back."

Sophia gestured to the chair across the room, still visible from the doorway where she stood. The agitated boy slammed down into it, crossed his arms, and slumped down, splaying his long legs out in front of him. With D'Vrae still in view, Sophia edged into the hallway next to Jerry.

"What happened?" she asked.

"I'm not sure. I heard loud voices in the classroom as I was coming down the hallway. I stuck my head in to check it out and saw the teacher with the phone in his hand and D'Vrae about four yards away staring at him, looking ticked, but also backing away from him. I asked if I could help and the teacher said he felt threatened, so I took D'Vrae out. That's when you saw us coming down the hall. So I don't know what happened before I got there," Jerry answered. "I didn't see anything that looked threatening, but when the teacher says he feels threatened, I know it's best to get the kid out of the room."

"Okay, thanks, Jerry," Sophia responded. "I'll see what I can find out and try to calm him down."

Sophia crossed back into her office, pulling her chair near D'Vrae, who was still sitting with his arms folded, looking out the window into a courtyard being tended by several workers. During summer the courtyard was alive with color, but now it was a drenched dreary, as though the sky had exploded a thousand cans of runny ashen paint. D'Vrae was a handsome boy of seventeen who prided himself on finding creative and unusual ways to fix his extensive hair. He created designs by braiding rows or circles, or put parts or all of it up in bands so that his head appeared to be topped with black mushrooms. When he did nothing to tame it, it stood a foot off his scalp in all directions, looking like a smoke plume. One could ascertain his attitude by reading his hairstyle--the more unruly and unusual the design, the more D'Vrae sought attention and recognition from others. Today's design was tidy lines of cornrows that began at his forehead and traveled down the back of his head. Today was not an attention seeking day.

"What happened in there, D'Vrae?" she began.

"Nothin'!" was the vehement reply. "I din' do shi'! Th'asshole jus' be trippin'!"

Some facility adults would have pounced on D'Vrae's colorful language, insisting he stop or immediately giving consequences, creating further eruption from him. Sophia didn't care how the youth expressed themselves as long as they did so relatively honestly and completely. She believed it released pressure so they could get down to solving the problem instead of adding a new layer to it.

"All's I was doin' was takin' a book to my homie 'cross the room and tha' piece of crap pick up the phone and gonna call security on me. I try tellin' him I jus' helpin' a homie but he don' listen. He trip and put me on blast," D'Vrae was incensed.

"Can we go back to the beginning?" Sophia asked gently. "What were you doing before you were trying to give someone a book?"

"We was doin' one of his dumb-ass pages. I was sittin' there and me and de homies were talkin' and one of my bro's 'cross the room said they din' have no book. I was takin' them mine 'cause I gots one next to me I can use. He turns 'round and sees me comin' tha' way and trips and star' yellin' at me to sit down. Tried to tell him I jus' takin' a book but he keep trippin' and screamin' at me to sit down. No one gonna yell at me tha' way!" D'Vrae twisted his head defiantly for emphasis. Having grown up in a tough neighborhood, D'Vrae had a hair-trigger on his pride and was not one to let a slight go unchallenged, even if that slight was offered by an adult. Sophia was somewhat amazed he hadn't become aggressive in response instead of backing away. A year ago D'Vrae might have handled that moment by pressing closer, proving his power when he perceived fear on the part of the teacher. Backing off and trying to explain showed the progress he had made in the last two years.

"So is that when Jerry showed up?" she asked.

"Yeah, and it's a good damn thing he did! I mighta give th'asshole a reason to call security!" D'Vrae replied. "I din' do nothin' but he gonna go speakin' on me and I prolly gonna have sanction now." Sanctions varied from having to sit alone without talking, being confined to a particular place, going to bed early, or doing some assigned chore.

Sam Gibson was new to the facility and was known for being quick to perceive a threat and react accordingly. Students sometimes intentionally tried to provoke him in a play for satisfaction and power. Mr. Gibson's reactivity was poorly suited to this work, but since the facility did not have people lined up at the door waiting for a chance, there was little choice but to help him be successful. Sophia spent many hours calming and debriefing youth who escalated during school, as well as time consulting with the teacher to build his skills and increase his understanding.

"I don't know if that is automatic here, D'Vrae." Sophia attempted to calm and reason with him. "In the first place, you didn't get aggressive. And secondly, it sounds like there was a misunderstanding between you and the teacher that can be cleared up with more information. You also came willingly with Jerry, which you might not have done a year ago. That's all important in how you handled this situation." Sophia looked for successes, no matter how small. Her clients having had more criticism than encouragement in their lives came in with defensive armor expecting arrows and bullets. "I can explain to your unit what I think happened, and I think Jerry will back that up. I can also see if I can help with how the teacher interpreted you. So let's not get ahead of things, and try to assume the best for now. Okay?"

D'Vrae's relaxed posture indicated he had calmed considerably. He trusted Sophia and knew she would do what she promised. He also knew she would be fair in her assessment of what happened and would listen without judging him. He smiled at her. "We hella tight," he offered as an acknowledgement of the trust they had established.

Sophia smiled back. He was a likeable kid, despite an outlook and behavior that reflected growing up in a poor, rough neighborhood. D'Vrae's mother had died of a drug overdose, and his father had spent most of D'Vrae's life in prison for gang-related offenses. D'Vrae had been raised by a combination of aunts and his grandmother, moving from home to home depending on the stability of the person he was with. The males in the neighborhood were often absent; imprisoned, dead, gone making money through the underground economy, or simply moving on to new relationships that did not include parenting children. The women did their best, but socializing head-strong male children as they aged and keeping them safe from the temptations beckoning in the street was a battle they often lost. D'Vrae talked fondly of his aunts and grandmother, feeling some attachment to them, but saw himself as a fully grown man who could take care of himself.

Sophia thought of D'Vrae and others like him as puppies with guns. Children on the inside, acting like adults on the outside, they carried lethal weapons to feel powerful and safe in an unpredictable world. They wanted to party and hang out, wear current fashion and hang with girls, just like most teens their age. They did impulsive things that sometimes came back to bite them, just like their peers. Only these boys hid a knife or gun in their clothing that could be pulled out and used, changing the course of their lives irretrievably. Because the streets had an unforgiving memory, any deed could be cause for retribution. There were eight gangs in D'Vrae's neighborhood, which meant any of the others could be gunning for him at any time, not because they had a beef with him personally, but simply because he was a member of the gang they had a beef with. D'Vrae knew five people who had been killed in the neighborhood in his generation alone. If one added his father's generation, the number increased to twenty-seven, some of them relatives. Control of drug dealing, theft, and prostitution were part of the constant war for economic survival in this world.

Despite all the violence, and scorn for more traditional, law-abiding ways, D'Vrae could be child-like in his views and desires. Much to his proud chagrin, his eyes glistened with tears when he was told he would miss summer fun with his friends upon entering Dalton. Realizing there would be no barbecues in the park, no swimming with friends, no mall trips, he struggled to remain stoic, but was betrayed by leaking coffee-colored eyes. Those were the signs she looked for when she met the boys. Signs of humanity beneath the inhumane behavior, evidence of vulnerability beneath the uncaring toughness, pliable soil beneath the crust hardened by unmet needs and pain, fertile ground upon which to build. She could usually find it in most of them. Even in D'Vrae, with his cocky, tough-as-nails attitude and tendency to pack a gun. Sophia worked tirelessly on the "us versus them" yardstick used to measure their worlds.

"Would you steal my car, D'Vrae?"

"Hell no, Miss Sophia! You tigh'. You be nice to me. I don' steal from no one I know."

"Would you steal a car if you knew it belonged to my family or a friend?"

"No!"

"Would you steal a car from someone if you knew they had worked for three years to save up enough money to finally buy a car so they didn't have to ride their bike to work anymore, or from someone who was being treated for cancer and needed the car to get to their treatments?"

"No. Tha' ain' right."

D'Vrae's moral compass allowed him to mistreat faceless strangers, particularly if he saw them as better off than himself. Making the victim more personal and visible allowed compassion buried inside to float to the surface and influence his choices. Sophia searched for that compassion as she continued to discuss his removal from class.

"So what do you expect when you go back to the classroom with the teacher?" Sophia asked.

"Hell, I don' know. He scandalous! He racis'. He pick on me 'cause I black," snorted D'Vrae.

"What makes you think that?" Sophia frowned slightly.

"He think I out to get him when I don' do nuthin'. He think I a punk who lookin' to jump him. All I wanna do is do my time. I don' wan' no trouble. Just wanna get out and go back to my hood." D'Vrae twirled the end of a small braid near his ear as he spoke.

"You know Mr. Gibson is new here. And you and I both know what the kids say about him. Do you think it's possible that his nervousness and newness are just making him a little jumpy about understanding you guys? Maybe he needs more time to be better at judging what's going on when people do things? Do you think you have enough information about him to know for sure his motives are racist?"

Many of the minority youth felt mistreated by the system and were quick to level the racist charge against an adult. While sometimes true, Sophia always tried to talk them into giving the person the benefit of the doubt, and to look for other possible explanations. She hoped her positive relationship with D'Vrae would help him make that leap.

D'Vrae regarded Sophia skeptically as his respect for her clashed with his life experience on the street. Sophia watched him, fully aware of his struggle. He was often picked out of a crowd to be stopped and questioned, had his bus pass torn up, and had been required to produce identification for no apparent reason. If what D'Vrae had previously shared with her was true, it indicated that racism was alive and well in the town of Parkerville. Even factoring in his reputation and past law violations, some of the contacts rang of harassment. Sophia did not assume all police were free from prejudice, or that all those who went into law enforcement were free from power and control issues. What she tried to guard against was the reverse form of racism, not assuming questionable behavior was the result of racism when there could be other explanations.

"I don' know. I just wan' him to lay off me. He leave me be, I leave him be," offered D'Vrae as a form of compromise without agreeing as to the nature of Mr. Gibson's motives.

"That's fair," Sophia agreed. "That's all I'm asking, if you can return to the classroom and let this be done, not do anything to restart it or draw attention to yourself."

D'Vrae smiled mischievously. "I do it for you, Miss Sophia."

D'Vrae could be charming and he knew it. His probation officer joked about the multiple broken hearts that had been left behind when D'Vrae was locked up. Even D'Vrae made comments about his "ladies", as in plural, another example of what was considered normal and acceptable where he'd grown up.

"Do it for you, D'Vrae," Sophia deflected. "You are the one having a lot riding on how things go. You are really close to getting out and I'd hate to see you mess that up now."

D'Vrae made a smacking sound as he tilted his head backwards, nodding agreement. "Awright then," he agreed.

Sophia escorted D'Vrae down the hallway and watched as he re-entered the classroom. Mr. Gibson glanced at her and watched as D'Vrae took his seat. His face initially tense, he appeared to relax as he saw that D'Vrae was going right to work on the worksheet still on his desk. Mr. Gibson nodded in Sophia's direction and resumed showing the boy next to him how to solve the math problem the student was confused about. Sophia stood in the doorway long enough to feel comfortable that D'Vrae was keeping his word and then withdrew. She made a mental note to connect with Sam during the lunch break to keep her word to D'Vrae.

RELATIONS

Sophia steeled herself as she knocked sharply on the door. Chilled by the winter air, she pulled her coat more tightly around her, adjusting the wool scarf wrapped around her neck. Rocking from foot to foot, she muttered impatiently, "Come on for crying out loud!" She briefly considered taking advantage of the delay to flee, but decided to stick it out for the sake of propriety. Having accepted the invitation, she felt an obligation to appear, even as everything introverted and sad in her pulled in the opposite direction. It didn't help that the yard and house-front were overflowing in Christmas, lights everywhere, animated reindeer pulling a sleighed Santa, and a nativity scene front and center. Sophia had not even put up a tree this year. Surrounded by this cheer, she felt increasingly unhappy.

The door opened suddenly, revealing a thin woman with black hair highlighted with blond streaks. She looked younger than her 44 years, and dressed the part, wearing black skinny jeans and a tight-fitting yellow sweater. The two inch heels on her knee-high boots brought her to eye level with Sophia.

"Oh, *there* you are!" the woman gushed as she wrapped her arms around Sophia. "I was wondering if you were ever going to show up! Come on in, give me your coat," she said as she stepped backwards into the brightly lit house.

"Sorry, Jane, things just took longer than I expected," Sophia offered half-heartedly, as she handed over the coat and scarf. The aroma of roasted beef and fresh rolls greeted her, making Sophia aware she was hungry, even if hesitant about the impending interactions. Some people were quiet presences and she could be in their company and barely feel them. Others were so full of energy that even if they didn't speak, she could feel them infringing on the perimeter of her psyche; the difference between an old golden retriever, who could lie at her feet and be forgotten, and a young Jack Russell Terrier vibrating with energy, always on the verge of activity. Sophia could be with a golden retriever person for a long time, but the terrier people exhausted her quickly. Jane was a well-dressed, manicured terrier in very high heels.

"How have you been, Sophia?" Jane smiled brightly as she linked arms with Sophia, leading her through the living room and towards the kitchen. "Are you ready for Christmas?"

The question Sophia had come to despise. The question she heard at the grocery store, the pharmacy, at work, at the gas station, and on the phone when friends and family called to see what her plans were; the question causing an immediate tug-of-war between her tendency to be honest and her belief that others may not really know how to handle her honest feelings, or didn't really care what the answer was. How often had she been asked how she was, and how often had she answered fully and honestly?

What if the answer was she had cancer, or had a daughter in rehab, or just lost her job, or was losing her house because of a gambling addiction? She could picture the look of shock, followed by discomfort as the one asking tried to escape the conversation. No, more common to hide behind "Fine", "Okay", "Not bad" responses, both insincere and inaccurate, but allowed everyone to remain in isolation chambers and avoid real connecting; like trying to touch through a glass door, hands perfectly lined up on each side of the glass, finger to finger, palm to palm, and yet cold emptiness denying contact between the two. It looks close, but it's a swing and a miss. It leaves one empty no matter how close it looks like it came. Maybe even more so because you can see what you missed.

How was she? *Crappy? Miserable? Sad? Empty? Tired? Shall I go on?* Sophia studied Jane's eager face, decided to take pity on her sister-in-law and replied, "Okay. I think Christmas is here whether I'm ready or not. I've kept it pretty simple this year."

"Well, we are SO happy you decided to come have dinner with us." Jane's hands fluttered around as she talked, and Sophia instinctively stepped backward to protect her face from their flight path. "Marcus was quite insistent that we get you over here and not let you sit by yourself this year."

Marcus, Sophia's older brother usually went months without making any contact with Sophia. An insurance salesman who spent long hours at the office, he preferred to use his free time golfing, having drinks with friends or watching televised sports. Not having been particularly close growing up, their lives rarely intersected as adults, with the exception of perfunctory family gatherings. They had little in common other than shared ancestry. Marcus held strong opinions that bordered on bigotry, while Sophia was inclined to see people as complex and multi-dimensional, not categorizing as quickly as her brother. They were on different sides of the political divide and rarely agreed on how to solve the social and financial issues the country faced. Marcus attended church occasionally but showed little evidence of being influenced by what was discussed there.

Much of what Marcus did appeared to be for show; he liked to look good, but there was little depth to the presentation. Sophia thought of Marcus and his family as The Perfects in her head. Entering their home was like being sucked into the pages of Better Homes and Gardens; furnishings trendy in style and color, and fashionable art on the impractical tables and walls, all of which screamed "don't you dare put down that glass or your feet on the coffee table." Their children excelled in school and extra-curricular activities. Jane worked in real estate part time so she could taxi the kids to their activities and volunteer at their schools. Lexi and Drew were a stark contrast to the kids Sophia worked with, and while she applauded their success, she noted the advantages and lack of challenge they enjoyed. She wondered how either of them would handle adversity when life threw sharp edges their way.

"Sophia! Good to see you!" Marcus boomed as Jane pulled Sophia into the kitchen.

"Hey, Marcus. Good to see you too." Sophia responded. *Okay, meaningless platitudes done, now what do we talk about?*

Doubt was growing by the minute regarding her decision to endure this dinner. She really didn't like being someone's feel-good project, which is what this had felt like from the beginning.

"How about a drink?" Marcus asked, raising a bottle of wine in one hand and whiskey in the other.

"Sure, a glass of wine sounds good." Sophia welcomed the glass, knowing it would take the edge off the tension she felt and give her something to focus on. She swirled the burgundy liquid in an oversized glass before taking a sip. "How's work been?"

"Great, just great. Company has some terrific new products to offer, and people have been snatching them up. Can hardly keep up with the demand out there," Marcus answered, as he began slicing the prime rib Jane had set on the countertop.

"Marcus earned the best bonus he's ever had this year!" Jane contributed as she began putting mashed potatoes into a ceramic bowl. "It's going to pay for our next vacation with the kids."

Sophia smiled and nodded politely. "I'm sure that will be fun. It's good to know some of the businesses out there are doing well in this recession. I hope that starts to happen in other areas soon."

The economy had tanked several years before from a banking crisis, leading to widespread unemployment and foreclosures. Times had been tough, and many families were struggling. Marcus and Jane showed no evidence of being impacted by the recession. Sophia, on the other hand, had seen many co-workers laid off and units at Dalton closed, resulting in fewer beds for those in need. Good people with years of experience were forced to transfer, requiring that they move away from homes they couldn't sell in a soft real estate market, in stark contrast to her brother's world of bonuses and vacations, which turned up the volume on Sophia's unfairness meter.

"Things aren't as bad as the liberal media would have you believe," Marcus' tone and face derided. "You shouldn't believe everything you hear. Besides, most of the people who are out of work or lost their houses probably had it coming. If they'd been smarter, it would never have happened. It's a waste of your sympathy."

Sophia's hand tightened around the stem of the wine glass, as she fought the urge to throw the glass at her brother's smug face. How had they come from the same parents? How had they become so different growing up in the same house with the same rules and teaching? How did they still manage to spend time together and speak to each other?

Sophia regarded her brother and said, "That has not been my experience or what I hear from people around me. I happen to know people affected by this economy who did not earn or deserve what happened to them. I do not form my opinions based on what I hear in the news."

Jane glanced nervously between Sophia and Marcus. Conflict was something she avoided at all costs. She preferred superficial (even dishonest) peace and pleasantries to any conversation that exposed real issues but might ruffle feathers.

She would respond to direct questions with an avoidant waltz, or, when cornered, spin a plausible tale to avoid what she thought might be ugly truths or feelings. It was the greatest barrier to creating a closer friendship between her and Sophia. Sophia never knew where she stood, was uncertain how Jane really felt about anything, and had caught her in more than one lie, damaging the trust between them. In the beginning, Sophia had tried to get past what she thought was insecurity driving the dishonest avoidance. When sharing her own vulnerable feelings and thoughts, complimenting Jane's efforts and abilities, and having discussions to clear the air of misunderstanding only resulted in more self-conscious distance between them, Sophia concluded she and Jane operated from a different foundation and resigned herself to a distant but civil relationship without trust and openness.

"I think this is just about ready. Would you mind rounding up the kids?" Jane asked, discomfort raising the pitch of her voice.

"Sure," Sophia answered, grateful to leave the room for a moment. Climbing the carpeted stairway to the second floor, she breathed in and out deeply and deliberately, willing the anger out through her nostrils, as though she were a smudging stick, cleansing her ill will as she breathed. The arrogance permeating Marcus' tone rankled her. All their lives Sophia had felt looked down on by her older brother. Rather than asking her what she thought or how she saw something, he told her what she should think and do. When opinions differed, he mocked her point of view or accused her of being too soft, too sensitive, too giving.

It had been decades before Sophia felt able to stand up to him and hold her ground as he tried to format her thought process. More than once she wondered what it would feel like to be so certain of things that doubt was never a guest in one's mind. What a freeing place to be. Never trapped in the loop of indecision, never turning over every rock in one's mental yard, convinced something crucial has been forgotten or overlooked, never replaying a scene in one's head like a stuck record repeating the same two lines of a song, making you crazy until you can silence it by picking up the needle. Grimacing, Sophia imagined Marcus slept well at night, the snoring sleep of the unconcerned.

Reaching Lexi's door first, Sophia knocked, calling, "Hey, Lex, your Mom says dinner's ready."

The door opened quickly and the thirteen year old girl threw her arms out, embracing Sophia and exclaiming, "Hi! I didn't know you were here!"

She had earbuds and cords hanging like a necklace, and a cell phone in one hand. Her gray and black outfit looked like it had been caught in a glitter rainstorm. Lexi was a sweet girl full of energy and enthusiasm. She was quick to laugh and showed a talent for imitating others' vocal patterns, leading to some hysterical impersonations.

"One sec, Aunt Soph," she said. She put the cell phone up to an ear. "Gotta go, talk to you later," she blurted, and then shut the phone off without waiting for a reply. "I'll be right down."

Continuing down the hallway, Sophia knocked on a second closed door.

Christmas, and they are all in separate rooms, she mused. That's not how we used to do it. We would all be working together on a puzzle, playing a game, or watching a movie together. I wonder how typical it is these days for kids to be in their separate rooms, with their technology instead of each other?

The door opened revealing Drew, a handsome boy of fifteen. He was taller than Sophia now, thin like his mother, with an expression that suggested he was solving a difficult math problem or was about to chastise workers in the lunchroom for taking too long on break. When younger, Sophia worried he was too serious and responsible; instead of enjoying plays he attended, he tried to figure out how things worked backstage. Instead of playing games with peers, he invented ways to earn money, making and distributing business flyers to the neighbors. As he aged, he seemed to develop a sense of humor, much to Sophia's relief, and even took the occasional short-cut in getting school work done, something he would never have done when younger.

"Hi," he greeted. Drew was not overly talkative unless you got him alone and he happened to be in just the right mood, or had something stuck in his craw.

"Hi, Drew. Your mom says dinner is ready. How are you?" Sophia asked.

Drew shrugged, "Okay."

The two walked together down the stairs. As they reached the bottom, Lexi came bounding down behind them and all three entered the dining room together, taking their places at the table, covered with an elegant green and gold tablecloth, fancy china plates, and crystal glassware. There were two candles flickering, and the lights had been dimmed.

I feel like I'm in the middle of a greeting card, Sophia thought.

As she ate, Sophia's thoughts drifted to Christmas dinner with Zach, which could not have been more different from this one. Sometimes those dinners had been quiet ones alone; sometimes they gathered with friends, becoming their own misfit toy island in the ocean of holiday commotion; other times they ignored it entirely, finding an isolated beach to wander or lakeside to enjoy, cozied up to a fire. She missed those days.

Jerked from her reverie by sudden silence, Sophia found eight eyes staring at her, questioning her without words.

"What?" she asked.

Marcus laughed loudly. "Where did you go? I asked if you were still trying to save hopeless delinquents."

Sophia stiffened, pausing before answering. "If you mean do I still try to help damaged kids find a more positive path, then, yes, I do."

One of the chasms between Sophia and Marcus was their view of people, their worth, their influences, their possibilities. Marcus would dismiss a person if they showed a trait he didn't share or value, while Sophia saw people as shades of gray with moving outlines, showing countless possibilities to redraw the boundaries of who they were.

Marcus laughed dismissively again and stuffed mashed potatoes into his mouth. "Seems to me you're swimming up an impossible stream. Don't know why you bother. Those people are going to be a drain on society the rest of their lives."

Sophia took a carefully deliberate sip of wine, slowly wiped her mouth with the green cloth napkin from her lap, and regarded her brother with barely contained anger.

She replied coldly, "A lot of these kids are able to benefit from what the program offers. They're able to figure out what influenced them getting there and they learn skills to do things differently when they get out. The recidivism rate from the program is really pretty good, better than a lot of similar programs across the country. People who don't work with the program often aren't aware of that. And these kids are *damaged*, not worthless. There is something to like in almost all of them. They haven't had the perfect, entitled lives that a lot of their peers have had. They come from challenging circumstances."

Sophia looked down at her plate, pushing the food around without eating any. What little appetite she had arrived with had evaporated and she considered how soon she could make her excuses and leave.

Marcus made a derisive sound as he gulped whiskey from his glass and loaded his fork again.

Jane chirped, "Oh, I'm sure there are reasons to like them. Let's just talk about something less depressing." Looking anxiously from face to face she zeroed in on Drew. "Drew, tell Sophia about the play you're in!"

With a bored look suggesting she had just asked him to memorize the phone book, Drew sighed and started to respond, but was cut off by Lexi, who blurted, "Hey Aunt Soph, did you know I made a cushion for my cat with my new sewing machine? It's really cute! I can show you after dinner."

"Oh, that's right!" Jane exclaimed, relieved at the diversion. "Lexi did a great job on that and picked out all the fabric herself."

For the next hour Sophia listened distractedly to Jane, Lexi and Drew talk about their various activities, adding the occasional "Uh-huh", "Really?" and "That's cool" at the obligatory times, her mind elsewhere. Marcus finished his meal and flopped into the recliner in the other room, turning on the television. Although the sound of gunfire and squealing car tires jarred her nerves, Sophia was grateful Marcus was in a different room and unable to jab at her further.

As angry as she was with him, she was more angry with herself; angry that her initial response to those jabs was self-doubt and feeling small, just as she had as a child. When faced with someone disrespecting her beliefs or criticizing her (even if unjustified), her first response was to doubt her own assessment of the facts, doubt her own worth, and doubt herself. Regardless of what she had accomplished or learned, she had difficulty fending off doubt, as though it crouched at the center of a spider web of well-meaning deeds, like a secret, the fragile connections torn at the slightest breeze.

No one could break the strands more quickly or easily than Marcus. Sophia had lost track of how many times she had restrung the web. Knowing she needed to do so once again, she made her excuses, said goodbye, gave half-hearted hugs, and walked into the cold night, feeling even more chilled than when she had arrived. Marcus regarded her clients as hopeless and inferior, yet she felt like one of them, like she might have become them if things had happened differently in her life. She was the lucky one.....or was she?

FACELESS

Lights flickered color as the thudding cadence of boots echoed. Frozen fingers jammed into his pockets, shoulders hunched against the chill. Walking…walking…walking, past brightly lit homes, Christmas trees sparkling through glass and the scent of pie and bread stoking his hunger. Driveways overflowing with cars, families gathered together, reminding, taunting, clawing at the shell of his isolation. Hating holidays the most. Why was he out? He should have stayed where he was. Realizing…it didn't matter. In, out, here, there, all the same. Empty. Restless in his own skin, which followed him wherever he went. Thud, thud, thud as he walked.

Dropping his head as the car approached and turned into the driveway in front of him. Pulling his hood more tightly to muffle the sound of laughter as the occupants walked from car to home, arms piled with gifts. Stiffening at the sight of joy, unfairness welling, drenching him with rage. Why him and not one of them?

CRASH! He had thrown the rock before being aware of holding it. They would find it within window fragments when they returned to the car, unfairness shared, but there would be no sign of the figure in black, merging with the darkness.

MSU

The heavy door clanged shut as Sophia made her way down the hallway to MSU, the wasteland offering only brief hints of life through office windows; a personalized coffee mug, a framed motto cheerily reminding of something positive, a woolen sweater to soften the chill.

Rounding the corner, Sophia arrived at the isolated cells. There were eight total, four on each side of the open space measuring twenty feet across. Today there was a full house. Here to check on Quinn, transferred from the restraint bed once he had calmed enough to be safe to transport, she glanced through the windows on the upper half of the doors as she walked by, looking for his cell.

"You here to see me?" the excited voice stopped Sophia in her tracks, as a freckled face pressed against the glass in front of her. Sophia recognized Jasper, a boy of twelve relatively new to the facility. Young in age, Jasper was even younger in development. If he were a dog, he'd be an exuberant puppy, frolicking across the grass, tumbling ass-over-teakettle into some kind of trouble. She could almost see the wet nose print he was leaving on the glass as he tried to get her attention. Everything Jasper did, he did with passion, as though he were a human exclamation mark.

Sophia paused and opened the food tray door, allowing them to talk without raising their voices.

"I wasn't, because I didn't know you were here. What got you here, Jasper?" she asked.

"Oh, you know. I was being annoying," Jasper remarked, smiling broadly as though that was not only normal but completely adorable. He pressed his face against the opening in the door as if trying to push his head right through the slot. Sophia was sure when the conversation ended he would have indentations on his forehead and chin to remind him of the visit.

"How do you get your teeth so white?" Jasper quizzed enthusiastically. "Mine are yellow…see!" He pointed to his teeth as though she might not know where to look for them. "I had five cavities last time the dentist looked at them. I hate spitty letters. You know, the ones that make you spit when you say them? I hate that." Jasper continued to grin, his expression contrasting starkly with his words, making Sophia realize she had never seen him angry, only overly talkative, hyperactive, and sometimes momentarily sad.

"What did you do that was so annoying to others Jasper?" Sophia attempted to bring him back to the topic.

Jasper's grin expanded and he answered, "I went crop dusting!"

More than once Sophia had been in a room full of boys and would hear the cry, "Ahhhgg, I've been crop dusted!", and one by one, like a row of dominoes arranged for a sequential topple, shirts jerked up over noses and accusing eyes sought out the boy who passed gas and walked away.

Jasper had a reputation for seeking attention and could easily stir up a unit like he had poked a hornet's nest. Unable to adjust to feedback or correction, he continued to poke in a variety of ways until he was removed for his own safety and the well-being of the unit. Isolation created the sadness associated with being genuinely clueless about how things had gone so awry. During one of his MSU stays, Jasper had sighed dejectedly and shared, "I feel like licking a frog's butt." Sophia was reasonably sure it was a statement indicating his distress, not a genuine culinary desire, but she didn't delve into it for fear she could be wrong. Some things are best left unexplored.

"Are you are still doing that, even after getting in all kinds of trouble for it?" Sophia shook her head.

"It's just gas. It doesn't hurt anyone," was Jasper's unremorseful response. He giggled as he pushed his head more forcefully against the opening.

That has to hurt, thought Sophia as she considered his point.

"True, but it is unpleasant. Remember our discussions about how there has to be balance between what you want and enjoy and what others want and enjoy? It can't just be about what you think is fun and funny or you will keep ending up places like this. And you'll keep having difficulty making those friends you say you want." Sophia often felt these conversations were like trying to swim up a waterfall with a boy who seemed to have no control over his impulses.

Jasper's face fell and the smile disappeared. "I know," he countered, "I just can't make myself stop. And then those bees steal my life!"

Jasper had difficulty connecting that his behavior caused his loss of freedom and privileges, preferring to blame those in authority. It was one of the things Sophia worked hardest on with him…good old cause and effect, while believing he might have neurological issues that made those connections more difficult for him. He could get there, with lots of discussion, but would lose it again as soon as he moved into the next moment. It was like watching a leaf, caught in an eddy, unable to extract itself in order to move downstream.

"Well, it sounds like you and I have more work to do on that, don't we? I'll come see you when you get out of here and we'll talk more about it." Sophia stepped back as she prepared to move to Quinn's room.

"Okay, see ya!" the smile was back on Jasper's face; the momentary dark feeling was gone, like dissipating fog. "Hey, how come your eyes are cracked?"

Thanks for letting me know, buddy. Sophia made a mental note to use drops for bloodshot eyes as she closed the tray door, continuing until she found Quinn in the last room. Looking through the glass she saw him lying awake on his bed. She opened the tray, bracing against the smell of a locker room with overflowing toilets, and waited for him to approach the door. Quinn was a boy of slight build, skinny really, and bony facial structure, suggesting the possibility of native blood somewhere in his lineage. His hair was dark and his eyes darker. He carried scars on both hands and the side of his face from previous fights, as well as multiple scars inside. Quinn nodded silently in greeting.

"How are you doing?" Sophia began.

Quinn shrugged and looked away, feeling awkward about his previous meltdown; he had a great deal of pride, and nothing felt weaker than being strapped against his will to a restraint bed.

"Do you have a book in here?" she tried to find something to discuss that was less emotionally charged.

"No," Quinn answered quietly.

"Deck of cards?"

"No," he said, still not looking in her direction.

"Do you know when you might have one or the other?"

Sophia tried to keep her anger in check, knowing how important it was for Quinn to have something to occupy his mind and hands when he was isolated.

"Told me I could have something after dinner if I don't cause trouble," was the response.

Well, that was something, Sophia thought. She wouldn't have to go rattle cages and risk making the staff angry if he'd be getting something soon.

"I'm glad," Sophia said supportively, "I know that will help."

Quinn rotated his head slowly and gazed at her, lips parting into a slight smile. "I have a pet beetle."

"Pet beetle?" Sophia's face shifted into a quizzical frown.

Picking up a paper cup covered with a piece of paper, Quinn showed Sophia the contents. Inside was a black and red beetle, the kind Sophia referred to as lady bug. "I call it Dot." As he talked, Quinn regarded the bug with curiosity and concern.

Quinn liked animals, and he and Sophia had talked about his pursuing a course of study allowing work with animals when he was released…veterinarian, vet's assistant, dog grooming or kennel. There was a cat cared for at Dalton, but it lived on a unit that housed those more stable and ready for release, not where Quinn was assigned. Sophia wished she could bring a cat or dog or even a bird in for Quinn to care for. She knew the healing effect animals offered those who were sick, lonely, or elderly. There was something about caring for another being, a more vulnerable being; not only was it calming, but it socialized and humanized people, giving a sense of purpose and value.

"What do they eat? And how long can they go without food?" Sophia peered at the bug.

"They eat aphids. Sometimes they eat other insects that hang out on plants. I don't know how long without food. Used to see them in the foster home I had in the country."

They both stared at the bug. Quinn had found his own diversion, without any help from staff, something to focus on, to think about, and to care for in his rudimentary way.

"Horticulture."

"Horticulture?" Sophia replied, puzzled.

"That's my word of the day. It means the art or practice of gardening," Quinn grinned knowingly.

Quinn had set the goal of learning a new word each day about three months before. He had come up with some good ones, unknown even to Sophia, his quest linked only to the self-satisfaction of expanding his vocabulary. Passing Quinn in a hallway or seeing him on a unit, Sophia would ask for the new word and then continue on, impressed at the depth that hid beneath the damaged exteriors she saw around her.

"That seems particularly pertinent given your new pet! So, Quinn, do you know how long you will be in MSU?" Sophia directed the conversation back to her purpose, now that Quinn seemed calmer.

"They told me if I don't cause more trouble I can maybe go back tomorrow after dinner."

"Do you think you can be here and not have more problems?"

"Dunno. Depends on who's working and if they run their mouth. They mess with me I ain't gonna just take it lying down. I don't want trouble, but they need to stay off my ass."

Of all the young men Sophia worked with, Quinn was the most easily set off and tended to react the most intensely when fired up. His wiry frame becoming all elbows and knees, it could take four or five adults to subdue and control him. Adrenaline was the equalizer when it came to physical ability, and his went into overdrive when he took offense or felt threatened. Light fixtures, tables, windows, and even metal pipes exposed in bathrooms were destroyed during his rage-filled attacks. When limbs were pinned, he funneled the adrenaline through his mouth spewing invectives at those around him. Reprehensible comments occurred when he was feeling mistreated, inciting staff and leading to escalations as a wretched game of get-even occurred. Even the most patient adults could find themselves reacting to the effortless insults Quinn could generate.

"Is that what happened before, Quinn? Did you react to what someone said?"

"Called me a punk-ass kid and told me I was never gonna get out of here, or if I did I'd just come back. Told me no wonder my parents beat me." Quinn clenched the hand not holding the bug cup. "Told him he was a sorry piece of crap and it was no wonder his wife looked for it everywhere but him. He got pissed and told me to hand over my book. Told him to come take it from me. Wimp had to call three other guys to come help him. Bloodied his freaking nose when they opened the door. Worth it too. Got no business taking my book. He thinks he can say anything he wants, and then he takes away my book when I say something back. It's bullshit!"

Sophia agreed but couldn't say so out loud. She had heard some of the comments made by staff and knew it was possible that this exchange occurred exactly as described. Even so, when she raised the issue with management she felt it had fallen on deaf ears. Tough job and few people lined up to do it seemed to create a culture of acceptance and ignoring. The comments by adults were frequently unheard by other staff, so it became an issue of one word against the other with youth being at a distinct disadvantage.

"I know how much you hate losing your books, Quinn. And I know you really react to situations you think are unfair." Sophia tried to keep the discussion focused where she could offer support without making it appear she was being critical of the staff involved. "My concern is to help you handle those unfair situations in ways that don't hurt you further. Do you remember us talking about the moth to a flame idea?"

Sophia tried to help the boys understand how their behavior drew them into outcomes that hurt them more; like a moth is drawn to light, and in seeking that light it is singed by the flame attracting it, the youth were drawn to things that were dangerous or harmful and ended up injured. Empathy for others did not influence their choices as much as self-preservation instincts. She had to convince them they were moths about to be singed if they were to think about their actions and what they wanted as outcomes.

Quinn sighed and looked away. "Yeah. Sometimes I just don't care. Sometimes I get so pissed off that I want to hurt them back. I want them to feel what I feel and I don't think about any of that." Quinn put the cup onto the floor and turned away, hitting one fist into the palm of his other hand.

"Who or what are you mad at?" she asked gently.

"Myself!" Quinn spat. "I know we talk about this stuff and it makes sense and I try to remember it, but when something happens I forget it all! Then I'm stuck here again and I don't think I'll ever get out!" Quinn turned back towards her and Sophia could see the frustration in his eyes.

"You can do this, Quinn. It just takes time and practice and doing it just a little better and sooner each time you try. If you can remember it after you get through being mad and think backwards in time about things you could have done differently, then eventually you will be able to choose differently at the time it is happening. You are great at processing it after it happens and coming up with different ideas. The more you practice that, the more those options will stay stuck in your head and the easier it will be to think of them when you need them. And remember, doing it that way is in a direct tug-of-war with your programmed instincts right now. It's no wonder you don't always remember or still lose that battle. You've gotten good at making them feel what you feel, but that lands you in the flame. You need to protect yourself from that."

Quinn nodded silently, pondering what she had said.

"So what can you do today, tonight and tomorrow to keep out of the flame, no matter who is working or what they might say?"

Quinn thought for a moment, picking the cup back up. "I'm gonna think about this beetle. I'm gonna ask Mandy if she'll get me some grass for it. I'm gonna think about the book I was reading and the characters in it, and I'm gonna write the next chapter in my head until I can get it back. I'm gonna try to put some of them new words I've been learnin' into it. And I'm gonna try not to listen to any crap the bees or them over there might say." Quinn nodded in the direction of the other isolation cells.

"Sounds like a good plan. I hope you can carry it out and get back to your unit tomorrow," encouraged Sophia. She knew Quinn could come up with a plan, the question was whether or not he could adhere to it once things started happening around him. There were so many good qualities in him that were held captive by his emotional reactions. She could only cross her fingers and hope that the individuals working the night shift were not those who delighted in tormenting him or lacked the patience required for his occasional neediness. Mandy was one who seemed to have a soft spot for him, and if she was working, she would bring him the grass he wanted. Little things like that helped him feel seen as a human being, not just a worthless thug.

"I'll check with you tomorrow. I'm going to hope for a peaceful night for you in here."

"Okay. Catch you later, Miss Sophia," Quinn gave her a crooked smile. "Thanks for coming to see me."

Sophia closed the open hatch and moved towards the exit. Jasper peered through his window and flashed a wide grin, waving his hand high above his head.

"Bye, Miss Sophia!" he yelled from behind the door.

"Good-bye again, Jasper!" Sophia shook her head as she pulled open the heavy door, letting herself out. She imagined him glued to that window all night, greeting each passerby with a question or a comment. He was really pretty adorable in an exasperating kind of way

GROUP

"You're crowding my world!"

Sophia's head snapped up in response to the shout, looking where it came from and saw Jasper leaning away from Quinn, but being impeded by the table on his other side. Quinn gave Jasper a quizzical grin and shifted his chair a few inches in the opposite direction.

"Chill, little man," Quinn soothed. "How much room one mini-dude need?"

"Is everything okay over there?" Sophia asked.

Quinn looked at Jasper, his expression inviting him to respond to the question.

"It's all good, Miss Sophia," Jasper beamed, rearranging himself in his seat until he was comfortable, feet intruding into the center of the five circled chairs.

Seated along with Quinn and Jasper were Sophia, D'Vrae and Aiden. Once a week, the five met to discuss issues and work on skills designed to improve their self-control and help them transition back to the community. To Sophia, it often felt like wrestling jello and she never knew what group would bring out. She had just arrived with Aiden after a delay in the showers when the shout had occurred.

"So what caused the delay, Aiden?" Sophia asked.

D'Vrae snorted. "He crazy! He fraidy cat!"

Aiden regarded D'Vrae with a look of disdain, his head tilted backward. "Caring about where I am walking in the showers makes me neither afraid nor crazy, you insipid imbecile," Aiden snapped back.

Sophia held up one hand, reminding, "Whoa, remember how we talk to each other here. Everyone needs to be respectful, even if they see things differently or disagree on something. What do you mean about caring where you walk in the showers, Aiden?"

Aiden sat straighter in the chair, chin defiantly extended. "One must remember who I share living space with in here. I see how these people live and I know how they smell. Most of them are filthy pigs. I'm not going to walk where they just dripped!"

There was a unified chorus of laughter from D'Vrae, Jasper and Quinn. "You serious, man?" derided D'Vrae as Jasper doubled over, bouncing in his seat. Quinn shook his head at this unexpected news, an amused look on his face.

"Who knows what vermin are hanging out on these hairy beasts? Who knows what I'm being exposed to every day? And the state soap is hardly adequate even if I can be assured they use it!" Aiden sneered in his defense.

Sophia attempted to silence the laughter again with an "I mean business" look and a slow wave of her hand. She managed to stifle their giggles but could not wipe the grins from their faces, nor clear the sparkle from their eyes. "Jasper, I need you to sit quietly over there," she admonished as he continued to rock back and forth grinning widely.

"I can't, Miss Sophia…I sit LOUD!" he giggled, checking to see if the others were equally amused. "Okay, I'll try," quickly followed as he saw a "you are about to be asked to leave group" expression on Sophia's face. He wrapped himself in both arms, trying to physically restrain his exuberance.

"How exactly do you try to avoid that, Aiden?" Sophia asked as she turned her attention back to him, preparing for whatever amusing or illogical response he might offer.

"I watch where they've been, and count to one hundred while the water is rinsing the spot clean. If someone comes through that spot, I have to start all over. That's why I was late. I had to count to one hundred three times before I could come out of the shower because those morons kept walking through dripping all over and…" Aiden stopped as the others howled again. He jumped up, his fists clenched.

Sophia, who was sitting next to Aiden, rose in response, putting a hand on his arm. "Aiden, stop and think," she cautioned. She scanned the faces of those seated and said, "You are all being unkind and disrespectful, not just to Aiden, but to me."

D'Vrae, Jasper, and Quinn made a valiant effort to contain their hysteria. They all liked Sophia, and while they had less concern for Aiden, they did not want to disappoint her or cause her to stop group. They enjoyed coming, to break the monotony of the unit routine and because they learned helpful things.

D'Vrae spoke for the trio, "My bad, Miss Sophia, but tha' scandalous! Who think like tha'?"

Sophia explained the unique thinking common to someone on the autism spectrum accompanied by a touch of obsessive-compulsive disorder, equating it to a sneeze or cough, something your body felt compelled to do and was impossible to hold back at times, a mental cough that might occur over and over again. It was difficult for someone who had never experienced it to really understand the power it had over thinking and behavior. As she explained, and Aiden sulked, the other three appeared to relax and get past their uncontrolled amusement. Uncertain she had actually accomplished true understanding; Sophia was relieved to see she had at least gotten them to discontinue their mocking. Her gaze rested on Jasper as she realized he was digging fiercely in one ear.

"Jasper?" she quizzed.

Jasper extracted his finger, regarding it soberly. "Thought I had an ear booger," he offered as he wiped his finger across his jeans, drawing a disgusted look from Quinn, who likely would have put more distance between them, had there been room to do so.

"Okay, so shall we move on?" Sophia asked, determining the best response was no response. "I think we were going to have D'Vrae share his timeline today. Are you ready for that, D'Vrae?"

D'Vrae tipped his head backward in assent. He had parted his hair in the middle and tied each side in bands, creating large lollipops sprouting from his head. D'Vrae's assignment was to generate a sequence of important events in his life and how he had been affected by them, a task each of them would eventually complete and discuss.

D'Vrae's account began with his birth to a woman with a drug addiction which she fed through prostitution. Having no education or skills, his father joined a gang when he was 16 and became part of the underground economy by dealing drugs and stealing cars. D'Vrae saw his father rarely, between prison terms or when he avoided streets that had become too hot. When he was three years old, his mother died from an overdose and he and his younger sister spent the next several years with a variety of aunts until placed in the care of their maternal grandmother. D'Vrae described his "Gram" as a strong woman who would "wup my backside when she mad at me" but who also "show me love" in a world where love was scarce. Gram fed, clothed, and tried to guide her grandchildren, but struggled to get compliance from young D'Vrae. "I's a man now, I say wha' I do," was his justification for running the streets against her wishes.

D'Vrae hung out at the parks, shopping malls, and neighborhood street corners with his "homies", was stopped by police and asked to produce identification if he was out after dark, and had to have eyes in the back of his head in public places, always on guard against rival gangs. He had uncles who were in gangs, and some who had gotten out. He was thrown out of multiple schools due to his tendency to speak with his fists and to swear at teachers trying to redirect him. Multiple friends and family members had died from drug overdoses or gang violence, and he had been locked up for fights, stealing, and being in possession of a gun.

Listening, Sophia was struck by how dissimilar their two lives had been; she wondered if he had any idea how atypical his life had been, how twisted his sense of normal had become, how cheated he was by circumstances beyond his control? While she couldn't imagine living in a state of constant alertness and lack of safety, she was certain that D'Vrae could not imagine living the relative peace and calm that she had.

D'Vrae paused, having finished his narrative, looking at her expectantly.

"Excellent job, D'Vrae" Sophia encouraged. "I can see you put a lot of work into that. Let's focus for a minute on the losses in your life. Which of those do you think was the hardest, or had the biggest impact on you?"

D'Vrae paused, looking down at his notes. He raised his head, swiveling slowly, assessing the faces of each group member around him. Sophia knew she was asking a lot from him. He disliked giving out personal information or talking about feelings, and answering this question was going to require both. A year ago she could not have asked it of him, but he had come a long way, and she was hoping it was far enough to tackle this.

D'Vrae's appraisal of facial expressions appeared to give him what he needed to continue. "Tha' easy. Kiah's."

"Tell us about Kiah and what happened to her," Sophia prompted.

D'Vrae took a deep breath, letting it back out slowly. He focused intently on Sophia as he responded.

"She my frien' fo' a minute. Grow up in de hood. I know her Mama and brothers, we all friends. We hang at de park and go to de mall. We party and barb'que. She braid my hair fo' me. She smar' and she gonna go to college someday. She tigh'."

"And what happened to her, D'Vrae?" Sophia gently probed.

"Candy-ass kill 'er. Cap her right in de head." D'Vrae's jaw clenched as he spoke, veins in his temples bulging.

"Where was she?" asked Sophia.

"We at de mall, just chillin'. I checkin' some bling in sto' winda, thinkin' how good it look on me and next I know I hears a pop, pop. I duck down and look and see she on de groun'. See tha' piece of shi' runnin' 'roun' de corner. My homie come over and we try to hep her. Pick her up some but blood be squirtin', jus' like in de movies. Put her back down and star' hollerin' fo' someone call de amblance, but they all jus' runnin' away." D'Vrae's head had slowly lowered, until he was looking down at his own lap, eyes hidden. "They jus' runnin' away. She their homie, too," he whispered.

Jasper, Quinn and Aiden remained motionless, enthralled. Sophia quietly cued, "What did you do next?"

"Hear sirens and see cops runnin' with they guns out, so I ran." D'Vrae's voice was barely audible.

"You WHAT?!" shouted Aiden. "You RAN? Your friend bleeding to death and you RAN?!" Aiden clearly incensed at a choice he would have been loath to make.

D'Vrae leapt up, taking a step towards Aiden. Aiden nervously pushed his glasses higher up his nose and leaned backward, bracing himself for an assault. Sophia rose just as quickly and stepped between the two. She raised an open hand near D'Vrae's chest as they locked eyes. She knew this was difficult for him, knew it had killed him to leave Kiah behind, dying. Aiden's black and white thinking about the "right" thing to do was incapable of seeing the massive gray in that moment for D'Vrae.

"It's okay, D'Vrae. You can handle this. I need you to sit back down and take a minute to get yourself back under control," Sophia guided. D'Vrae stood stiffly erect, jaw muscles clenched and grinding as he battled with his desire to break Aiden in half, the memory surging recklessly through him.

Jasper watched from the side, frozen, like a puppy knowing it has displeased its master and is afraid to move until clearly forgiven. Quinn regarded Aiden with a mixture of disgust and pity. Quinn understood D'Vrae's dilemma more than the others, given his own gray life moments. Violence and pain had taught him there were few absolutes in the world, that sometimes it was a choice between bad and worse.

D'Vrae backed up and took his seat, scowling at Aiden. "You don' know shi', so shu' the fuck up!"

"I know I wouldn't leave my friend to bleed to death!" was Aiden's unwavering retort.

Sophia's sharp tone stopped D'Vrae mid-rise as he again sprang upward, "AIDEN! I need you to stop talking for right now!" Her expression matched her tone as she turned to face him. "Your comments are not helpful, and I will have to ask you to leave group if you continue to make them. Right now I want you to focus on listening and not speaking, no matter how important or relevant you think what you have to say is!"

"Muzzle tha' dog, or I give him my ones," D'Vrae spat as he reluctantly sank back into the seat, his expression conveying a willingness to follow words with action as he glowered at Aiden.

Knowing that giving ones meant a one on one fight, Aiden sat straighter in his seat, crossing his thin legs, causing one pant leg to ride up slightly, exposing a white shin covered with scabs which he began to rub. Among his compulsions was the need to pick at any imperfection he found, which caused unsightly scabs and scars and led to infection at times; his need to engage in such unclean behavior, even as he fixated over the germs of others, proved there was nothing rational about obsessions. While Aiden stopped talking, the nature of his offense was anything but clear to him; he had only pointed out the obvious to everyone, and weren't people interested in the truth no matter how stupid or ugly? He shook his head silently. As much as he liked Sophia, he begrudged that she was just too easy on some of these inane jerks!

Sophia appraised D'Vrae to see if he could continue. In contrast to her external "I'm in control" demeanor, her heart was pounding and she was developing a headache from the stress of sitting on this powder-keg. Discussing difficult things was a challenge under the best of circumstances with people who liked and trusted each other, it was even more trying when those involved were limited in their skills and didn't like or respect each other.

"Okay group," she began, "I am going to speak with D'Vrae for a few minutes and I want all of you to watch and listen until I ask for your input." She looked around for agreement, seeing each head nod in response, some more agreeably than others.

Sophia gently prompted D'Vrae to continue by asking, "Why did you run when you did, D'Vrae?"

"You see cops with guns in my hood, you run. Don' ax no question, you jus' run. They like as not gonna cap you as look at you." D'Vrae snorted, still visibly upset by the previous interaction with Aiden. "I know they gonna blame me and it ain' my fault. They not gonna help Kiah neither. They don' care."

"So where did you go?"

"I run 'round de co'ner and throw up. Then I keep runnin' till I get home." D'Vrae dropped his head, staring down at his lap. "I be weak, man. Tha' jus' WEAK!"

A glisten appeared at the corner of his eye as he spoke, a crack in the tough exterior he struggled to maintain. He smacked one fist forcefully into his other hand. He had been unable to forgive himself for that moment, and it continued to haunt him.

"It's not weak to care about your friend, D'Vrae. It's not weak to feel helpless in helping her at an overwhelming moment. You followed your instincts, and your instincts told you that you needed to get away," Sophia persuaded gently.

Jasper and Quinn regarded D'Vrae with a mixture of sympathy and concern, while Aiden continued looking skeptical but abided by the order to keep silent. He rubbed his exposed shin absentmindedly.

"I maybe coulda hep her…call a amblance or sumthin'."

"What do you think might have happened if you had chosen that?"

"Cops probly throw me on de groun' and frisk me and make me sit and not move. They al'ays do that when they come bus' up a beef," came the angry answer.

"So even if you had stayed, you might not have been able to do anything more to help Kiah. You might have felt just as helpless, and just as frustrated, and the result might have been exactly the same," countered Sophia. "Do you know who fired the shots?"

D'Vrae raised his head, meeting her eyes. Street code was you didn't give up information like that. You didn't name names, you just took it to the homies and retaliation was handled in-house. "Can' say."

Can't or won't? Sophia asked herself silently. Chances are won't, but she wasn't going to push that with him. "Okay, do you know who their target was?"

"Not Kiah. She not hurt anyone. She not even in a gang." D'Vrae squirmed in his seat as he answered.

The question hovered in the air as each of them considered the possibility that D'Vrae was the intended target. Bad enough that he had seen his friend killed, worse that he felt he needed to run to protect himself rather than stay and help her, and worse still that he may have been the reason for the shots in the first place. How does one live with that, Sophia mused? Where does one put that kind of experience as they try to go on with their lives? How many sweaty, thrashing nightmares were created by that one event? How do they survive streets that become a war zone, molded into something twisted and misshapen, not unlike coastal trees battered by wind and driving rain, creating limbs gnarled and barren on one side and tenacious tufts of defiant leaves on the other as it leans away from the onslaught?

Sophia tried again, "Do you think they were after you?"

"Don' know," D'Vrae responded, shaking his head slowly. "I wasn' only one there tha' day. Goin' ta find out though and cap they ass. They not gonna come into MY hood and take out my homies withou' hearin' from me!"

Revenge, hurting back, maybe harder and deeper than what you received, a never-ending cycle of violence leaving a trail of blood, damaged psyches, and broken or dead bodies. Children with guns…puppies with pistols…powerlessness vanquished by cold metal in their hand, loss only partially eased by the momentary thrill of seeing the enemy fall in the street. How do you ask them to give that up when what you have to offer instead seems a poor substitute?

Sophia sighed as she regarded D'Vrae, who had defiantly thrown his head and shoulders back, as though preparing to get up and follow through with his threat at that very moment. "What do you think Kiah would think of that? Would she want that to be your response? Would she want you to risk getting yourself killed to avenge her death?" Sophia queried.

D'Vrae considered for a moment before answering. He looked genuinely torn as he responded, "Prob'ly not. She din' like guns and she din' wan' me on de streets. But a man gotta do what a man gotta do. Ain' gonna let it go. Ain' gonna look weak. Couldn' hold my head up no mo' if I did."

Sophia turned to the others at this point and said, "OK group, now it's your turn to help D'Vrae see all the possible options he has in how he responds to this very difficult loss. But I only want you to speak if you have something *kind* and *productive* to offer…there will be no second-guessing or criticism here or you'll be excused from group." She scanned each of them in turn with an "I mean it" look that lingered on Aiden.

Quinn cleared his throat and turned in D'Vrae's direction. "I'd want to make them pay for what they did too. But if she didn't believe in that kind of thing, it seems like it would be killing her twice if you got yourself hurt or in trouble by doing something to get even. Seems like it pays more respect to her if you did something she would like you to do instead of something you know she wouldn't like." Quinn made brief eye contact and then looked back into his lap.

"Yeah!" Jasper piped in enthusiastically, "You might feel better at first, but then I think you'd be sad about your friend again and maybe be guilty about what you did." He grinned at Quinn, looking for validation that Quinn approved of his effort.

Jasper would leap-frog onto whatever idea-lily-pad someone else offered, having more difficulty coming up with something novel on his own. It was one reason the older youth used him as a torpedo; manipulating him into doing their bidding, sending him out to cause damage or create problems with others. Jasper was so desperate for approval he would do just about anything he was asked to do, suffering the consequences willingly, believing it meant he was liked.

Quinn continued to focus on his lap, ignoring Jasper. Quinn had no use for torpedoes; he did his own work when he thought he needed to, including working hard at relying on no one for anything.

D'Vrae shifted in his chair, clearly uncomfortable with the emotional tug-of-war he felt in wanting revenge when he knew it dishonored his friend. This angst was the only portal Sophia had discovered to the tenderness hiding beneath the psychological calluses rubbed by street programming and mistreatment. Create discomfort, encourage gray thinking, challenge assumptions and automatic reactions, dig, dig, dig, and maybe, just maybe, the soil would open up and a new thought, realization, or feeling would find its way into the light.

"I don't see the logic in killing someone for killing her," added Aiden, staring directly at D'Vrae as he spoke. "What does that help? It won't bring her back to life and it leads to more death, maybe even your own." He slid his glasses up with a finger from one hand while scratching his leg more intensely with the other. "Besides, how can you be sure you would even have the right person? It's not like you've done an investigation nor have any facts to go on. That's what we have police officers for."

D'Vrae scowled at Aiden, "I don' rely on cops to take care of my bizness. They don' care nothin' 'bout wha' goes on in de hood 'cept if it happen to whiteys. You pro'ly never had to worry about tha' where you come from. You call cops and they come runnin' to save you sorry ass, and wipe you runny nose."

D'Vrae's distrust of the white community, and especially the police, led him to seek his peers first if there was an issue to resolve.

Sophia, wanting to deflect another confrontation between D'Vrae and Aiden, and needing to wrap things up, interjected, "Okay guys, we need to end this for today. D'Vrae, I want you to think about what you shared today and what the other guys had to say, and come back next time with at least three things you could do to honor Kiah that don't involve violence or getting even with whoever you think may have been responsible. I hope you all have a good, non-eventful evening, and I'll see you tomorrow."

Jasper burped loudly. Grinning as he stood to leave, he said, "Whoa, that food came all the way up to my voice! Guess I ate too much lunch!"

Sophia shook her head as she watched the guard lead them all out of the conference room. Feeling she had dodged a bullet herself, she slumped in the chair with fatigue. The work with these boys was so intangible she wondered if what she did made any difference at all. It was easy to see her effort as wasted when she watched repeated mistakes, clients being released only to return a few months later. She constantly had to remind herself of the story of throwing back beached starfish. She wanted to give them all a chance, but knew that helping even one made the effort worthwhile. All she could do was try to get them back into the water. The rest was up to them and fate.

GHOSTS

In weaving, there are two sets of threads which create the pattern seen in finished cloth. They are the warp and weft, one strung vertically while the other travels horizontally between the vertical threads. The beginning threads and how one interlaces them determine the ultimate pattern. Sophia had dabbled with it, finding the finished product did not always match the vision she held in her imagination before she began. Initially annoyed, she grew to value the discovery process, watching the fabric self-create with minimal help from her. She considered herself a fabric of interwoven threads, her mother's warp and her father's weft creating a unique blending of each that shared this color or that shape, this texture or that design, yet was clearly different from both. Human cloth with personality fibers, hues infused through life experiences, and occasional rips and stains from trauma. Life the ultimate weaver, the completed result remaining a mystery until the end arrived.

Looking into the mirror, Sophia searched her features for what appeared more like her father or her mother in what looked back at her. She believed she more closely resembled her mother, but had been chagrined when rarely seen relatives could recognize her due to the likeness to her father. She hoped the similarity ended at the epidermis, as it appalled her to think it might run any deeper. Navigating the complex relationship with her father had been like walking through an emotional minefield. Explosion after explosion had blown so many parts off the relationship there was nothing recognizable left but a spongy mass of raw nerves and charred intentions. Eventually choosing to leave the minefield, she had had little contact with him until her brother called to tell her he was dying, his call shifting her focus from her clients' issues to her own.

Dying. How did she feel about that? Initially, perhaps a dispassionate mild interest, something akin to noting a spring rainstorm has suddenly stopped. Years of burying all signs of connection kept her from fully processing the news initially; she had to search for a reason to care. When an artichoke leaf is pulled through teeth, we experience emptiness until the last moment when a small burst of taste awakens the mouth. There's nothing but dry, rough blandness until that final surprising second when you discover something is there after all. Pulling through the rough memories in her mind, she recognized there was something hiding there after all, that the weft in her fabric had torn loose and become frayed.

"Are you coming?" Marcus had asked.

"I'm not sure why I would."

"You aren't going to get another chance, that's why. Why can't you just forget the past? He's dying, Sophia!" had been the exasperated reply. Marcus had never understood how Sophia could just turn her back on their father. Despite his own history of ugly interactions, Marcus appeared to have shrugged them off, deflecting penetration, an insignificant flesh wound to rinse and ignore as it scabbed over and morphed into a pale scar. Sophia always wondered where all his hurt got buried—in the nooks and crannies of his pursuit of things? Under the stack of money he talked about earning and spending? Embedded in the know-it-all bravado used to bludgeon those who were meeker? Was this the bling that distracted from the festering sores?

"I'll think about it," Sophia had offered.

And she had thought about it. *If I go will he think it means I forgive him? What new things might he say or do to further hurt me? Do I want to give him that satisfaction? Will my absence be the final statement of how I feel about who he has been and what he has done? Will I be sorry if I don't go? Is this not a false gesture to a failed relationship?*

In the end, she had decided to make an appearance, despite the breath-stopping anxiety it created in her. She had once told him she was afraid of him. He responded with the ironic inconsistency of reassuring her he would do everything in his power to change that, and to remind her that his savage intelligence could destroy anyone. No one was more surprised than he when Sophia pointed this dichotomy out to him. Russ was perpetually confused by his inability to connect dots despite a brilliant mind, a mind more suited to memorizing notable passages and pontificating philosophical concepts than observing and understanding the simplest of social proprieties. That interaction had been their last, followed by years of distance and silence, until now.

Sophia turned so she could see the back side of her outfit. The black pants selected provided side pockets, knowing she often did not know what to do with her hands, giving them a place of refuge, like ground squirrels hiding in the dark. A red cardigan sweater over a black turtleneck and large red earrings jutting boldly through the curls of her hair completed the ensemble. Red was the power color she wore to combat vulnerable feelings. Peeved that she felt the need to "power up", she still complied with the urge, wanting every advantage when it came to sparring with her father.

She made the drive to the farm slowly, in no particular hurry to arrive, unaware of her surroundings as she worked to mentally prepare for the sight and sound of him. Startled out of her numbed autopilot, Sophia barely recognized the house in front of her and wondered how long his health might have been failing; causing a disregard for what once had been sacred. He had always taken great pride in tending his five acre parcel on the edge of town. Boasting frequently of the bounty his garden produced, he shared it with neighbors and colleagues, entering some of it in the local county fair. He toiled by day, weeding, pruning, mowing, raking, building and hoeing. By night he gazed from the porch, whiskey in hand, rocking in the wicker chair, satisfaction occasionally darkened by the overcast shadow of something else—something inscrutable from deep inside.

Now, the rock wall built by hand was crumbling, nearby hedges were unruly and overgrown. Blackberry vines snaked their way through rhododendron plants, obstructing walkways, while tree boughs threatened from above. The stones paving the way to the front door were cracked and slick with moss. Sophia shuddered making her way down the path to the doorway, reminded of the sinister look deliberately given to haunted houses. *Seems fitting, a haunted house for a haunted man.* Knocking on the door, she realized she was holding her breath and made a point to exhale slowly, trying to calm her over-amped nervous system.

The door opened, revealing Marcus, hair somewhat disheveled above his navy polo shirt and jeans. Marcus' tendency to show stress by running his hands through his hair, and even twirling it with his fingers, resulted in hair that looked like it was combed with an egg-beater. Often the only outward sign of his inner feelings, he appeared oblivious to it.

"Ah, Sophia, it's good you are here. He's not doing very well," he greeted, backing away from the door to let her in.

As she stepped inside, the room closed over her like a slow drowning. Stacks of newspapers, books, and magazines covered all horizontal surfaces. Thoughts scribbled on yellow notepaper littered the room, as though a gust of air had given them flight before crash-landing. Dust bunnies lapped at dried spills of food and drink, while coats languished on chair backs and slippers interrupted the floor dust. The house had always been dim from wood paneled walls and few windows, but today it had the added layer of nefarious memories to darken it further. Sophia had to fight the impulse to open the windows and find a mop.

"It looks like a stroke," Marcus continued. "He's had cirrhosis for a while and has been told he doesn't have long, but I found him in bed not able to move one side. The home health nurse and hospice have been out to check on him, and he's adamant he doesn't want to go to the hospital. His medical directive states that he doesn't want to have treatment to keep him alive if he is unable to function on his own. He doesn't look very good and is in and out of awareness, but he can still talk and seems to know who I am. He asked if you were coming." Marcus' hands fluffed through his already tufted hair as he paced back and forth before her.

Again, Sophia realized she was holding her breath. Angry with herself, she willed the air in and out of her lungs, reminding herself she did not need to be afraid of him anymore. She nodded at Marcus wordlessly and turned, passing through the kitchen and entering the poorly lit bedroom on the other side. The smell of imminent death, both sweet and acerbic, with a faint overlay of warm urine, engulfed her. The lump under the comforter moved, drawing her attention and she forced herself to walk closer to it, trying to make out the shape hidden in bedcovers. As her eyes adjusted to the dim light she began to recognize her father's features, or what remained of them.

Once a tall man with a massive build, imposing presence, and piercing eyes, her father now lay gaunt, yellowed, and dull, his vital essence removed, only the chaff remaining. The hand he could move appeared to tremble slightly as it rested on his chest. As a child Sophia had imagined seeing ghosts and monsters in the dark. In daylight, it was clear those monsters were nothing more than shadows created by the evening moon and dancing tree branches. But somehow each night, what was clear by day became smeary and unreliable, recreating fear as her imagination conjured up ever more frightening possibilities. Standing there, Sophia felt as though she was watching the rising sun bring the monster into focus as a pathetic old man.

"Who's there?" His voice was weak and hoarse, but still startling to her.

"Sophia," came the simple response.

"My Sophia?" his tone suggesting both surprise and wonder.

Yes. No. Sometimes. Maybe. Not anymore. Multiple possibilities simultaneously held up their hands, as truth and empathy duked it out. Empathy won as she responded, "Yes."

"Sophia, I'm glad you came. How are you?" he ended his question with a dry cough.

"I'm good. Looks like you aren't doing so well," Sophia answered awkwardly. How do you chat with someone after so many years of not speaking? What do you say to a person on the brink of dying?

"I'm preparing to die," came the matter-of-fact reply.

Russ raised his trembling hand, inviting Sophia to take it with her own, which she did. Flesh and emotion reacted strongly to the sensation of skin on skin with this ghost from her past, engulfing Sophia in a wave of revulsion and fear; not because he was dying or his physical appearance, but because it pierced the self-protective walls she had built psychologically and geographically over the years to shield her from remembering, from feeling. She stifled the urge to jerk away, feeling grateful his grasp was so weak it was easy to pull away gradually after a moment, pretending she needed that hand to scratch an itch on her opposing shoulder.

"Are you sure you don't want to go to the hospital? Or shall we call a doctor to come here," she offered.

"No," he responded resolutely, "No doctors. No hospitals. I'm ready to go."

"Have you been eating?" The answer was obvious, but wasn't this the kind of thing one asked in a situation like this?

"Not hungry--unless you can make me a blueberry pie!" Blueberry pie was one of his favorites, even though he had never won the county pie-making contest with his version. Unfortunately, blueberries were not currently in season, and pie-making was a skill he had hoarded rather than sharing it through the genetic chain.

"Out of luck there, I'm afraid. I bake cookies, not pies. You sure you don't want some soup or something light?" she tried again.

"No, tired now." He had closed his eyes without warning and seemed to drift off almost immediately.

Sophia regarded him for several minutes as he slept, struck by how much he had changed on the outside, wondering if a similar change had occurred on the inside. It had been impossible to tell in their brief exchange. She backed away from the bed and returned to the kitchen. She was in need of something to drink, her mouth dry from tension. Opening the refrigerator, she found only beer. Finding a glass from the cupboard she drew water from the tap and went to find Marcus in the living room.

"Yes, Jane, that's right. It's in the bottom drawer of the filing cabinet and clearly marked. Bring it with you when you come back." Marcus nodded in Sophia's direction as he talked with his wife on his cell. "Okay, I'll see you then," looking up as he clicked off the call. "Jane's bringing our copy of his medical directive and will over later. I figure we should talk about what it says."

"So we're going to jump right to that? He's not dead yet." While there was no love lost between Sophia and her father, she still reacted to what seemed a speedy jump into predatory behavior by her brother.

"It's only a matter of time, according to the hospice people." Shrugging as he spoke, Marcus waved his hand in a dismissive gesture. "He's showing all the signs considered classic for being near the end of life. He named me executor of his will, and I see no reason to wait to have this discussion."

Biting down on the urge to slap the hand that had waved her off, Sophia looked out the sliding glass door at the deck in need of power-washing and new stain. It had begun to rain, and she watched droplets trickle down the glass. As she pulled her cardigan more tightly around her to combat the chill in the air, there were two quick knocks on the door, which then creaked as it opened. *The haunted house even creaks, she thought.* A figure hidden under a black raincoat with a large hood stepped into the room and shut the door. Hands reached up to remove the hood, revealing a blond-haired stoutly built middle-aged woman.

"Sophia! Marcus! It's good to see you." The woman smiled broadly, crossing the room to give them both a welcoming embrace.

"Hello, Annie. Good to see you, too," they each replied.

Annie, half-sister to Marcus and Sophia, slipped off the wet raincoat and draped it across the back of a chair to dry. While they were both tall and thin, Annie was a foot shorter and built sturdily; a thick and strong build that brought to mind pioneer days of chopping wood or wrestling a plow behind a mule. The gray sweatshirt and jeans, lack of jewelry, and chore dirt under fingernails highlighted the differences between the siblings.

"I got here as soon as I could," she said. "How is he?"

Marcus filled her in while Sophia listened. She did not dislike Annie, but they had little in common and had never established much relationship in their years of living in separate worlds. Marcus saw more of Annie, as they had continued to have contact with their father. Sophia's parents had divorced when Sophia was four, and Russ had married a co-worker *("How cliché", Sophia had always thought)* and had two additional children.

Initially, Sophia had occasionally spent time with her father and his new family, but as she aged, those visits decreased in length and frequency, and she had largely lost contact with her half-siblings when she had stopped interacting with Russ. There were occasional birthday and Christmas cards, but they said little and did nothing to keep the tenuous relationships intact. When contact was made it would be like seeing the flash of light a lighthouse beacon creates when rotating in your direction, only to be just as quickly gone when it continues on its path, returning the darkness. Relationships struggle to endure with only transitory attention and focus, and theirs had not. Sophia didn't really know Annie or her brother Dylan, although she had felt compassion for them; while she had endured the absence of her father, they had endured his presence, and Sophia had never been sure which of those was loss and which was gain.

"…so Jane should be back shortly. Do you think Dylan will be coming?" Marcus asked as he concluded filling in Annie.

"I don't know for sure. I let him know how things were, but you never know what to expect with him," Annie responded, shrugging. "Sometimes they were on speaking terms and sometimes they weren't. I couldn't tell from his answer which is the case right now."

"What is Dylan doing these days?" asked Sophia.

"He's been driving truck for a local company, over the road, but still home most nights. He's been doing that for about three years now. Seems to like it, and it pays pretty well. He's still living in the mobile home on the other side of town. He got divorced a year ago, and his ex-wife took the kids and moved about two hours from here. That was pretty hard on him."

Annie brushed her curly blond hair away from her face on both sides, tucking it behind both ears. She had remarkably large ears, and putting hair behind them made them stick out noticeably, as though they had been glued on as an afterthought. "How about you…are you still working with the messed up kids?"

Sophia affirmed that she was and started to give details when they were all startled by a loud thud coming from the bedroom. They rushed in, as a group, fearing Russ had fallen from the bed. He was at the edge of the bed, having hauled himself sideway, and had knocked a large book off the nightstand onto the floor. Sophia turned on a lamp in the corner of the room as Annie approached the bed. Annie picked up the book and replaced it, leaned down, and gave her father a kiss on the forehead.

"Hi, Daddy," she said sweetly.

"Hi, honey. It's good to see you," he responded, smiling wanly at her.

"How are you feeling?"

"Tired. I'm preparing to die," Russ said unemotionally, as if he were ordering salad with his steak.

Sophia mentally rolled her eyes while keeping the actual orbs stationary, a skill practiced to deal with the seriously mundane and overly irritating. Her father, the perpetual drama king, would land on an idea or phrase and build a condo there. Rinse and repeat ad nauseam until you were frantic for the remote to change the channel. Sophia was sure he had lain there, rehearsing the moment, coming up with the most perfect response to the question of how he was; the response he could be confident would elicit the most dramatic reaction from whoever asked it; the response that made him the most "Perfect Dying Man" on the planet, the one that would be talked about for months to come—*how serene he was, how magnanimous, how peacefully accepting*. Seriously!

"Help me sit up," Russ said, as he struggled unsuccessfully to shift himself backwards.

The three of them managed to prop enough pillows behind him to allow his half-useless body to lean against them in an upright position. Although still frail looking, he appeared more alert than when Sophia had seen him earlier.

"I'd like a cigarette," he announced.

"Where are they?" asked Annie.

"On the kitchen counter. I saw them earlier," Marcus said.

Annie fetched the cigarettes and returned, helping Russ to light one. He clutched it awkwardly in his good hand. Sophia stood as far away from them as possible while still remaining in the room. She detested cigarette smoke. She also was having a hard time believing he wanted one and that Annie and Marcus were fine with providing it.

Yeah, that's what he needs. A stinking smoke! Gonna offer him a drink next?

Russ moved his gaze slowly from one person to another, taking in the sight of his children. "Where's Dylan?" he finally asked between drags.

"Working. He said he might show up at some point if he could," Annie offered.

Russ nodded, a whisper of arrogant satisfaction on his face. He loved an audience, even if it was at his death. Watching from the corner as Marcus, Annie and Russ conversed about the ordinary topics of work, kids, and gardening, Sophia wondered if this was all a charade. Yes, he may have had a stroke, but people recovered from those all the time. Was this all just a grand production to entice her into showing up? Was he really going to recover and all this be a waste of time? Did he create a little drama for entertainment in his retirement years, having lost his classroom and students?

Feeling anger rising, Sophia excused herself from the room and returned to the living room. She examined the art work on the walls—a colorful Native American totem, an unassuming line drawing of an Amish homestead, a large black crow with red eyes, and several pictures of Russ, of course. A constant contradiction, her father embraced the serene and metaphysical even as he trampled mercilessly on the fragile life around him; mimicking the Amish by day in his garden, but drowning in alcohol each night, profanely berating those around him; delighted and amused by the antics of his geese, then viciously kicking a dog whose tail wagged in silent greeting knocking over a favorite plant; inviting students to visit his acreage, only to sulk when they arrived, hiding in his bedroom, pretending not to be home.

Confused by his disparities, stung by his unpredictable mood and behavior, Sophia had progressed from trying to please and gain favor, to disappointment, to distrust, to disdain. The disdain sometimes bled into other relationships when she saw siblings continue to patronize him, leading to heated arguments as they criticized her when she backed away.

She had stood her ground, until today. And today he was supposed to die. Imagining him recovering and having to start the process again, she felt overwhelming fatigue. *If there is a God, let this be the day. This is a better ending than he probably deserves. Please don't prolong it.* She knew as she thought it that her brothers and sister would hate her for it. But that was her wish, for an ending, a forever ending. She wondered if she should feel guilty for having such thoughts, but couldn't seem to muster any. It wasn't the first time she felt like something critical was missing from her psyche. Or maybe not…maybe others felt like this too when family members died, they just knew better than to say it out loud.

A burst of noise and cold air pulled Sophia from her reverie as Jane nearly blew through the door, pushed by a gust of wind, followed by Dylan and several leaves, just as Marcus and Annie emerged from the bedroom.

"Sophia!" Jane greeted, with a smile so wide she looked like she was trying to swallow a plate. "I'm glad you are here. Dylan is here, too, as you can see. I filled him in."

She dropped a large leather bag on the floor and shrugged off her coat, draping it across the nearest chair. Running a hand through her hair to fluff it, she crossed the room, giving Sophia and Annie a quick hug.

Dylan stood awkwardly nearby, shifting from one foot to the other. He was the tallest of the four, with lank hair that fell to his shoulders. Sturdily built, like his sister, he walked and stood slumped, as though trying to be shorter than he was, or perhaps stooped from the weight of an invisible burden. Still wrapped in his leather biker jacket, he was ill at ease. Quiet to the point of shy, Dylan stayed in the corners at what few gatherings they had put together in the past. While his eyes seemed to take everything in, he rarely offered an opinion or comment unless directly asked.

When they were younger, Dylan had borne the brunt of their father's mistreatment. Even with limited contact and visits, Sophia had witnessed the constant belittling and criticism Russ directed at him. It was not a surprise when Dylan struggled with drug use and had short stints in detention when younger, nor that he failed to finish high school, being led astray by the tangles of unmet needs and self-hate. Sophia was more surprised when he eventually pulled himself away from those temptations to become employed and relatively functional. She wondered how much past ghosts might have contributed to breaking his marriage. She had always liked Dylan and his quiet ways, and wished she'd had the chance to get to know him better.

A coffee pot gurgled loudly, signaling the end of the brew cycle, reminding Sophia of Jasper's description of the coffee drowning.

"Who wants coffee?" asked Annie from the kitchen. All four affirmed, and she brought five cups out on a metal tray, putting it on a coffee table permanently etched by drink and carelessness. As each of them took a cup, they chose a chair or couch to sit down on, cradling the hot cups in cold hands. Marcus' lap held the papers Jane had brought with her.

"I guess since we are all here, we should look at what this thing says," Marcus began. "This is the last will I know of that the old man had done. Basically it says to divide all assets four ways equally. The assets include this house---such as it is---a life insurance policy and his pension. I'm not sure what the value of the insurance or pension is, just that they are mentioned. I also don't know what's still owed on the house, although he has told me before it was almost paid for. We would have to pay that off, of course, which would come off the assets. He also has the car and a motorcycle, although I don't know what kind of shape either of those might be in. I might be interested in keeping the car for Drew if it isn't worthless. I'm sure it will take some work to get this place to sell-able condition, which will use some of the assets too." Marcus shuffled through the papers as he spoke. "He had appointed me the executor and gave me power of attorney in case something like this happened and he needed someone to make decisions for him. It looks pretty straightforward to me and shouldn't be hard to carry out."

"So how do we go about getting the house ready for sale?" Annie looked through the window at the overgrowth, mentally calculating how many hours of work there were in getting it in shape.

"Well, we can either all pitch in and work on it, or hire it out, or pay one of us to take it on if someone thinks they have time." Marcus responded. "I don't have the time or the desire to do it all, so my vote would be to hire someone from the assets."

Jane nodded in agreement, her hands twisting like two playful gerbils, as she spoke. "I think that might be best.

Marcus is busy with work, and I have so little time after getting the kids all the places they have to be."

Annie glanced at Dylan and Sophia trying to read their expressions. Sophia gave a quick shrug and offered, "I'm pretty busy at work too and don't own the kind of tools it would take to tackle that mess. I can follow orders if someone puts a tool in my hand and instructs me, but I can only do weekend work."

Dylan stared out the window, deep in thought. He enjoyed this kind of work and was good at it. He also had access to tools and was pretty sure Russ still had some around, even if he hadn't been using them. Now that his family was gone he often had trouble filling up his spare time. He wouldn't mind taking on the project, but also wondered what it would feel like to be here so much, with all the reminders of the past crowding him. Could he do what was needed without it costing too much? He turned to Annie and said, "I might be willing to take a stab at it, especially if you and Sophia are willing to help a little on a few weekends. If it gets to be more than I can handle, we can hire out the rest. Are you available to help?"

Annie replied, "Sure, at least some of it. Might be fun! I'd like to see what's buried under all those bushes! Maybe we'll find some old treasure Daddy had forgotten about."

"Since I'm executor, I need to approve of what gets done before you spend any money," Marcus stated. "So you'll need to make a plan and run it by me, complete with estimates."

Dylan tensed subtly, but not so subtly that Sophia missed it. *Back off Marcus.*

"A plan?" Dylan's voice was so soft it was barely audible.

"We need to treat this like it's a business venture. I need you to develop a list of what you want to do, what you think it will cost, and let me see it before you start to make sure I'm in agreement." Marcus' voice tended to get louder when he suspected he might get challenged, and it had risen a few decibels.

"Is that really necessary?" Sophia jumped in. "He's doing everyone a favor to take this on. It's not like we expect him to rip us off or anything. Geez, Marcus! Cut him some slack here!"

"Well, maybe that's why the old man put me in charge? He knew I'd look out for his assets and take care of business *like* a business instead of a laid back, anything goes arrangement. All I asked for was some accountability. Why is that so difficult?" Marcus' face was tight with self-righteous indignation.

Jane's hands went airborne, rearranging her hair, flipping through papers nearby, smoothing her already smooth blouse, and randomly changing direction, like plastic bags caught in unpredictable air currents. Her eyes moved quickly from one person to another as she appeared to want to speak but stopped herself.

Leveling a tensely calm gaze at Marcus, Dylan quietly stated, "I can make a list of things that need to be done, but I'm not going to have time to research how much each thing might cost ahead of time. And I'm pretty sure that once I get started I might run into things that weren't obvious from the beginning and may need to be added. I don't have a problem with keeping receipts to show what needed to be spent, but if you think I'm going to cheat you somehow, maybe you ought to just hire it out and leave me out of it."

Dylan continued to regard Marcus, his expression inscrutable, his hands slowly rubbing his thighs as though he were wiping off something unpleasantly sticky.

"I'm sure that's not what he meant, Dylan," Annie piped up, attempting to head off conflict. Closest to Dylan, she knew better than the others how easily offended he could be when he felt his integrity was questioned. "I can help with that part, too, keeping track of expenditures and making sure things get reimbursed. That's one of the things I'm pretty good at and it can be my part of helping."

"Oh, that sounds just perfect. It's all settled then," chirped Jane as she settled back into her chair looking visibly relieved, hands in for a landing. "Marcus is such a businessman it leaks from his pores sometimes!" Jane giggled while Marcus rolled his eyes.

"Dylan, I would be happy to walk around with you and help make that list if you want," Sophia offered, not wanting Dylan to feel he was alone in reconciling accounts with Marcus. "If something looks big or expensive, I can help make some calls for estimates too."

Glancing at Sophia, Dylan nodded once and said, "That would be fine. Between the two of us we should be able to make a reasonable plan. Wouldn't mind the company either."

Dylan still felt somewhat on edge. He could see that Sophia was trying to be helpful and appreciated Annie's speaking up on his behalf, but he always felt inferior around Sophia and Marcus, especially Marcus. Dylan was quiet and pensive while Marcus was loud and self-assured. Dylan enjoyed hiking and fishing and could not relate to golfing or televised sports. He had no particular political leanings or opinions while Marcus often told others how they should vote. Dylan had been unable to find common ground with his half-brother, which left him feeling the lesser of the two. He hadn't yet figured Sophia out. She seemed a bit remote--almost cold—and then she would suddenly surprise him with a comment that he found kind and reassuring, or an offer of help, like the one she had just given. Maybe working together on this place would help him know her better. Dylan was grateful he would not be working closely with Marcus. It would be tough to feel his work was monitored and second-guessed, especially by someone who didn't seem to know the first thing about manual labor.

"Well, make sure I see the list you come up with and any estimates you get. I'd like to get information on a weekly basis or at least every other week so I can track expenditures. I may take out a credit card for just this purpose, which will help track what gets spent and doesn't have to go on anyone else's accounts," Marcus stated authoritatively. "I can't check into the value of the pension or insurance until he actually passes so that will have to wait."

"Doesn't all of this have to wait?" asked Annie. "Until he's…gone?"

"I think it's okay to start cleaning the place up a little, especially those things that take labor but not much money. No reason to put off what looks inevitable," Marcus answered.

Looking out the window, Sophia saw that the rain had stopped and the wind appeared a bit less robust. Knowing a break from the intensity would feel good, as would the fresh air, she said, "I think I'm going to do a little walk-about to see what occurs to me for that list. Dylan, are you interested in joining me?"

Nodding, Dylan rose to his feet. Sophia pulled on her coat and the two headed out, as Marcus continued to read the will and Jane and Annie went to check on Russ. Once outside, Dylan seemed to relax. Sophia found a pair of rubber boots close to her size on the porch and exchanged them for the dress shoes she had worn. The pair ambled along the gravel road leading to the barn, noting what needed attention.

"I apologize on behalf of my brother, Dylan. Sometimes he can be a real pain. I'm used to it, but I can imagine how it might be more difficult for you to understand or tolerate," Sophia said as she briefly touched his arm. "He usually doesn't even know how he's coming across, and if he does realize it, he usually thinks it's necessary to manage a situation."

Dylan was quiet as he absorbed her words and then responded, "Thanks. I don't know him very well and he doesn't know me. Felt like he didn't trust me."

Sophia nodded in agreement, "That's what worried me. He thinks being executor means you have to micromanage everything, which might be the case with people you hire, but it doesn't work so well and feels kind of crappy when it's family. And Marcus isn't one to consider someone else' feelings before opening his mouth. He just goes full speed ahead and then is surprised when he sees the resulting collateral damage."

The two continued to walk leisurely, taking in the surroundings. Sophia shivered, uncomfortable here after so many years, and wrapped her arms more tightly around herself. While the air was moist and the sky dark with clouds, it was the chill of childhood ghosts that seemed to lower her temperature and create the sensation of being slowly choked as she passed once familiar things seeming unfamiliar in their disrepair.

They reached the barn and made their way through the entrance. The barn roof sagged and revealed holes where shingles had flown free during windstorms. The tops of stall boards were chewed away while green fingers of mold crawled down the front, reaching for the dirt below. Cobwebs hung like disintegrating sheets throughout. Coughing, Sophia recoiled as she was singed by the acrid stench of rat urine and feces, and male goat; an odor that lingered long after the last of the goats had died, as though it had permeated the decaying structure itself. Dylan picked up a piece of wood and, swinging it as he walked, cleared a path through the cobwebs to the middle of the barn, slowly rotating so he could see each angle.

"The old man hasn't done much with this place in years. This is going to take some work. Might be best to knock it down and burn it." Dylan noted the piles of unmatched wood, corroded metal containers, filthy canning jars, and an assortment of worn looking lawn and garden implements. "There's not much in here worth having except maybe these tools. Some of them will help with the work that needs to be done."

Sophia nodded, afraid to breathe too deeply for fear she might choke or vomit. She had backed up to the edge of the doorway to put distance between herself and the smell, and yet still feel she was helping Dylan assess the place--but it wasn't far enough. The memory seized her before she felt it coming, before she could deflect it.

'Put the dog down! Put it down or I'll shoot you along with him! I've told you not to take the dogs outside the property but you did it anyway and now it's your fault they got out. It's YOUR fault they will die. And so will YOU if you don't put it down right now!" Running into the darkened woods. Who's crying? KABLAM! KABLAM! KABLAM! Is he shooting at us? Did he shoot the dog? Running…running…running. Cowering beneath a canopy of lurking trees as the sunset chill set in, skin gouged by harsh scrub, shivering without words in the emptiness. Waiting until he had passed out and it would be safe to return.

Sophia was puzzled by the hand on her arm, gradually coming into focus. She stared at it, trying to place it, trying to place herself, confused fatigue consuming her. Blinking, she followed the hand up the arm to the face above it. Her mind fought to come to a place of quiet, like a spinning top gradually losing speed and coming to rest on its side.

The mouth on the face moved, while eyebrows knit together with concern, yet no sound reached her ears. *Have I gone deaf?* She continued to stare, willing herself to glue together the fragments of perception colliding in the centrifuge that a moment ago was her head. As she stared, the hand tentatively caressed her arm and a small voice from a distant place gradually increased in volume until she could make out the words.

"Sophia, take it easy. You scared the crap out of me. Are you okay? What the hell was that?"

Sophia finally remembered his name. Dylan, the brother she barely knew. She looked beyond him to the barn in the distance and remembered that she had been at the edge of it. She did not remember leaving it to be where she now stood. Sophia inhaled deeply, closing her eyes. Feeling his grip tighten in fear, she opened them again.

"I'm okay," although the voice coming from her throat was not the voice she usually heard when she spoke, and it sounded unconvinced. "I'm sorry I scared you. I'm okay."

She breathed deeply again, relieved to find no goat smell in her nostrils.

He's sick and in bed. He can't hurt you. And the dogs are dead and gone. You're ok…ok…ok.

With the centrifuge calming and logic returning, Sophia surmised she had run from the barn when the memory triggered. Dylan, regarding her with caution and [illegible] continued to wait for an explanation.

I can't explain it to you. I barely know you. I wond[illegible] saw…what I have to explain?

With control mostly returned, Sophia tried a half-hearted laugh, "I guess I'd forgotten how much I hated the smell of goats. And now there's the smell of rat crap added to it. Overcame me and I thought I was going to puke. I didn't think you'd want to see me do that so I high-tailed it over here[illegible] in case I did. Really, I'm fine. Sorry if it seemed worse than it was."

She patted Dylan's hand, trying to appear more light-hearted than she felt.

Dylan noticed that her hand shook as she patted his, and he heard the slightly-too-high tone in her forced voice. Withdrawing his hand from her arm, he recognized the face-saving pitch she had thrown and decided to catch it with grace rather than insist on a more truthful explanation. The distraught look in her eyes had faded and her flailing hands had quieted. He glanced briefly at the scratch she had put on her own hand, certain she had not yet discovered it.

Dylan knew secrets. He knew embarrassment. He knew when to let something go and focus elsewhere in order to survive. And he knew pain that was hidden so deep you didn't want to unearth it because it might bury you alive when you lost your grip.

Shrugging slightly Dylan said, "Well, shall we stay out of the barn for now? Do you want to follow the path around the back of the acreage to see how the fences are holding up?"

Relieved, Sophia nodded her assent and the two resumed walking without speaking, each lost in their own thoughts. Dylan felt drawn to the sister who had appeared so vulnerable and lost a moment ago, feeling a clenched part deep inside him relax a bit in her presence. Sophia worked to recover her outer calm and inner vice grip, as she appreciated this barely known brother sensitive enough to understand her need and fulfill it. What could have been an awkward silence felt tentatively comfortable and reassuring instead. They discovered the fences had survived the years of neglect better than the rest of the property.

Ironic, she thought. He was always good at putting up fences and walls. Keep people out rather than things in. No wonder he took the most care with that. No wonder they stand intact as he fades away.

From their vantage point the house and barn were no longer visible past the tangle of trees and blackberry bushes. The intersection of fences that marked the farthest boundary was just behind a year-round pond (unless the year was exceptionally dry). Absent-mindedly Dylan picked up a rock and tossed it into the water, watching the splash and ripples. Amused, Sophia wondered for easily the hundredth time if throwing rocks into water was part of male DNA, and how did all those rocks not displace the water to become rock piles instead?

"Did you ever come swim here?" Dylan glanced at her as he reached for another rock.

"No," she replied, "I came out here to sit but never used it for swimming. It always seemed peaceful out at this corner. You felt like you were alone in the world for a while."

Dylan hurled another rock towards the center of the pond as he nodded to a tree on the opposite edge and said, "I used to sit up in there. You could climb out on a branch and jump off into deep water along the other side there. My mom didn't like it much, but she wasn't here to stop me."

Sophia could see that the tree was perfect for climbing, with wide, long branches forming almost a seat near the trunk. The thought of jumping off into the murky water made her shudder, however, as she disliked the feeling of water on her face or submerging her head. When she swam, she eased in up to her neck and then swam with her head above water. In the shower she used a washcloth on her face and when it rained, she used an umbrella or hunched over to protect her face. She joked she must have drowned in a former life, but really didn't know why she had this sensitivity, which led to an affinity with those she worked with as she understood how assaulting the outside world could feel to them, even when they didn't know why.

"Looks like a nice place to hang out," Sophia offered. "Did you invite friends here with you?"

"No. I didn't bring a lot of people around here. Never knew what kind of mood he'd be in," was Dylan's subdued response.

Sophia glanced sideways at him. *Is this an opening? Does he want to say more about that?*

"Yeah, I know what you mean," she began. "I'm sure you saw more of that than I did, but I got to see more than I wanted when I'd come visit when you were younger."

Dylan slid the side of his heavy boot along a rut in the soft dirt, his breath creating little misty clouds in the cold air. "I barely remember you coming to visit. What I remember was good mostly. You used to play games with me. No one else ever would, except sometimes Annie when she wasn't busy with her horse. I never got told why you stopped coming. But I can probably guess."

"You probably can," Sophia debated how much to say in response. She didn't know how close Dylan was to their father and she didn't want to beat up on someone who was dying. "Had a lot to do with those moods and what would happen during the bad ones."

Dylan tipped his head back and inhaled deeply. He watched a hawk circling the tree he had spoken of for a moment before answering.

"He had his demons, all right. And you never knew when they would show up and take over. That affected a lot of people. I remember a party the folks were having with some of the old man's students. The party had been his idea, and he had decided who to invite. Everything is going fine and then all of a sudden he gets ticked off about something and dumps his drink onto his best friend's plate of food and starts yelling for them all to get the hell out of his house. I can still see the look on the faces of people who had never seen him other than in class. It was like he suddenly had three heads or had started speaking in Martian and drooling. It would have been funny if it hadn't been so embarrassing," he said, continuing to dig a trench with his boot.

"Yeah, that was what I didn't want to watch anymore. One of the last times I was here he had invited some new students out to see the farm. And before they got here he decided he didn't want company anymore but it was too late to stop them because they had already headed out. So he went to take a nap, and I was told to meet them at the gate and tell them he had an emergency and had to take the dog to the vet. When they got here they asked if they could drive through to see the place because it had taken half an hour to make the drive from town. I had to cross my fingers that they wouldn't see him as they drove past the house and barn on the way out. I'm not very good at deception, and I don't believe in it either, not to mention the disrespect to the students making the drive out. And that was just a mild example of how his moods drove everything."

Sophia tried hard to keep the scorn from her voice as she remembered the incident. *I could tell you so many stories, Dylan.* Standing still in the frigid air the cold began to seep into her. "It looks like it's about to rain again. Shall we wander back?"

Dylan gave her a quick glance of understanding, and then led the way around the pond in response, holding back overhanging branches and thorny tendrils so they wouldn't swing into Sophia. As predicted, the rain began just as they approached the house. Leaving muddy shoes on the porch, they embraced the warmth that greeted them inside.

They found Annie keeping watch over Russ, and Marcus and Jane napping on the couch. Dylan picked up a nearby notepad, settled into a chair and started making a list of things that needed to be addressed if they were to sell the property. Sophia went into the bathroom to put cold water on her face, still trying to regain her self-control. Patting dry her face and hands, she realized how exposed she felt being here, like she was a human nesting doll, the outer, more grown up dolls removed, leaving the vulnerable smallest one alone. No matter how long she was away, how much additional experience or education she had, how accomplished she was in her career or relationships, all she was in this house near her father was the smallest nesting doll, kidnapped into a science fiction movie and shrunken to a mini version of herself. Anger flashed as this reality sank in; anger at him for creating those feelings and anger at her for not having found a way to exorcise them. *Seriously? I will NOT allow you to continue to control how I feel! I am NOT less than you and I WON'T be afraid of you anymore!* The anger slid a larger nesting doll over the exposed one as she opened the bathroom door.

Seeing nothing had changed in the living room, Sophia returned to the bedroom where Annie kept vigil. Russ tossed fitfully in the bed, trying to will his paralyzed side to move. Annie murmured reassuring comments to no avail as she stroked his arm and head. Sophia pulled a chair against the wall on the opposite side of the bed, taking in the surroundings as her eyes adjusted to the dim light.

The furnishings resembled a consignment shop, a merger of cultures, eras and raw materials as though Russ couldn't quite decide what type of decoration he liked best, although much of what was there might have been chosen by her step-mother before their divorce. She wondered where Sharon was these days and made a mental note to ask Annie or Dylan.

Sophia didn't know all the reasons for the divorce, but could easily imagine how Sharon could have become fed up with her dad's unpredictable moods, self-centered choices, and abuse. One had to be a symbiont to co-exist with Russ, living within the tissues of his dreams and desires, being fed through his achievements and starved through his failures, giving up all sense of self in order to calm the marital pool. Sophia had decided she would rather maintain her sense of self even if it meant being alone; perhaps Sharon had as well.

A startling noise can yank one from a daydream; unexpected quiet can also suddenly capture attention. Aware that Annie had stopped talking and Russ had stopped moving around in the bed, Sophia shifted her focus to them. Russ stretched a trembling hand to stroke the side of Annie's face as she gazed at him with a mixture of compassion and longing. As his hand fell backward, Annie caught and held it. Turning his head to take in the rest of the room, Russ inhaled deeply as he and Sophia locked eyes. Russ continued to stare at Sophia as she struggled to maintain both eye contact and her resolve, fighting to keep both nesting dolls in place.

Annie's sudden gasp jolted Sophia into realizing that Russ had not exhaled, nor had he inhaled again. His eyes were open but lifelessly dull, as though someone had turned off the subtle backlighting that you weren't even aware was there until it was extinguished, as though a cloud has shrouded the moon.

Wow, just like that? Not even a wiggle or a moan or a comment on the way out? How do all those working, moving parts just stop? You were just here and now you're not?

Sophia tried to take it in. It seemed as though there should be more, some remarkable punctuation to mark the transition from is to isn't, here to not here, movement to stillness. Was it a trick? Was he pretending? Was he going to suddenly laugh and offer a smart-ass comment about how gullible they all were, or some caustic remark about how they'd have to wait longer for their inheritance and then demand a cigarette? They would learn later that the stroke was a precursor to a burst aneurism. The end had been not only quick, but without warning, even to Russ.

Annie began to weep, still clinging to the lifeless hand, and Sophia realized it was indeed real and Russ was gone. She rose and walked quickly to the living room. Dylan looked up from his list and, reading her face, knew without words. He rose slowly and moved past her, touching her lightly on the hand as he did. Crossing to the couch, Sophia gently shook Marcus awake.

Blinking several times and rousing himself from his prone position, he stated crossly, "What?" His movement and voice woke Jane who also moved to a sitting position, smoothing her hair and clothing automatically.

"He's gone," Sophia stated simply.

"Oh!" Jane's hands quickly covered her mouth.

"Shit!" Marcus sprang to his feet and jogged towards the bedroom with Jane trailing.

By the time Sophia made her way back to the bedroom Marcus, Jane, and Annie were all kneeling around the bed, each with a hand somewhere on Russ, a shoulder, a leg, an arm, each crying as they stared at the motionless form. Dylan stood against the wall, breathing deeply as though the rush of air might dry tears from the inside and deter them from leaking out. Obviously distressed, he was making every effort to maintain outer control, arms folded stoically across his chest.

Sophia stood against a wall as well, in need of physical support as the emotional tidal wave of others came at her. *Shouldn't I feel something? Shouldn't I be sad? Shouldn't I cry?* She watched the others, clearly distraught, and found her own lack of emotion somewhat disturbing. *Relief? Is that what I feel? Grateful? Grateful this chapter of my life is finally finished?*

Counting on the dim light to conceal her lack of grief, Sophia watched as her siblings reacted to the loss of him. When guilt poked her, suggesting how she "should" feel, she argued she had already grieved the loss years ago, crying many tears as she chose to stay away when it caused her nothing but pain. In the intervening years, the "shoulds" had been buried, the throb of loss lessened, as she understood that the real thing given up was not the relationship itself, but her hope and expectation for a loving, trusting relationship which had been impossible from the beginning. She believed more grieving is done over unfulfilled expectations or desires than loss of important beings or things; there are so many more opportunities to be disappointed, to create assumptions, resentments and judgments that choke the life from relationship and self. The life had been choked from her relationship with Russ long ago, leaving only the compassion she felt for anyone who was facing trauma or hardship, just as she would feel watching the news. She did not expect any of her siblings to understand the detached compassion she felt, so she hid in the darkness, counting on their own preoccupied grief to keep them unaware.

As shock ebbed into resignation, Dylan was the first to move. Uncrossing his arms, he shuffled into the kitchen and stood at the sink, hands clutching the counter edge as he gazed out the window at the falling rain. Fogged glass obscured the view of the back pasture, but Dylan didn't notice…lost in his thoughts. Sophia followed him, standing next to him, gently touching his back.

"You okay?" she asked softly.

A delayed reaction, one too many puffs of air into an already filled balloon, one too many pounds for the lifter, Dylan's resolve crumbled, his control burst, and Sophia found herself holding him as he wept, listening as he regretted the years lost to conflict.

"We were finally getting along," Dylan lamented. "I wasn't ready to have him gone yet, even though he could be such a bastard."

Dylan's arms around her back felt paradoxically both natural and odd as she tried to infuse comfort through the embrace. Knowing no words could fill the void he was feeling, she didn't offer platitudes that would skip uselessly across his anguish like the rocks he had thrown earlier into the pond. Feeling his arms begin to slacken and his heaving chest quieting, Sophia dropped her arms and took a step backward.

"I'm so sorry, Dylan. I know this was all so sudden and a shock. I'm glad there was peace between you before he was gone. I'm glad those memories are the most current ones."

Dylan nodded wordlessly and left to compose himself in the bathroom, as Marcus, Jane and Annie entered the kitchen with drawn faces. Annie filled a cup with coffee, offering it to Marcus who accepted it and took an immediate sip. Doing the same for Jane and herself (Sophia declined with a shake of her head) Annie led the way into the living room where they all took a seat. For several minutes they sat without speaking, each lost in thought, processing what had occurred. During their silence Dylan rejoined them, sitting on the hearth of the woodstove.

"I guess we need to call Hospice and let them know he's gone. They said they would take care of informing anyone who needs to know and help us follow the next steps," Marcus spoke first. Getting nods of support, he picked up the phone and moved into a nearby room to explain events and ask for assistance.

Jane twirled the cup around and around in her fingers. Dylan stared out the sliding glass door. Annie focused on her lap, hands gripping the sides of her legs. Shell-shocked was the word that seemed to describe them, as Sophia looked from one to the next. It was hard to know what to do or say. She wondered if the others felt the same strained tension she did, or if this was another example of how she differed from them.

Seeking deeply rooted connections, discovering the fears and joys hiding in fissures, intertwining experiences to weave lives more tightly together; Sophia absorbed every emotion, expression, and nuance from the others in the room. Watching them, she wondered if they were doing the same, or if they were unaware of anything but their own thoughts and feelings. It was odd how far away from people you could feel when sitting right next to them, or how family could seem like strangers. There was a surreal quality to the moment, like if you examined anything or anyone too closely, it would shift, pulsate, evaporate, as if trying to hold a cloud. The eyes see something but the skin can't quite feel it when you reach out to touch.

"Well, Hospice is on the way," Marcus reported as he entered the room and took a seat next to Jane. "The nurse will come out and do what's necessary to make the death official and also take care of arranging transportation to the funeral home." Marcus rubbed his hair back and forth, dislodging the invisible, with fatigue in his eyes. "She says she can confirm the death, and we can make contact with Harkin's Funeral

Home within the next couple of days to make whatever arrangements we want."

"I know he would want something simple," Annie spoke softly, still staring at her legs. "And I know he would want Amazing Grace to be sung. It was one of his favorites. I wonder if there is a music student from the college we could get to sing."

"Oh, that sounds perfect!" offered Jane, who continued to spin her cup, although Sophia had not seen her take a single sip from the swirling liquid.

"Dylan, do you have any ideas about what to include?" Annie asked, finally lifting her head to look at her stoic brother, who continued to stare outside.

The only part of Dylan that moved in response was his mouth, which offered a barely audible "No." Looking like a marionette, sitting woodenly unless the appropriate string was manipulated; someone had pulled the string on Dylan's mouth while the rest of him remained frozen.

"Sophia?" Annie turned in her direction.

"Not really. I didn't really have enough recent contact with him to know what might please him. I'm okay with you guys deciding how to proceed."

Marcus stood abruptly and started to pace. "I can talk to the funeral director tomorrow and get some idea of what's standard protocol and then let you know. We need to decide who to have run the service, where to have it, who to let know, and what to put in the paper. I'll do some preliminary work on it and get things started. Unless any of you object, I can write up the obituary and run it by you for input. It makes more sense to have one person put the main notice together…more efficient that way."

For all the times Sophia resented Marcus' tendency to take charge, this was one time she felt some relief. She was grateful she didn't have to put time and energy into trying to balance disparate needs to give their father a proper send-off. The nods and "okay's" indicated they all felt that same sense of relief. Sophia also knew she would have difficulty coming up with an obituary that was devoid of sarcasm and resentment. While she was pretty good at keeping unkind thoughts to herself most of the time, it was another matter to pretend or express something she did not feel. This task was better left to Marcus and the others.

In time the hospice nurse arrived and did the necessary checking to confirm the death. She was followed by the transport vehicle, and within minutes they watched their father's body being moved for his last trip down the gravel drive. Dylan finally moved and helped lift his father onto the stretcher that took him to the car. His hand was the last to touch Russ as the door closed. Brushing the back of his sleeve against wet eyes, Dylan disappeared briefly into the house, returning with his jacket to say goodbye in quiet, terse tones. Sophia also exited, overtaken by a sudden need to be alone. Watching Annie, Marcus and Jane in the rear view mirror as she pulled away in the continued drizzle, she felt like she was trying to hold onto a handful of smoke; the thing she wanted just outside her reach or disappearing as she tried to embrace it, a mirage, life shape-shifting like the aliens on the science fiction shows she liked to watch, people appearing to be one thing and suddenly becoming something else. Who were these people really?

FACELESS

Pulling the pillow over his head did not stop the pounding…did not still the trembling walls…nor soften the taunts and din of breakage. Restless squirming as though a thousand fire ants were burrowing out from the inside. Life closing in, squeezing, his world a vise, his lungs filled with sand. Fists clenched, slamming against ears, shutting out the moans, unsure of the source…was it him or them? Wanting to move, to leave…feet anchored, paralyzed…trapped in this box…this box inside a box…this dead inside the living. Twirling to the edge of the tornado, hoping to be thrown clear…hope sizzling away as it hit the parched earth, leaving nothing, not even an indentation to show it existed. Shielding…enduring…reaching the edge of the abyss…

RAMPAGE

She heard the rhythmic pounding long before she reached the source. Panting from the exertion of running up a flight of stairs, Sophia leapt the remaining two steps and quickly opened the door with her key. Rushing into the staff observation room, she tried to catch her breath while scanning the scene through the glass.

Beyond the wall Quinn slammed a chair repeatedly against the wall. THUD…THUD… THUD echoed through the unit as the plastic chair quivered with each contact. The doorway into the unit was barricaded with a bookshelf and couch. Books and papers lay strewn across the floor between upended chairs, sogging in water from an overturned cleaning bucket. The unit's television lay on the floor among glass shards.

Four of Quinn's peers huddled in the corner farthest away from the staff window, their faces reflecting a mixture of excitement and trepidation as they stared at Quinn. Stripped of power, the residents were impressed when one of their own rose up to seize control. But, like a tornado a safe distance away which suddenly changes course to come your way, they knew rage's funnel could shift without notice and touch down on whatever was near and accessible. None of them wanted to find themselves in the crosshairs of his emotional rifle, having witnessed his previous escalations with staff.

"Come on you rent-a-cops!" Quinn taunted. "Come on in. What's stopping you?" THUD…THUD….THUD. "Bunch of sissy girls? S'matter….you afraid of a plastic chair? Who's big and tough now? Hiding behind that glass like fucking pussies…you ain't NOTHIN'!"

The yellow blur of plastic chair smashed against the window, making Sophia jump. Quinn's hand followed the chair and slammed against the glass as he glared through to those inside. Spotting Sophia, he stopped abruptly as they stared at each other for a frozen moment; Sophia, hoping her presence might make some difference for him, and Quinn, startled enough by the unexpected that his fight momentarily froze. His face contorted as a tug-of-war ensued between years of pent-up rage and hatred, and his desire to earn his freedom from places like this, people like these. An avalanche of thoughts tumbled…images, feelings, experiences… screaming voices; the smell of burnt flesh, feces and stale beer; the welting pain of belts on his body; unable to move, or to breathe; and fear, overwhelming, paralyzing fear. Quinn's entire body trembled as he covered his face with his hands and turned from the window. An anguished roar erupted as he paced through the unit, head down. Passing items in disarray on the floor, he kicked them aside, but did not pick any up to throw. As he paced he gave a wide berth to the four continuing to watch warily from the corner.

"I want to go in and talk to him," Sophia asserted quietly to Eliza, the unit manager.

"Are you NUTS?" Eliza's reply was immediate. "Absolutely NOT! I'm responsible for safety here, and no one is safe going in there to talk to that lunatic. I've already called for backup from MSU. He's going into lockdown!" Eliza crossed bulky arms over her chest with an expression that dared disagreement.

"I don't think he will hurt me, and I'm not afraid of him," Sophia countered. "I can already see he's coming down, and I think I can help him continue to do that. If you bring in staff from MSU he's likely to escalate again."

"Well, if he does, it just proves what I've been trying to tell everyone; he's dangerous and he doesn't belong here. Maybe now someone will listen, before someone else gets hurt! I'm not going to try to open that door without backup!" Eliza replied stubbornly.

"Can I try to talk to him through the med slot?" Sophia knew when she was in a standoff. Although not ideal, talking to Quinn through a small opening was preferable to not being able to talk to him at all, and this was a critical moment for him.

Eliza raised an eyebrow at Sophia and made a small derisive noise, but simultaneously nodded in consent. "If he throws something at you through there, just remember that I warned you."

Next to the window was a small hinged door that opened to allow items such as medications to be handed out from the staff office. Moving to it, Sophia unlatched the door and squatted down, allowing her to see through the opening, recoiling from a burst of unit air even more pungent than normal. Quinn continued to pace, nervously pushing his hands through his hair or squeezing them into fists. She called his name quietly. No response. She tried again, a bit more loudly, but still trying to maintain a tone and volume that offered calm comfort.

Years earlier, Sophia worked with neglected and abused horses, where she learned the importance of moving slowly and quietly to avoid making them frightened and suspicious. It was the same with aroused kids; the nervous system was the nervous system, whether it was a horse or a human. Kindness and calm helped no matter what kind of being one was dealing with. Quinn glanced toward the sound, body tensed, until he recognized Sophia's nonthreatening eyes looking at him through the slot. His shoulders gradually relaxed and his pace slowed. The inner struggle continued to distort his face.

"Quinn, can I help?" Sophia queried gently.

Quinn closed his eyes briefly and took a deep breath. Dropping his head, his pacing brought him closer to the open slot, but he continued to walk back and forth on the opposite side of the opening. The whirl of images and feelings had slowed and dimmed, but his heart continued to pound so hard he wondered if his head would explode. The muscles in his body felt like a clock that has been wound so tight the smallest tap might shatter it into a thousand pieces. He made a deliberate effort not to look through the window at the others standing near Sophia in the office. He especially avoided making eye contact with Eliza.

"I don't know," Quinn replied tensely, "I don't know," as he took another deep breath.

"You're halfway there buddy. You can get the rest of the way if you keep working at it. Just try to remember what we've talked about and what you've been practicing. Deep breaths, relax those muscles, choose what you want to focus on to bring you back down. Focus inside, not outside. Remember why you are doing this and what matters to you more than this moment. This moment will pass," encouraged Sophia.

Because of Quinn's horrific history of abuse, his system often became dysregulated at the smallest thing. He lived with heightened arousal all the time, requiring little stimulation to fire him out of control, much like a car having the engine gunned, while the brake is on and the clutch disengaged. Once you take off the brake or engage the clutch, the car lurches forward. Quinn had the misfortune of living with a chronically gunning nervous system. He was just beginning to understand how that affected him and how he might change it so he did not lose control so readily, but he still needed encouragement and reminding to make use of his new understanding.

Sophia watched as the muscles in Quinn's face softened and his breathing slowed. His pace became more measured and he paused at times as he passed in front of her. Sophia found her own muscles relaxing in response to Quinn's increased calm, becoming aware of her own discomfort in squatting. *I'm too old for this!*

She shifted positions to put her weight on the other leg without taking her eyes off Quinn. Behind her she heard the door to the office open and MSU staff entering. She tried to remain focused on Quinn despite the briefing behind her between Eliza and the security staff. She could see that he was almost there and was hoping she could buy him the time to get there without MSU taking over and possibly re-escalating him.

"You're doing great, Quinn. Just keep working at it…you can do this."

Quinn stopped directly in front of the slot and looked squarely into Sophia's eyes with an exhausted expression of pain and gratitude. "It got away from me again," he said with resignation. The avalanche stopped, leaving behind a bone-deep fatigue and ache; like the ache felt by those who've had a limb amputated but still feel the phantom pain when nothing is there. When you can't find the place from which the hurt emanates, you can't make the pain stop; you just have to find a way to live through it. For Quinn, the aches were never-ending.

"Yeah," Sophia replied gently. "It did."

"Dude! That was epic! This room is thrashed!" a congratulatory shout from the corner, as one of the onlookers saw it was safe to go back into the proverbial water.

Crap! Sophia cringed as the stallion reared, eyes blazing, on alert, for the unexpected threat. He glanced around the room, taking in the overturned chairs and scattered materials he had previously been oblivious to. At that moment the MSU staff and Eliza decided it was time to force their way through the barricaded door.

"Wait! Give us a few more minutes! He's almost there, and I think he'll remove those things if you give him a little more time!" Sophia pleaded.

"We need to get in there now that he's calm to get this situation under control," Eliza responded. She unlocked the door as the four security staff began pushing in unison against the barricades. Panicked, Sophia looked back at Quinn who had moved to a corner away from the door and picked up a chair.

"Quinn!" she called through the door. "Quinn….they aren't going to hurt you. You need to put the chair down. Please, Quinn, you know what this is. Try to control it! Don't give up…you were almost there!"

But Sophia could see in his eyes he was gone again. The demons were back, his instinctual terror palpable. Sophia shut her eyes and dropped her head so she would not see what she heard; couch scraping the floor, bookshelf tumbling, chair smashing the wall, grunts and scuffles and shoes squeaking against the polished floor, bodies falling to the ground, shouted commands, swearing, panting, screaming, the clanking of metal handcuffs, anguished sobbing, and finally, relative silence as they carried Quinn down the stairway; a frightened abused stallion learning again to trust no one.

She thought she might vomit; the sounds and sights of violence so familiar that she needed a moment to regain her composure, to free herself from the tide of helplessness that swamped her. She wanted to take Eliza by the hair and shake her until she managed to put sense into her. She wanted to storm into management's office and shout at the superintendent about everything unfair and unwise at the center. She wanted to save them, to help them, to protect them. Instead, she rose slowly, surprised she could still do so with the increased gravitational pull, and descended the stairs, making every effort to practice what she preached no matter how discouraged and angry she felt. Five minutes might have made all the difference…

STAFFING

"I think the kid's dangerous. I think he'll always be dangerous. I think we'll all be better off if he's locked up his whole life. He's unsalvageable."

Sophia sat at the corner of a large meeting table. Sitting across from her was the manager of the facility, Jeff Colton, a hefty man prone to wearing flamboyant shirts, making the song "Don't Worry, Be Happy" pop into Sophia's head. Next to Jeff sat the staff psychiatrist Dr. Blain, a man who wore thick black glasses and polished suits, but often had crumbs from whatever he'd eaten on his lapel. Compassionate in his work with the kids, his interpersonal style was unassuming and genuine, in contrast to his well-dressed appearance. Eliza Bennett, who had spoken, sat at the opposite end of the table. In her early fifties, Eliza was plump, with graying hair that appeared untended, as though she had better things to do than find a comb. The only expressions seen on Eliza's face were contempt or bored disgust, making Sophia wonder what life experiences had created such a relentlessly unhappy demeanor. *"It's as though they think you've come to put poo on their porch,"* Zach used to say about personalities who seem to expect the worst in every situation. Sophia wanted to ask Eliza who had put poo on her porch, but Eliza was not one to talk about herself....ever.

"Can you explain why you think that?" asked Jeff, oozing diplomacy.

"He's ready to explode at the drop of a hat. He will go after anyone at any time and won't quit until he is physically overpowered. He's broken more things and hurt more people than everyone else on the unit put together. And he won't talk to anyone or work on anything." As she spat the information, Eliza wore an expression of spitting out a bug that had crawled into her mouth while her attention had been elsewhere. "I've done all I can with him. He can't be reached." She tossed her head backwards, indicating the end of the discussion.

Jeff looked expectantly towards Dr. Blain and Sophia, "Do you agree?"

Dr. Blain adjusted the front of his jacket as he sat forward in his chair, brushing off the remnants of a cheese cracker. "Well, we have tried a number of different medications with him. We've tried stimulants to help with impulsiveness, mood medications, and antipsychotics for calming his nervous system to reduce the aggressiveness. Some seem to help in the beginning but none continue to work long-term. His chemistry appears complex and may even adapt to what we do so it becomes ineffective. I have begun to wonder if he is developing a personality disorder that will be a life-long challenge. He is still too young to call that one, but his lack of response to pharmaceutical intervention is less than promising. And he doesn't always want to follow my recommendations." Dr. Blain flexed the fingers he had interwoven as he spoke, looking in Sophia's direction.

Jeff also looked at Sophia, waiting. Sophia sighed, "I know Quinn is challenging. And I know he doesn't always respond as we would like to the medications. But there is so much history here that shaped him. He has a lot of instinctive responses that are driving his bus right now. I've actually seen him be far less aggressive and more functional when he comes to school than what he seems to show on the unit. If we give him the right support and structure, he seems to do well most of the time. I think he's too young to write off. I think he can still grow. He has huge trust issues, but I wouldn't say he won't talk to anyone. He has talked to me some. It just takes a lot of work to build that relationship with him. And he has a hair-trigger on some of his buttons. And once triggered, he has no way to stop his reactions. Yet," she added.

Eliza snorted and morphed expressions from disgust to contempt. "He just put one of my staff in the hospital! And it's not the first time. He has no regard for rules or personal safety. And just because he talks about bugs with you doesn't mean you are changing him."

Eliza did not hide her disgust for the mental health component at Dalton. She saw anyone convicted of a crime as dangerous and hopeless, unredeemable bad apples, causing her to frequently bump heads with Sophia over treatment options.

And what did the adult say or do before he attacked them? What unnecessary corners was he backed into? And who put a stick up your butt so far that you take your discomfort out on kids? Jeesh, no wonder you're single. A couple of mistakes and you'd throw your husband out or make him want to find the nearest railroad car to jump.

Sophia turned to face Eliza, attempting an inscrutable expression, "I know he has his moments, Eliza. And during those moments he can be as dangerous to himself as he is to others. We talk about more than bugs, and he is trying to learn how to control his reactions, but it is an uphill battle to get rid of what he has learned and put something else in its place. I think he is trying. I think I've seen progress. I believe he can continue to improve with the right support. This place triggers him more than he would be triggered outside these fences, and if he could go off by himself when he gets frustrated instead of feeling cornered he might not get so aggressive." Sophia turned toward Jeff, "Jeff, it's my observation this place triggers the PTSD in him, and the structures here don't allow him to use strategies that would keep him calmer and help him cope. I'm not sure he would even be considered dangerous in the community because he'd have the freedom to leave situations instead of being trapped in them."

"Oh, you can't be serious!" Eliza bellowed. "Look, Jeff, I've worked with these law-breakers for years, and I know one when I see one. This kid is nothing but a future felon. His being here is a waste of time."

Swiveling in his chair, Jeff regarded the pen in his hand as he tapped it gently against the table, considering the conflicting opinions. Turning to Dr. Blain he asked, "Are there any other medications that can be tried to settle him down? Do you have any other ideas that might help reduce the risk of further harm to staff and help him control himself?"

Using a tissue to wipe the lenses of the glasses he had removed, Dr. Blain replied, "Well, there are some new things available I can try. He seems to have an unusual system so maybe trying something off-label and non-traditional will have a more long-lasting effect. I would agree with Sophia that he may be challenged more by being in this kind of environment than the average kid because of his abusive history. He's going to be more reactive due to that, and have more distrust, and need others to be aware of how they might be coming across when they speak to him or redirect him. Having some training for staff might help with that."

Bored disgust again blanketed Eliza's face, "I have some of the best trained staff in this facility. I don't know what you think they need to do differently. We hold kids accountable for their aggression so they can exist in society without causing harm. Are you saying we need to let him do what he wants so he doesn't explode? Lots of people have been abused; it doesn't give them the right to beat other people up. You can't just hold a pity party for them and expect it to improve their behavior."

Don't-worry-be-happy moved forward in his chair, the loud shirt contrasting the quiet but firm tone as Jeff spoke, "Eliza, I don't think we are saying not to hold him accountable. I think what we are trying to do is recognize that adult behavior can either keep things calm or add to his reactions. Why don't we give the Doc some time to try a new approach, and have Sophia do some training with your staff to help them know how to best approach him. You might be right about where he is heading, but I want to make sure we have tried everything possible to settle him down before we give up on this. This might be the last opportunity this young man has to turn things around. Would you and Sophia connect on when that training can take place, and we'll plan to meet again in a month to see how things are going?"

Eliza begrudgingly shared the date of the next unit staff meeting with Sophia and stomped out of the room. Sophia sighed inwardly. It was hard enough to talk unit staff into seeing new possibilities or trying new approaches; she knew it was going to be like pushing toothpaste back into the tube to convince people if Eliza was there to belittle and undermine what she said. But, she cared enough about Quinn to give it her best shot. She turned to Dr. Blain who had risen, preparing to leave the room. "Thanks for backing me up and not giving up on him yet."

Dr. Blain nodded, "You made me ask myself if I'd done all I could. I confess to feeling a bit frustrated by his lack of progress and his unwillingness to listen to my advice or take what I prescribe. But I have to remember how distrustful he is of others, and I need to work harder on gaining his trust so he will try what I suggest. He does trust you so perhaps you can encourage him to follow my advice?"

"I will certainly do my best," Sophia assented as she shook his hand and said goodbye.

THE FUNERAL

Caw! Caw! Caw!

Piercing the silence, the crow's insistent call drew Sophia from her pensive reverie, pulling her eyes upward to its source. She watched it circle the clearing of trees where they stood, manic flapping wings replacing gliding dives. Crow, a symbol often seen as meaningful; on the negative end, a sign of death or a troublesome omen; more positively, the presence of magic, intelligence, and fearlessness; somewhere in the middle a mischievous trickster; symbolism seeming both ironic and appropriate in representing the riddle of Russ to those present. His students remembered an intelligent cantankerous teacher, prone to taking up lost causes and supporting the underdog. His ex-wives, with the acute vision of hindsight, would describe a troublesome omen and dash in the opposite direction. Sophia shivered slightly with a sudden feeling of foreboding, without knowing why. Looking back on this moment later, she would believe she had been brushed by the ghost of the mischievous trickster.

Caw! Caw! Caw!

Gliding onto a tree branch overhead, the crow settled wings against its body and quieted, appearing ready for the proceedings about to begin in the rural cemetery. Choosing to stand on the edge of the gathering beneath a large oak, she was able to see those who entered and keep one side free of people, ensuring she could avoid any claustrophobic reaction to being surrounded. She watched now as young and old, stricken and impassive, disheveled and manicured filled in the empty spaces near the casket.

There were only a handful of chairs for those unsteady enough to need them, as the ceremony was expected to be brief. While Russ was prone to talking non-stop, he couldn't abide listening to others for long, so the consensus was to keep the service short. Marcus and Jane arranged large photos of Russ near the casket while Annie tended vases of flowers sent by well-wishers. Dylan stood alone on the other side of the clearing, staring at the ground before him, his face concealed by a black beret and sunglasses. Sophia knew his ex-wife and kids were there somewhere, too, but must have chosen to stand elsewhere. *Dylan looks like he feels as awkward and uncomfortable as I do*, she thought ruefully.

The small crowd must have included faculty members and students, as Sophia did not recognize many of them. Having been estranged for so many years, she really didn't know who was connected to Russ or how. Sophia's ex-stepmother, Sharon, was there and had nodded briefly to Sophia and then disappeared, which was fine with Sophia. It was hard to feign real sorrow, and yet, isn't that what people expected? How do you respond when someone approaches, clasps your hand with tender concern and regards you with eyes oozing sympathy? What do you reply when they tell you how sorry they are he is gone? Sophia had actually practiced different looks and statements in the mirror that morning to prepare for this role. *"Thank you so much for your concern and for coming. I know he would have been pleased."*

Yes, best to keep it about Russ. Hide behind the smokescreen of pretense and civility. Hope you don't choke as you bite down on the words that float unbidden through your mind.

Few approached her as she lounged in the shade of the oak tree. The relentless rain had subsided, and several days of sun had dried the ground, grass, and trees to allow an outdoor ceremony, which all had agreed would be more consistent with who Russ was than a church or mortuary. No one could remember him ever gracing the inside a church and a sterile funeral home setting might have caused him to fling open the casket and shout, "Get me out of here before I kick someone's ass!" No, outdoors with foliage and birds was more Russ; he would even appreciate the memento of muddy shoes, or a splotch of bird poop on someone's shoulder, chuckling from the afterlife. In moments of insecurity, seeing others as envious of his accomplishments, Russ believed there was always someone waiting to do him harm. He might see a bird's missile as a glorious karmic moment.

"Amazing grace, how sweet the sound, that saved a wretch like meeee."

Lilting soprano fusing with rich, reedy bagpipe brought the crowd to reverential silence as the harmony swam around bodies and scaled barren oaks, released into the sky by praying branches. The sea of bodies parted to allow the piper and woman in flowing red dress to pass, then eased back together.

"I once was lost, but now I'm found; was blind, but now I see".

Having always loved this song and all it conveyed about hope and healing, Sophia's throat tightened and her eyes moistened as her body reacted viscerally to the bagpipes and melodious voice. For a few moments, she was lost in the music, forgetting all else about where she was or why. The sudden silence was as startling as the abrupt musical onset had been, as though the sky had inhaled all sound. Marcus turned to face the group as the musicians moved to the side.

"Thank you all for coming. I'm sure my father would have been pleased. You all know how much he enjoyed being the center of attention!" Scattered laughter echoed through the trees. "It is always a difficult thing to lose a person you are close to, and a parent can be especially hard. They have been a force in your life for as long as you can remember. My father was proud of his accomplishments…."

Marcus droned on with a bleached rendition of Russ' accomplishments, promoting the more positive things he had done during his life as the crowd laughed, sniffed, blew noses and shifted on their feet. Several students and faculty members made brief statements as well, telling stories or offering appreciation for the man they knew.

Sophia's mind wandered as she began to imagine her own funeral. Who would come, what would they say, and what would they remember about her? She wondered if death wiped away the bad and ugly, or if people just buried it to focus on the positive. She imagined a service where she heard, "I'm glad the old coot is dead", "The planet is better off without him", or "She made Cain look like a saint". Sophia contemplated organizing a service of her own before she was actually gone, to hear and see what might be said, but only if they all told the truth. She wanted to hear, finally, just how others saw her. No games, no sugar coating, no filling the room with verbal air-freshener to camouflage the stink of unspoken resentments. Would she be surprised? Aghast? "Pleased" is not a word that first occurs, she noted wistfully. Would anything she had done in her life be remembered? Would the things they valued about her be the things she valued in herself?

"…Thank you again for coming and paying your respects. The college is planning a celebration of life for any of you who wish to attend next week. Details will be published on the college website for those who are interested," Marcus offered as a conclusion to the service.

As if on cue, the crow, which had remained silent since landing, issued a final "Caw!" and jetted into the azure sky. As people began clustering into small groups to share final thoughts or exit, Sophia noticed a woman dressed completely in black standing alone a short distance away, almost behind a tree. *Human crow* flashed as she stared, intrigued. The woman's face was obscured by large sunglasses and a tightly wound scarf, her presence tentative, as though hiding from notice. She stood immobile, hands in the pockets of a woolen jacket, shoulder-length auburn hair hanging in soft curls. She made no contact with the people strolling past her to their cars but seemed to be scanning the crowd.

Are you a student groupie? A past love? Some secret admirer? An angry jilted left-over? Although mildly curious, Sophia turned and walked around the edges of the few people left to join her siblings near the casket, standing together in a half circle near the pictures and flowers. As she reached them, a final glance revealed the woman was gone. *Probably never know,* she shrugged.

Sophia loaded flowers into her car to be dropped off at a care center on her way home. Marcus made arrangements for the final disposition of the casket while Jane and Annie took care of the rest of the flowers and pictures. Dylan seemed ill at ease, shifting his weight from foot to foot, repeatedly removing his hat, only to replace it. As the rest of them prepared to leave, cars loaded and arrangements made, Dylan indicated he was going to stay and help with the interment process. His expression deterred any well-meaning objections, and even Marcus appeared to recognize his need to do something concrete to close this chapter.

Sophia hugged him briefly and then said, "I'll be in touch about continuing the work on his place."

A silent nod was his reply. As she drove away from the empty parking lot, the rear-view mirror reflected Dylan, coat removed, picking up a shovel. She wondered if demons could be buried along with a body, one shovel at a time, as he faded from view.

EXIT

D'Vrae's wide grin almost disappeared around the back of his head as he leaned through the doorway of Sophia's office. "I gettin' out tomarah! I goin' home to de hood."

Sophia smiled broadly in return. "The moment you've been waiting for! Congratulations!"

Today's hairdo, a mixture of braids and ponytails, resembled a manicured yard with rows of trimmed hedges mingled with small trees. D'Vrae strutted across the room, head bobbing and body pitching as though unbalanced by small waves. He dropped into the chair opposite her, crossing his arms.

"What are you most looking forward to?" asked Sophia.

"Fried chicken and sweet potato pie," was the immediate answer. "My Gram gonna fix tha' fo' me my first nigh' out. She say all the aunties and uncles and cousins gonna be there."

"That sounds like quite the homecoming for you. I'm glad you have family to go back to."

And she was, even though some of them might be of questionable influence. If she could, she would have transported him to a different town, a different family, a different reality, to give him a fair shot. Seeing someone released mixed hope with terror. Could they hang on to the new skills and understanding within the gravitational pull of old environments, familiar people, and ingrained habits? The new behaviors were as fragile as the crust on a crème brûlée…so easily broken, allowing the mushy past and long-established patterns to ooze out.

"Yeah," D'Vrae nodded in agreement, "I gonna have ta see how dem BG's doin' since I been gone. Migh' need to lace 'dem up."

Okay, that's a new one. "What does lace them up mean?" asked Sophia. D'Vrae had already taught her the older generations were called the OG's (original gangsters), while younger members were YG's (young gangster), and those newly initiated were BG's or baby gangsters.

D'Vrae grinned. "Tha' mean teach dem baby G's how to presen' theyself. How they gotta dress and walk with they head up so no one mess with dem." D'Vrae enjoyed the moments he could teach something to Sophia, even if it was street language and culture.

"D'Vrae, are you going to remember what you worked on in here and do things differently when you get out there? Do you think you can stay out of trouble and not come back here or worse, end up dead?" Sophia asked.

"You come to my funeral if I dead?" D'Vrae's crooked smile contrasted starkly with the content of his question.

D'Vrae had no idea his question created a tempest in Sophia; her biggest fear was hearing one of the youth died once released, falling victim to the whirlpools of risk that suck them down before they're even aware of danger. She had never grown accustomed to their casual discussion of death, as though they expected it on a daily basis, instead of seeing it as a distant unlikely abstraction.

"I don't know, D'Vrae. I might be too angry that you are dead to come," answered Sophia. "I expect you to use what you've learned to make different choices and avoid putting yourself in a situation where you might be killed. What do you think you will do once you're home?"

D'Vrae shrugged, watching a maintenance worker blowing leaves from the wet sidewalk across the lawn. Hearing the distant whine as the blower pulsed on and off, he watched as new leaves floated to the ground behind where the man worked, wondering why he bothered; one would have to stand there all day because once the path was clear, another leaf found its way down.

He looked back at Sophia, waiting patiently for his answer, her expression a mixture of concern and encouragement. He trusted her and knew she genuinely cared. She helped him look at things differently and to feel more empathy. She helped him understand why he was so angry, and to recognize and appreciate the love and help some had given him, like his grandmother and sister. She planted a seed he might be able to have a different kind of life than he had thought if he worked at it, one free of violence and death. He knew if they continued to meet, he might be able to resist negative influences in his life; she would be his leaf blower, there to blow aside the temptations, to remind of choices, to encourage when determination waned. But he also knew that the center's regulations did not allow contact with staff after release. They had already discussed it, and Sophia had given him the names of other counselors in his home area.

"But if I could kick it wich you, I know I could stay outa trouble," he pleaded.

"You know I can't do that D'Vrae. We have to follow the no contact guidelines after you leave," she answered, disliking the answer as much as he. What sense did it make to establish that trust only to sever it completely because of geographical distance? Sophia could only hope that D'Vrae would develop trust in another person to continue his progress.

"I gonna stack paper," he finally offered in response to her question.

"Stack paper....collecting money? What plan do you have for that? Something legal I hope?"

D'Vrae's eyes twinkled as he replied, "I try to find me a job."

They discussed the jobs he might qualify for, and the application process. They identified possible temptations and how he might avoid or resist them. They made a list of what he could do for entertainment to avoid frequenting dangerous places or getting into trouble. The discussion revealed how overwhelming the odds were against successful transition and change.

Sophia wrapped up the session by saying, "I have thoroughly enjoyed getting to know you and seeing your progress over these past two years D'Vrae. Please be careful and safe out there. I don't want to read about you in the papers, unless it's for something good!"

"I miss you a'ready, Miss Sophia. We go back fo' flats on a Cadillac. You put sense in my head," he answered as they regarded each other, the connection between them as palpable as interwoven threads.

Sophia learned as much from D'Vrae as he may have learned from her. Prior to D'Vrae she regarded gangs as a refuge for soulless sociopaths deserving lock-up; in D'Vrae she saw ground fertile with possibility. Watching him leave with his escort, she made a silent plea to the universe to protect him, giving him a chance to change.

TRICKSTER

The message was short and angry, "We have a problem. I need everyone at the farm for a meeting at 10:00 Saturday. This is a priority!"

Sophia briefly considered telling him to shove it, but Marcus was not in the habit of insisting people come to meetings, even if he did believe he could order people around. Extracting the more conciliatory of her multiple layers, she made the trip to the farm, wondering what all the fuss could be, hoping it was not Marcus finding ways to harass Dylan, or make his commitment to getting the farm ready more difficult. They had just gotten Russ into the ground, and work on the property had barely begun. *If he's going to be difficult about this, he's going to have to go through me!*

Sophia wasn't sure why she felt so protective of a half-brother she hardly knew, but she did, sensing vulnerability beneath the guardedness. A school project from childhood involved soaking strips of newspaper in a solution and wrapping them around a balloon to dry, allowing the outside to appear strong and solid for decorating. But push too hard on the coating, get too enthusiastic in your creativity and you could have pieces of shredded balloon in your lap. Dylan, like those decorated balloons, was a paper-thin hardened crust hiding a barely contained eruption.

Crunching gravel signaled her arrival as the trees gradually gave way, revealing the others were already there. Letting herself in, she found them standing in the kitchen. Anger and disgust clouded Marcus' expression, "Good, you're here. Let's move to the living room."

Annie, Dylan and Sophia glanced at each other with confusion as they complied with Marcus' suggestion. Jane appeared unusually nervous, even for Jane. "He wanted to wait until you were here," offered Annie to the unspoken question as the group took their seats.

Marcus cleared his throat and took a deep breath, "As you know, Dad left me as executor of his estate. You also know he had a copy of his will here that I read and took to the lawyer who created it to ask questions, making sure I understood what needed to be done to follow his wishes. It seemed pretty straightforward and directed the assets to be divided equally among the four of us." Marcus paused.

The others looked at him expectantly. *Yeah, we already know this. Why are we here?* Sophia nodded, encouraging him to get to the point.

"Well, when I went to ask those questions, I found out there is a new will that replaces this one, one none of us knew anything about." Marcus paused again, obviously fighting back intense anger. "And the new one is nothing like the one we've discussed." Marcus waved the folder he had been holding in the air. "Not only is there a new will with different directions, but we also get to find out that we have another sister none of us knew about and who has been made a substantial part of this estate!"

Crushing silence permeated the room as Marcus stood abruptly, threw the folder down on a side table, and began to pace back and forth.

Pivot: the central point, pin, or shaft on which a mechanism turns or oscillates; a sudden, rapid change of direction; a thing or person on which something or someone functions or depends on vitally. Synonyms: rotate, turn, swivel, revolve, spin. There are moments in life that are pivotal. Some happen with advanced warning, like Russ' decline and ultimate death. Some occur spontaneously and without notice, like a plane crashing into a house, ending unsuspecting lives watching TV. Some pivotal moments are obvious as they are happening while others may be recognized in hindsight. Some wear the appearance of a bigger-than-us plan while others are costumed as capriciously random, like deciding to turn left instead of right and into the path of an intoxicated driver. But in that pivot, that tornado-like spin, your lungs freeze for a moment, and you instinctively know that the next breath you take will be different. Like breathing invisible dust, something feels clogged, heavy, and claustrophobic as you try to move forward. The memory of clear sweet air trying to pull you backwards in time as the pivot's current propels you reluctantly forward. These are the moments that move at a different pace, forever instants that can be recalled in microscopic detail years later; a lifetime that fits on the head of a pin.

A sister? Sophia shook her head slightly as she tried to absorb this news. *How is this possible? Why had they not been told? When? How? With whom?*

Numb with disbelief, Sophia felt betrayed by the dishonesty of it, as well as mild curiosity about the person and her story. What did she look like? What did she do? Where did she live? What kind of a person was she? How fascinating to know there was another human being who shared half of her biology out there, but was kept a secret her entire life. *Wow. Leave it to Russ.*

"Are you sure this is genuine?" Annie's quavering voice penetrated the stunned silence as tears glistened. "No way this could be faked or a mistake?" She struggled to accept the possibility that Russ had kept such a secret from them, from her.

"It's no mistake," was the heated reply. "The lawyer had copies of birth certificates and other verifications in the event that was questioned. He was fully prepared to defend the new will."

"Why weren't we told….ever?" Dylan asked, staring at the floor.

"That's something I can't answer. The attorney either could not, or would not, provide any explanation other than this was Dad's wish. This will was created quite recently, when Dad knew how sick he was becoming. I don't even know if Dad was always aware he had another daughter or if he found this out more recently. I just know he's revised how he wants things done, and this person is a major player now." Marcus continued to pace, ruffling his hair continuously as he did.

"Does "this person" have a name?" Sophia asked, wanting to put flesh on this family ghost, to apply color to a black and white portrait.

"Elizabeth Walling, but she goes by Beth. I don't know if it's a married name or not. I was given her name and a way to contact her. The attorney says she also has a copy of the will and my number. It appears the attorney met with her before I got there. Dad must have given her a copy so she could follow up. I'm guessing he told her about us, even if he didn't tell us about her. I don't know WHAT he was thinking!" Marcus slammed an open palm against the glass door he had been walking past.

"Oh now, Marcus, please calm down," the high-pitched admonition beseeched by Jane was answered with a snort as Marcus flopped onto the couch beside her.

"Calm down? Calm DOWN? I find out I have a sister I never knew about and have to cut her in on this inheritance whether I like it or not? Whether I think it's RIGHT or not? Whether I've been put in charge or not? Did she have to put up with him all these years? Was she here to take care of him as he drank and smoked himself to death? Does she deserve a DIME of his money? I don't think so!!" Marcus was churning inside; outside his arms waved and his body bounced around on the couch. Sophia felt mildly sorry for Jane as she bounced along with him, looking like she'd rather crawl to the corner and cower.

"What do you mean by major player, Marcus? What was changed?" Sophia tried to move the discussion to something concrete.

A second snort escaped, "She gets a third and we divide the other two thirds among the four of us!"

Annie gasped and Dylan slowly rolled up his head to make eye contact with Marcus, the look on his face unreadable. Annie's previously glistening eyes overflowed, and she quickly wiped her face, making a valiant attempt to contain her reaction.

"Wow!" was all Sophia could muster. *Must be a heck of a story behind this one.*

"I don't understand any of this, Marcus. How could he do such a thing? WHY would he do such a thing?" Annie was clearly struggling with the new information and all it seemed to convey.

"I wish I knew! I think it's bull and can't believe it myself. The only way to sort out what happened and why is to meet this woman and ask questions. Not that I want to, but I don't see we have much choice. I also haven't found any way to fight it yet, but I intend to continue to look for that possibility. Obviously I couldn't go any further until you were informed of the situation. This may mean everything we've discussed and decided on so far has to be put on hold until we determine what this means. I'm not sure it even makes sense to work on the property until we have some kind of meeting with this woman."

"Her name is Beth, Marcus" Sophia prodded.

"I don't care what her name is, Sophia. You may find it interesting and fun to suddenly discover you have a new sister, but I find it appalling and offensive. She will be no sister of mine, especially after this rip-off. Once I've dealt with this mess I want no part of her in my life."

Well don't ride the fence, Marcus. How do you REALLY feel about her! Sophia resisted reacting outwardly to her brother's tirade, knowing this was hard news for all of them.

Annie dropped her head into her hands, moaning softly, rocking back and forth. "I can't believe this is happening. He never mentioned any of this when he talked about what would happen after he was gone. I just don't understand."

"What are we going to do about meeting Beth and sorting it out?" Dylan interjected. Sophia silently thanked him for using her name.

"I suppose I can call her and set up a meeting. I'm assuming you all would want to be there too?" Marcus received nods from all three. Jane did not vote but they all knew she would do what Marcus asked of her, whether that was to participate or stay home. "Do you want to meet in town somewhere or out here?"

They discussed the pros and cons of various options and settled on meeting Beth at the farm. If she was going to be a player in the negotiations, it might be best for her to see what the property consisted of, if she hadn't already secretly had that opportunity. The thought that she may have wandered through these rooms, roamed the grounds, sat in one of these chairs, had a cup of coffee with Russ, all without their knowledge left each of them with an uneasy feeling, as if someone had come into their private space and subtly rearranged things. It looked and felt familiar but wasn't quite the same. Once the decision had been made, Marcus and Jane departed with the promise to let them know when the meeting was scheduled.

"You haven't said much, Dylan. What do you make of this? Are you doing OK?" Sophia probed.

Dylan rubbed his hands together slowly, back and forth, hesitating before answering. Looking out the window, he said, "I'm not sure what to think. Somehow it doesn't surprise me all that much. The old man was always a womanizer. For all we know, there could be more of them out there." Annie groaned. "What does surprise me a little is she's part of this picture now. Makes me think she's someone important to him, and I want to know why. And why is she this important now, but wasn't important enough to tell us about earlier?"

"And neither of you ever heard or saw anything that would have suggested this was possible? You two have spent the most time with him recently…nothing was ever said that hinted at it?" Sophia grasped at phantom straws.

"Absolutely nothing," Annie replied. "I thought I knew him. I thought I knew everything there was to know about him. And I just can't believe this. I feel so..." she trailed off as a deep sob overtook her. In a moment she continued. "It's not even the estate or the money involved. It's the dishonesty. It's the secrecy of it. There's a person out there that is related to all of us! How do you NOT share that? It's so….I don't even know the word that describes it!"

Annie's struggle with their father's inconsistencies filled Sophia with compassion. Resigned to them long ago, nothing surprised her anymore about Russ. He fell off his fatherly pedestal so hard he exploded into slivers and floated away, leaving a shadowy outline of what once was. Initially stunned by the existence of an unrevealed sibling, it took only a moment to see it as completely consistent with his character, he may have even delighted in the secret. Remembering well the disappointments leading to estrangement, she patted Annie's hand, attempting to comfort her.

"I don't have any way to explain that either. Perhaps if we meet Beth she can answer some of our questions and help us understand. I know this has been a shock and it's going to take some getting used to. I'm going to keep an open mind about her and see what she has to say. We may have no choice but to accept what the will states, but it will be up to each of us whether or not we accept her as a sister or what we do with her appearance."

"I don't know if I can. I resent her already. I feel like she stole something from me, from all of us," Annie covered her face in her hands.

"It's not her fault, whoever she is and however she came to exist," Dylan contributed. "I don't know what the story is behind this, but I know who is responsible. I'll hear her out."

"I think that's all we can do to begin with. Hear what she has to say and see what happens," Sophia was grateful for Dylan's objective stance. Having been so distant from Russ and the farm, she did not feel particularly attached to the place or his personal belongings, but she knew Dylan, Annie and perhaps even Marcus felt differently. They would have stronger reactions to the notion of having to share with a stranger. Hearing Dylan's willingness to put off judgment relieved her; not for the mysterious sibling's sake, but for his own and perhaps Annie's.

Emotionally depleted and needing to process, they left for their respective homes, knowing they would soon gather again to meet the stranger thrust into their midst. Driving home, Sophia wondered what Beth might be feeling about the prospect of meeting the four of them. How daunting that must seem. What might Beth make of each of them and their unique personalities? What a mess Russ had created with his final act.

FACELESS

Turning the key in the lock, he raised the lid as the inside pins released their grip; corner light giving just enough illumination to glint off the stony metal he lifted and embraced. Caressing the sleek barrel against the rough of his hands, as soothing as aloe on a burn, he smelled its power as he pointed it at nothing, and everything. Inner typhoon ebbing, losing energy as it spins against his imagining, hardening thoughts which became glow-in-the-dark islands marking the way out of this life storm. Soon…..soon…..

Beth

Despite expecting it, the doorbell chime still made them all jump. *Nothing like good old anticipation adrenaline to put nerves on high alert*, Sophia mused.

Marcus strode to the door and yanked it open, his entire body emanating tension, if not hostility. The remaining three (Jane had gratefully accepted Marcus' decision she not be present for this meeting), without realizing it, had momentarily stopped breathing. The last remnants of a setting sun cut through the shadows as a tall, slender woman stepped across the threshold. Briefly a two-dimensional silhouette in the dimming light, she morphed into human form as she moved into the center of the room and Marcus closed the door behind her.

A stunned gasp caught Sophia by surprise as she made eye contact. Standing before her was a close replica, a near-twin. She might have been looking into a slightly distorted carnival mirror. The woman was a bit shorter than she was, but the hair was almost the same color and the facial features so similar that there was no mistaking the common genetics. Even the eyes were a familiar green. She was close in age too, perhaps a few years younger. Beth's expression telegraphed recognition and reciprocal questions in the visual exchange.

"Wow," Dylan exclaimed quietly from his side of the couch, voicing the reaction they all felt seeing the resemblance. Annie remained speechless, motionless.

Dylan's voice nudged Sophia from her stunned inertia. She stood, extending a hand to her duplicate. "Hello, Beth. I'm Sophia."

The return grasp was firm and the voice soft, "Hello, Sophia. It's nice to meet you."

"This is Dylan, that's Annie, and Marcus let you in," a gesturing hand accompanied the introductions.

Dylan stood and shook Beth's hand. Annie waved from her seat and Marcus nodded as he returned to his place at the desk along the wall. Indicating a nearby vacant recliner, Sophia said, "Please, have a seat. Would you like something to drink? Coffee? Water? Might even be a beer in there if that is more what you like."

"Thank you but I think I'm fine," Beth responded, lowering herself into the chair offered.

Dylan and Sophia returned to their places on the couch, creating a circle thick with tension.

"I guess you know you've been included in our father's will. We want to know who the hell you are and why that happened, especially since it was just recently changed," Marcus' sharp tone accentuated his hostile expression.

"Whoa! Hold on, Marcus!" Sophia jumped in. "What the hell?" *Why do you have to be so nasty?*

No discussion had occurred regarding how to conduct the meeting, no meeting of the minds regarding an agenda or how to tease out the desired information, no decisions about whether someone tried to lead it or not. Anticipating it, Sophia couldn't decide what to start with or how to proceed. There were no blueprints for annexing a sibling halfway through your existence, no cookbook for blending your history with new ingredients to create a revised outcome. But she did know beginning with a cannon blast was likely to sink the entire effort.

"Hold on for what?" Marcus shot back. "I want an explanation. As executor of this will, I am owed an explanation!"

"I agree we all have questions and a need to understand the situation, what Russ was thinking and why. But I think we can do that without being rude and unkind. Beth may have as many questions about this as we do. Can we give her a chance to speak before she's attacked?" Addressing Beth, she added, "This is a tough situation for all of us, and we are confused, surprised, and somewhat upset that we just found out about you. We aren't sure what to make of it or how to understand it. We're hoping you can help with that."

Cold expression on his face, Marcus nodded towards Beth as he said, "Well? So what's your story?"

Taking a deep breath as she looked at Marcus, Beth began to speak, "I know this has to be a shock, and probably an unpleasant one. I wasn't sure if I should even come today. I haven't been sure how to handle any of this either. I wanted to meet you but wasn't sure you would feel the same. I don't know if it helps or not, but I haven't known about your existence for very long either. All of this happened rather recently, and I'm also trying to sort it out."

"How long?" barked Marcus.

"Several months."

"Obviously you are Russ' daughter. Who's your mother?" Marcus continued to grill.

"My mother's name was Marie. She died recently, too, of cancer." Beth paused, eyes glassy, struggling with the disclosure.

"How did our father know her?" Marcus continued relentlessly, unconcerned with Beth's discomfort.

"I'm sorry for the loss of your mother," Sophia inserted. "I'm sure that was very difficult." She glared at Marcus in a silent attempt to rein in his unbridled malice.

"Thank you," Beth directed a slight smile at Sophia. "As I understand it, they met when she took a class from him at the university. They had a short relationship, and I was the outcome of that relationship."

"Did he know about you?" Annie spoke for the first time.

"Yes. But he did not maintain contact with my mother and made no effort to see me or have any contact with me. My mother raised me as a single parent until she married when I was two years old. I grew up believing that man was my father because I was too young to know the difference. They divorced when I was fifteen. My stepfather made some initial efforts to see me and stay in touch, but that eventually faded, and it was just me and mom after that."

"So you didn't know about Dad or any of us until a few months ago? How did you find out about him? And us?" Dylan interjected. Somehow, the fact she had not known much sooner than he made Dylan feel better, like they were on more equal footing, like he hadn't missed half the movie she had seen entirely.

"When Mom got sick and knew she was going to die she told me. I think she wanted me to know the truth before she was gone. Although they had not stayed in touch, she knew where he was because he was still teaching until recently, and he apparently has lived in this house for a very long time. I was able to find him through that."

"I'll bet that was a fun meeting!" grunted Marcus. "The old man doesn't like surprises, and if he hadn't chosen to stay in touch he was probably not thrilled to have you show up out of the blue."

Beth looked quizzically at Marcus. *I wonder how a person gets so jaded and angry. I wonder what happened to you.*

"Actually, it went okay, and he seemed happy to have the opportunity to know who I was and how my life had been. I was glad I had a chance to meet him and have a little time getting to know who he was before he died. I would have liked more time for that, but what time I got will always be precious to me. I'm glad I could be there at his service."

Flashing back to the unknown but familiar looking figure in black standing under the tree, and the goose-bump moment she had experienced, Sophia realized that must have been Beth.

"YOU were at the service?" exploded Marcus. "Wow, don't you think that's a bit bold?"

"Okay, knock it OFF, Marcus! How can you be so insensitive and rude?" Sophia was instantly incensed. It was one thing for her to put up with his belligerent attitude over their lifetime, it was quite another to see it showered upon someone he had just met and who had done nothing to deserve it. "It hurt nothing that she came!"

"Really? I think it's disrespectful to those of us who actually knew the man. How much can you know about someone you met a few months ago? How much can you care about his death? Why would you attend, knowing the real family is going to be there dealing with so much? Why would you risk adding all this crap to the feelings already going on?" Marcus countered.

"Perhaps it was a mistake to come here," Beth stood as she spoke.

Dylan and Sophia both rose in response, Dylan speaking first "Wait. Marcus obviously has some strong feelings about this. I think we all do. But I want to hear more, and I don't necessarily agree with what Marcus is saying. I think we all have had different relationships with our dad so we all come at this from different angles."

"Yes, please don't let what Marcus says make you think he speaks for all of us. He may speak the LOUDEST, but his feelings and way of looking at this are not true for all of us. Please stay, we'd like to hear more." Sophia added as she put her hand on Beth's arm, confirming her interest and openness. She looked towards Annie, who had continued her silence. "Annie?"

Despite a constricted look on her face, Annie nodded in agreement, "I would like you to stay."

After hesitating a moment Beth sat back down, trying to calm fragile nerves. This was more difficult than she thought it might be. "Perhaps it was wrong of me to have gone to his service. I tried to be respectful and unobtrusive. I wanted to get more of a sense of him by hearing and seeing the people who chose to come, to fill in more blanks and understand him better. Perhaps that was selfish of me. It would never have been my intention to cause any harm or more pain."

"You said you got in touch with him and had time to get to know him a little. How did you do that?" Annie asked, finally finding her voice.

"I wrote to tell him who I was and that Mom had just died. I asked if he would be willing to meet me, and he said he was. We had coffee once a week after that until he got too sick to do it anymore. I came out here once, at his invitation. He told me about all of you, and teaching, and farming. He wrote me letters, too, after we had met for coffee. He seemed to keep thinking about things after the conversations and wanted to write things down in case they were forgotten before we saw each other again. That's how I knew about his will changes. He wrote me about it and gave me the name of the lawyer and a phone number for Marcus. He told me how proud he was of all of you and how much I would like you. He thought you would like me too. I didn't see him or hear too much from him once he got really sick. The last contact was him calling to tell me he was going to die. Then I saw the obituary in the paper."

"Do you know why he didn't tell us about you?" Dylan asked.

"I don't know. He talked about us all meeting, in a sometime-in-the-future kind of way. Maybe his illness progressed too quickly and there just wasn't time. I'm not sure. You all know him far better than I do and may know better his reasons. He didn't say he intended to keep it a secret."

Perhaps he was afraid to bring the closet skeleton into the light for all to see? Didn't want to tarnish his precious image? Didn't want to have the evidence of his tomcat ways known by his family and friends? Not to mention his total abdication of parental duties. Sophia could think of multiple reasons Russ might have been disinclined to share this part of his life with them. *Do you hate him? Do you resent being ignored your entire life until a few months ago? Are you angry about what your Mom experienced because he took no responsibility for you? How hard was your life?*

"Well, you know the old man," Marcus offered. "Whatever the reason, it would have been all about him, not any of us." For once Sophia agreed with Marcus, although she did not voice that thought aloud.

"So, where did you grow up and what do you do?" Sophia thought it was time to know something of this woman and the mystery of her existence. Clearly she had no other siblings given her comment about it being just she and her mother most of the years. There was no wedding band visible, which could suggest no significant other either.

"I grew up in Butteville."

An unknown sister thirty miles away this entire time, went through each mind, although each mind had a different reaction to that concept. The world was simultaneously large and small.

"I still live there. I work for a youth transitional program that helps foster kids who are aging out of the system find work and get set up to live on their own. I have an apartment on the edge of town," Beth replied.

"Are you…in a relationship? Have any kids?" Dylan hesitantly asked.

"No kids. The kids I work with keep me busy enough. I've had relationships in the past, but there is no one special at the moment. I've never been married." Beth understood the curiosity they felt. She wanted to ask them questions in return, even though Russ had given her some information about them during visits. Marcus' hostility kept her from following that impulse, however. She didn't want to risk further ire and instinctively knew now was not the time to satisfy her own curiosity. Perhaps if things went well she would get a later opportunity to know more about these stranger relatives.

"This is all very fascinating, but can you tell us why Dad would decide to cut you into the will, and for such a large portion of it?" Marcus cut in, eager to move the discussion to what was most pressing to him.

Face flushing red, Beth became quickly uncomfortable. While she had wanted the opportunity to meet her siblings, she knew this part was going to be potentially unpleasant. Having been as surprised as they were, she had no idea what to expect from them in response.

"I'm not entirely sure," she began tentatively, "All he said to me was that he felt bad about not being a father to me and he wanted to make it up to me. He wanted to make things easier for me now, especially since Mom died. I didn't expect him to do this, even though he said he wanted to. People say things when they feel bad, but that doesn't mean they will act on what they say."

"Well isn't that just rich! He's trying to make up for being a lousy father! Welcome to the frigging club of poorly treated children. I wonder how much he thought we needed for the lousy childhood we had WITH him? I wonder how much THAT is worth…what kind of price tag THAT comes with!"

Anger contorting his face, Marcus leapt from his chair and began stomping along the wall, hands almost pulling the hair from his head. "What a nightmare!"

Beth shrank back into her chair in silence, while each of the others absorbed the news through the filter of their own relationships with Russ.

Dylan… Guilt money. I wonder if that works. I wonder if her living without you was any worse than us living with you. I wish I had known this before it was too late to ask questions. I wonder what it was like to know she was out there all this time and not have any contact? The hardest thing in my life was losing daily contact with my kids. I can't imagine just turning my back on one from the beginning. How did you live with that? Maybe this did make you feel better when you knew it was the end. Maybe you needed to do this to ease your guilt.

Annie…I thought I mattered. I thought you loved me. You promised me so many times, why have you abandoned me after all this time. I don't understand. I don't know why this girl matters more than any of the rest of us. I just want this to go away. I want things back the way they were. Daddy, how could you?

Sophia…As you were lying there dying, were you thinking about her? Were you feeling smugly satisfied you righted one wrong in your life? Did it cross your mind at all what everyone else would feel or how we might react? Did you actually feel less guilty? Did you know you were poking a hornet's nest as you faded away? Typical, Russ, so typical.

Marcus…You ass. Leave me with this mess after all the things I've put up with. Leave me with almost nothing after all the things I've done for you over the years? Selfish to the bitter end, huh? Maybe I'll just resign as executor. Maybe I'll let your newfound daughter figure it out and do all the work. Would serve her and you right! I'm tired of trying to fix what you break. Actually, to hell with that. I'm going to defend my own rights here! If you thought I'd take this lying down, you were dead wrong!

Marcus broke the silence, "Did you give him some song and dance about how awful your life had been and convince him you needed a handout? Did you make him feel guilty for getting your mother pregnant even though she obviously owns part of that blame?"

Looking like she had been struck, Beth's eyes widened, then moistened. In imagining this day, she had never expected to be treated like the enemy. If she had, she would not have come. She opened her mouth slightly, and then closed it again, having no idea how to respond. She was beginning to wonder if she would be able to like this brother, or any of them for that matter.

"I think you need to take it easy, Marcus," Dylan leaned forward as he attempted to rescue Beth from the tirade. "We all know Dad did what he wanted, and sometimes he wanted conflicting things. Don't blame Beth for what he decided. If he hadn't wanted to do it, he wouldn't have."

"Agreed," Sophia was grateful to have Dylan's assistance. "Russ made decisions based on fantasy much of the time, not reality. There's no telling what he told himself about the situation or why he wanted to do it this way. Regardless of his reasons, Beth is not responsible, and you shouldn't be treating her so poorly."

"I'm not treating anyone poorly. I'm just trying to wrap my mind around the absurdity of this mess! We have been his children our entire lives and we have been half erased by this woman who met him a few months ago. Tell me how that's fair! Tell me how that's right! Tell me why I should put up with it. Why ANY of us should put up with it? Blood or not, she hasn't BEEN his daughter until a minute ago. We are the ones who grew up with him. We are the ones who put up with his crap all these years. We are the ones who looked after him when he got sick and buried him. And we are the ones who are entitled to have what he leaves behind. Not some distant memory of a daughter he ignored until now."

"You know, Marcus, what a person does with his will is his own business. It's not up to you or me or anyone else to decide what Russ does with his assets…it was up to him. And if he wanted to send it all to an orphanage in China, that was his right. We have no business getting angry about it or punishing Beth for what he decided," Sophia tried to insert logic into the emotional storm.

"I agree with Sophia," Dylan added, "I have never understood how Dad decided things, but I know he has the right to decide. He's helped me out before…helped me get set up in my mobile after my divorce, and paid for me to get my trucking license. And he didn't have to do either of those things. I know he's helped Annie out too, hasn't he, Annie?"

Continuing to sit motionless, looking stricken, Annie nodded tentatively, "He bought me a car when mine gave out on me. And when I was off work for a while because of a surgery, he covered my house payment for me."

"Yeah, I know he was pretty generous to you two, more than to me or Sophia. I worked my ass off to not need his help, and I know Sophia paid her own way through college. He took care of you two while he forgot about or ignored the two of us. I figured this would finally settle that score, even things out a little. I thought maybe I'd finally feel like he treated us all the same, and now this! Now we ALL get to feel like second class citizens to a stranger!" Marcus punctuated his statement with a furious glance in Beth's direction.

Remaining silent throughout this exchange, Beth finally summoned the courage to speak, to defend, "Obviously this has been hard for everyone involved. I didn't mean to cause this by getting in touch with Russ. I just wanted to know who he was. I had no idea he would feel moved to change his will to include me. I know he cared about all of you because he told me and I could see it in how he talked about you. I never told him my life was terrible because it wasn't. My mom was a loving woman who always supported me. I have a job and support myself now, and have for years. Russ knew that. This was not done because I had some kind of horrible life because I didn't. I did wonder for years why the man I thought was my dad drifted away and out of contact. Now I know why. Although I believe he cared for me, he always knew I wasn't his, and I guess the bonds we had gradually faded. After the divorce, maybe he didn't feel the same connection, or maybe he thought I'd find out about Russ someday. I was just trying to figure some things out about my own life. I never meant to bring any harm into yours."

Beth paused for a moment looking in turn at each of them. Sophia and Dylan returned her look, nodding encouragingly. Marcus and Annie stared at the ground as she continued, "I was excited to hear that I had half-siblings out there, being an only child. I was hoping each of you, or at least some of you, might share that excitement and be open to meeting me. Mom couldn't tell me much about any of you. She knew a little about you older two but not the younger ones."

"How did she know anything about Sophia and me?" demanded Marcus.

"I….I…." Beth stammered for a moment, suddenly uncertain she should continue.

"Come on…HOW?" he repeated.

"My mom was his student when you and Sophia were little. I guess he was actually married to your mom at that time…it was about the time your sister Addison died. I know it was wrong of her to be involved with him, but…." Beth trailed off, seeing the change in expression for both Marcus and Sophia.

Some explosions are instant and loud, erupting and spewing, slicing through solid matter to leave shards and ashes of what once was. Others suck all sound and breathable air from the room first, a pre-tsunami wave of suctioned silence, followed by a surge of overwhelming force that casts you along a path not of your choosing. This explosion began with the loss of sound, the loss of air, the loss of reason. This explosion began with a suffocating moment of emotional implosion.

GHOSTS FROM THE CRIB

Buzzing, annoying buzzing, gasping for air, gulping, trying to breathe, spinning. Sounds, from outside, or inside? Am I thinking or is someone talking to me? Whirling as if in a wave, end over end, air, must breathe, choking. Am I going to vomit? Who's crying? Can't find the surface, clawing, finding nothing, giving up. Floating downward, darkness, cold, ice cold, shivering, stillness, emptiness.

"Hey, hey, it's okay," he murmured. His instinctive response, driven by compassion, immediately led to his feeling awkward and clumsy, and he was uncertain what to do for her. He continued to make soothing sounds as he watched for signs she was coming out of it, like she had at the barn.

Staring in horror at Sophia, Beth stammered, "I…I…I'm so sorry."

Marcus, shaking free from shocked immobility, moved to the couch and knelt down, his face near Sophia's. "Sophia? Sophia? It's okay Soph. Come on, it's okay," stroking her hair as he spoke and placing a hand on her knee.

"Can I do something, Marcus?" Annie asked. "Should we get a blanket? Glass of water?"

"No, just give her a minute."

Skin tickling, ocean waves, am I at the beach? Where's the water? Tingling, who's talking? Swallowing, I can swallow. Bee sounds, am I in a hive? Is the sun coming up? Darkness becoming light. Ringing, whispering, what did you say? Is this a dream? Am I asleep? Cold, shivering, bee sounds, bee on my knee, get it off….

Sophia pushed Marcus' hand off her knee, lifting her head enough to look at the knee. The choked cries had stopped, as had the rocking. Her downcast eyes slowly came into focus and she found herself staring at a rounded knob. Recognizing her knee, she looked for the second one and found it where it belonged.

Why am I sitting here staring at my knees? What's on my head? And my back?

Raising her head farther, Sophia looked at Marcus. Brain still swimming, she stared for a silent, confused moment. Marcus allowed the hand caressing her head to drop to his side as he watched her pupils begin to shrink and the face coated with perspiration began to relax.

Nodding slowly he said, "That's right Soph. That's right. Come on back." Glancing at Dylan he bobbed his head slightly, signaling Dylan could release his hold.

Dylan eased his grip gradually until he could shift his weight to move away, watching her carefully as he did, grateful for Marcus' assistance.

Sophia shuddered, hugging herself again, feeling chilled, struggling to assemble the missing pieces, her mind taking this part and that one to find which lines matched, which colors coordinated. The buzzing had stopped, the twirling slowed, and there was enough light to see again. She looked around the room in search of bearings.

Dylan, quiet, kind Dylan. Annie, why do you look so frightened and small? Marcus, my thorny brother. And who are you? Why do you look like me? Oh wait, I remember…Beth, my new sister. The sister born while Russ was married to my mother. Sister. Oh. OH! I remember! Oh my God! Addie…

Sophia's stomach somersaulted as she remembered what had preceded the black hole that swallowed her. Inhaling sharply, she stared at Beth who continued to look stricken.

Marcus and Dylan instantly tensed in response to the sound, but relaxed again as Sophia continued to regard Beth without further reaction.

"Sophia?" Marcus checked.

Sophia nodded wordlessly, telegraphing a silent plea to Marcus with her eyes.

Message received, Marcus turned to Beth, whose expression conveyed both regret and bewilderment, "I think this meeting is over. We will be in touch if and when we think we need to be. For now, you need to leave and let us decide what comes next," his tone unyielding, but without its previous malice.

"Are you sure about this, Marcus?" asked Dylan.

"Very sure. You need to trust me on this."

Beth stood slowly, unsure if she could trust her instincts. She wanted to apologize, to explain, and to let them know she had not meant to cause harm. But she already had, according to what she was seeing, even when her intentions had been good. She certainly didn't want to cause any further trouble.

Torn and unsettled, she offered, "I am truly sorry. I just wanted to meet you. I never wanted to cause any problems. I'm so sorry."

Tears welling, she let herself out the door, closing it gently behind her, fully aware this might be the last time she saw any of them. Entering her car, she cursed herself, wanting a rewind, a do-over. Driving out the gravel road, barely able to see through smearing eyes, she filled with anger, at her mother, at Russ, at her own clumsy attempts which had tripped over hidden mines strewn through the past she was just learning of.

ADDiSON

Fighting nausea, Sophia worked to still the buzzing sensation that prickled at her skin like a light dose of electricity, the ride was over almost as soon as it had begun. Feeling inside out physically and mentally, she was grateful for the silence Marcus had maintained as he drove her home. She briefly resisted, then succumbed to the plan, knowing Dylan would bring her car, and Annie would follow to take him back to his own. Feeling caught in a time warp with disturbed dimensions, she had difficulty focusing on objects and their relevance, even as a passenger. Like a fly buzzing randomly around a room, bouncing off windows, her mind seemed unable to land on a train of thought. Sophia was certain that her mouth would have similar difficulty forming words, as her mind careened on without waiting. Marcus had looked sideways in her direction a couple of times, but had not tried to engage her in conversation.

The familiar shape of her apartment building loomed before them and Marcus parked the car before it, "I'm going to walk you in."

"That's not…," Marcus' look stopped her mid-try. "Okay," she said vacantly, "But I need my keys to get in."

Marcus retrieved the keys from Dylan, thanking him and Annie for helping to get Sophia's car home. Returning to where he had left Sophia, he opened the door and followed her inside. Marcus found a bottle of wine and poured himself a glass as he waited for Sophia to change into pajamas. When she emerged, he held up the bottle with a quizzical expression and received a nod of assent. He poured a second glass and handed it to her, then sat on the nearby sofa. As he stroked the fabric, he noted many colors subtly hidden in what appeared to be black from a distance. Fine lines of pink, lavender, light green and blue appeared as he moved his fingers back and forth, shifting the nap. Lifting his eyes to look at his younger sister, he realized how much she was like this fabric. She could appear colorless, remote, and controlled until you got closer, peeling back layers to reveal the underlying patterns. He knew they had differences, argued, believed different things, but she was still his little sister and he felt he had to look out for her. Always had, especially after all that had happened; it was the responsibility he accepted at a very young age.

Sophia fell heavily into the nearby chair, taking a long drink from her glass, "You don't have to stay, you know. I'm fine." Still trembling hands suggested otherwise, a fact not lost on Marcus.

"What do you remember Soph? I think we need to talk about this a little," Marcus gazed intently at her.

What if I don't WANT to talk about it? What if I want to forget this whole stinking mess? What if I don't want to think about it or remember it or have other people talking about it? What if I want to sit here by myself and figure out how to put it all back in the box so I don't have to feel it anymore? Maybe you aren't the person I want to discuss this with anyhow. What about THAT Marcus!

Sighing loudly, Sophia shifted in her chair and drew her legs into a curl. She took another long sip, feeling the warmth of the liquid and the calming sensation it offered.

"I don't remember much. I remember talking with Beth about how her mother knew Russ, and she mentioned Addie, and the next thing I remember is everyone staring at me and feeling like I'm going to vomit. How does she know about Addie? *What* does she know about Addie? I *hate* that she knows about Addie! We didn't even know about *her*!" The words came out in an unfamiliar rush. To stop them from continuing, Sophia pressed the wine glass against her lips again.

"I don't know the answers to any of that yet," Marcus responded. "Maybe at some point we can find out more if we want to, but you were in no shape to ask any of those questions tonight or hear any answers. I thought it was best to stop the conversation and take some time to sort this out. You were kind of a mess at that point."

Sophia had a vague memory of Beth leaving but it was indistinct, incomplete. With a sincerely puzzled look she said, "Mess?"

When they were young children, Marcus had seen these episodes in his sister from time to time, but had not seen it since they'd become adults. If it was still occurring, it was not in his presence. He had forgotten about it, assuming she had put it behind her, mastering it. Today he was ricocheted back in time; back to pink rooms and cradling the mute, rocking, six year old, open eyes blinded to his face, ears deaf to his pleas, skin indifferent to his touch; back to the unresponsive eleven year old scratching crimson grooves into her luminescent skin; back to the unreachable fourteen-year-old, retching sobs leaking from dark closet corners.

Although the passing years faded the memories, instinct propelled him when they resurfaced like a corpse from murky depths. Suddenly it was yesterday and she was six, eleven, fourteen, lost inside herself once again, needing someone to throw her a lifeline. He had never been sure what she remembered afterwards, for they never spoke of it. They just found the other side together; Marcus, waiting breathlessly for her to grab hold; Sophia, finally grabbing and pulling, easing her way back to the surface, holding tight in silence until each could breathe again, until her spinning stopped and his clenched hold relaxed.

An unspoken pact formed between them in the awkward stillness that followed each time. A pact of silent acceptance that some things can't be spoken, because the sounds needed to speak the awful truth were fragile as butterfly wings and might be torn apart on the way through one's lips; or worse, might be picked up and flung like daggers to slice apart the world they knew. Both knew that once said it couldn't be unsaid and there would be no way to control the outcome. No, silence was better. Silence offered protection. Silence kept them safe.

Sophia, looking small with her feet curled up behind her, reminded Marcus of how fragile she had seemed as a child. Was it time to break that silence? Could they handle it? Would it bring something good or bad into their lives and the already troubling circumstances? Needing time to think, to respond, he stood and retrieved the wine bottle, refilling both of their glasses.

Handing hers back to her he began, "Sophia, when Beth mentioned Addison you kind of had a fit. I don't know how else to describe it. You were shaking, twitching, scratching at yourself and sobbing. It was like you were somewhere else and not able to hear or see us. This isn't the first time I've seen you do something like that. I'm not sure you remember them once they are done. Do you….remember any of that?"

Frowning, biting her lower lip, Sophia shook her head slightly, "I kind of felt like I lost time….like I was watching a movie and it skipped a few scenes. But I don't remember doing any of those things. My ears were buzzing and I remember feeling confused, like when you wake up from a dream and there's that moment when you aren't sure if what's going on is still a dream or if you're really awake. It takes me a minute to sort that out sometimes and figure out what I missed. And then I'm just really tired."

"Takes you a minute…you make it sound like this has happened more than I realized? Have you?" Marcus frowned in concern.

Eyes downcast, finger caressing the glass rim, Sophia could feel the edge of the abyss lurking behind her, words sticking to the inside of her throat as she tried to force them upward. "It was worse when I was a kid, but, yeah, sometimes it happens. Not too often," she minimized, as much for her own sake as to not worry her brother.

This conversation was uncharted ground and the potential grenades were palpable to her. This was not who she and Marcus were together and the lack of trust she felt kept her from wanting to disclose too much about something she barely understood herself.

"Really, I'm fine Marcus. She just took me off guard and after all the emotion of what's been going on with Beth and Russ it just triggered me. I can imagine what they all think of me now. Probably think I'm a freak," she added a mirthless laugh.

"I think you just freaked everyone out. I've seen it, but I don't think any of them knew what to do, or what was going on. I doubt anyone thinks you're a freak, they were just worried. And they can't possibly understand any of it. The good news is they didn't ask a lot of questions, just focused on helping me get you here. But we need to figure out how to deal with the Beth situation, especially after this. I'm thinking we need to deal with her through lawyers and avoid any more direct contact. If she is going to have this kind of effect on you, we need to be more careful. I don't have any desire to add her to my life, so we just need to get through this estate ordeal and put all of it behind us."

Sophia fought to stay coherent, to sort through conflicting feelings churning within her, confusion, fear, and the feeling that boxed up puzzles were trying to escape and re-form.

"Marcus, I appreciate that you brought me home and are concerned about me, but I don't want to decide anything tonight. I need to think about what we heard and to know what Dylan and Annie think too. I know today was hard, harder than I thought it would be, but I don't know how I feel about any of it yet or what I might want to do about Beth. I guess I hadn't really thought about how her mother was connected to Russ, or when, or what that might mean in terms of our own lives at that time. I just wasn't ready for what she said and I need to let it settle and think it through before I decide anything. Can you please just give me some time?"

Marcus gulped the wine remaining in his glass and set it down on the table beside him. "If that's what you want. I don't have to make any decisions yet, but I also know that so far she hasn't endeared herself to me, and I see no point in creating more headache or trouble just because she wants to know who we are. It's just not worth it, Sophia. She's really no one to us. She was barely anyone to Dad. We don't have to turn our lives upside down just because she got shoved into it. And I won't stand by and watch her hurt YOU either."

Sophia was surprised at the level of his concern. Growing up, he had occasionally been kind and protective, but mostly distant and pursuing his own interests. As adults, they had drifted farther apart as their personalities appeared to lead them in opposite directions. While she felt somewhat touched by his behavior she also was puzzled and not sure how to understand or respond to it. This was not the Marcus she knew sitting before her.

"Okay, why don't we both get some sleep and give this some time for processing?" Sophia countered.

Marcus nodded. She let him out and locked up behind him. Outside movement made her pause as she began to close the drapes to her window. A hooded figure stood in the shadows, just outside the circle of light thrown by the streetlamp. Sophia was momentarily concerned for Marcus, but then heard his car start and drive away, reassuring her he was safe. She watched for a moment, wondering who this person was and why he or she stood there, alone. *Maybe they came out for a smoke. Maybe they have a night job they are heading to. Maybe they are waiting for someone.*

Realizing how tired she was, she closed the drapes and decided to call it a day, even though it was hours before she typically went to bed. Barely having the energy to brush her teeth, she fell into bed and succumbed to a restless sleep within minutes.

Images, falling through holes in a wooden bridge, arms helicoptering to catch the air, still falling. Trying to scream, no voice, plunging into ice cold water, choking, drowning, desperate scooping for solid within liquid, floating. Airborne, flying, water-logged cloud gliding, people below, crying, silent screaming. Fingers pointing up, fingers becoming crows, chasing, biting, flogging. Falling, darkness, inside a box, fingers scratching to get out, pounding, kicking, trapped, exhausted blackness.

ADDIE IN THE BOX

The human body protects itself from pain by going into physical shock; so does the mind. When events become too painful, when we are overwhelmed by emotion that threatens to swallow us whole, we separate…dissociate from our surroundings and self. We seize those events, shove them into our mind's darkest corner, pound the lid shut and run as far away as we can. We put up mental wall, we numb, we pretend until a new reality is formed. We adjust memory storage to camouflage any hints of concealed recollections. As time passes, the disowned pages fade, yellow, crinkle, and disintegrate. Or do they? Perhaps they lurk, biding their time, waiting for a fleeting fissure to open, allowing trapped energy to surge, to demand long-overdue audience, not unlike a jack-in-the-box toy. Life cranks the handle until an unpredictable pressure pops the lid and out comes that which was thought to be safely tamped down. Addie, the doll in the tin box.

Addison was the younger sister who died before she was a year old, leaving vague memories and few pictures. Being only three years old at the time, Sophia was little help with the baby when she was born, but was fascinated with the squalling lump prone to leaking white nectar from her tiny mouth. She watched her mother feed, bathe, and rock Addie, petting her downy head and tummy and kissing her feet when she was allowed to. Addie was just beginning to sit up and crawl when she died. Her body able to fit through the bars of her crib, but not her head, she was found after a nap, lifeless. Sophia didn't understand what happened to the baby until years later. Confused, asking questions, being hushed, Sophia learned to miss her in silence, to move on without knowing, and to swallow grief. Sophia practiced those skills for years, as the baby's death was the catalyst for the collapse of her family and additional loss.

Their father's unpredictable and violent temper became magnified in his grief. Before Addie, her parents occasionally had shouting matches that led to slamming doors or thrown objects. After Addie, the closed doors did little to soften the sound of their raised voices and crying. Puddled and weeping on the floor outside the door, Sophia pleaded for them to come out until Marcus dragged her away.

Locked doors and cursing eventually gave way to stoic silence and unanswered questions about where her father was, which gave way to boxes, packing, and driving for hours to a house in a new neighborhood, where her toys and bed covers bore the same resemblance but seemed inexplicably different and she was afraid to touch them. Days became weeks and weeks became months and Sophia began to forget about Addie, and Daddy.

In time, there was contact with Russ, when she learned she had another brother and sister, which puzzled her. Eventually, there were visits to meet them and to visit with her father and stepmother. Sophia liked both of her new siblings well enough, but always felt she had been replaced by them, which never allowed her to feel solidly at ease with them.

Initially, Sophia tried to rebuild the lost relationship with her father, but his violent explosions and tendency towards monologue over discussion created a chasm too wide to bridge. They had no common ground, other than heredity. She stopped visiting. She stopped writing. She stopped talking. She stopped caring. And she put Addie into a mental box, locked, stuffed away and hidden from view, until Beth turned the crank that unexpectedly spilled her out.

Sophia had not spoken to Marcus about Addie after the divorce and move, nor had she ever discussed her with Annie or Dylan. She had not talked to her mother about it once she understood as a child that the subject was off limits; first, because she thought she wasn't supposed to, and later out of compassion for her mother's loss. When indistinct memories occasionally surfaced she was quick to send them back into the shadows without looking too closely in their direction.

Beth's casual mention of her death was a lightning rod, sparking half-formed visuals and muffled sounds which smoked through her mind. Unsure why the mention caused her reaction, she was reluctant to share what she remembered with anyone, particularly Marcus. Although able to see his concern and uncharacteristic tenderness, the years had taught her to be wary and self-protective. The scale had been balanced too heavily on the side of derision and judgment for her to have faith that the vulnerability inside her was safe in his hands. She was unsure it was safe in her own hands.

Sophia stared at the mug circled within her fingers. Marcus had made it clear he wanted nothing to do with Beth. Sophia, on the other hand, had been curious before, and was even more curious now, about who she was and what she knew. Beth had said she was the outcome of an affair between her mother and Russ around the time Addie died.

So that would have been before he got together with the co-worker? Or was he seeing both at one time? Did mom know about them? Was that what the fighting was about? Is that what split them up?

Sophia had always thought the parental split occurred in response to the grief of losing a child, but what if it hadn't? What if there was more to the story? Did the disintegration begin with losing Addie and evolve into finding comfort in the arms of other women? What if Beth knew things that could put some pieces firmly into place and shine light into the shadowy corners of that history? Would that help, or would it make things worse?

Since Addie had re-emerged into her conscious mind, Sophia was having difficulty stuffing her back into her box. Having come back to life, she was resisting the pressure to fit where she previously had. Sophia had questions. She had fragments that she couldn't understand. She wanted to know. But she was also afraid. Afraid of what she might hear, of what the truth might be. While her intellect wanted to put the puzzle pieces together, another part of her was inexplicably terrified. *Of what? What could possibly be so scary about what my parents did that led to divorce? It's not like Addie can die again.*

Although unable to shake the ominous feeling, Sophia decided to meet with Beth again, with or without Marcus or the others. Something was pulling her in that direction, even though she didn't know what or why. The urge to follow was irresistible.

UNEARTHING

Stomach in knots, Sophia pushed the buzzer, hearing the chime announce her presence. Within seconds the door opened, revealing the woman more twin than not. An awkward greeting followed as Beth ushered Sophia into the living room, softly furnished with cloud-like couch cushions, and mushrooming potted plants confirming tender care.

"Please, have a seat," Beth invited, as she sank into a nearby recliner.

Sophia sat on the loveseat, feeling the overstuffed pillows wrap around her like welcoming arms. Although a small room, Beth's furnishings and decorations made it feel expansive, as though the walls would politely step back as you approached. Multiple photographs of scenic places enhanced the effect, as she took in waterfalls, mountains, oceans, and wildflowers. Nodding towards a particularly striking sunset photo Sophia said, "That's very pretty."

Following her glance, Beth smiled slightly, "Thank you. I took it when I was on vacation in California. It's the only time I've been out of this state so it's memorable to me."

"It's very nice. Did you take the others also?"

"Most of them. I have a friend who also likes to take pictures so a few are from her. It's kind of a hobby."

A strained silence ensued as their eyes swiveled from the pictures to each other. *Where does one begin to unravel a tightly woven past? What loose thread does one pull first?*

"I'm glad you called," Beth began tentatively. "I didn't really think I'd hear from you again. Thank you for giving me the chance to apologize again, and in person. I'm really sorry to have caused you such pain. It was never my intention and would never be my desire to do that. This is all so awkward and difficult. I try to be honest and straightforward and sometimes don't realize what I say may be hard for others. I had no idea."

"I know that. How could you have known? This has all been upsetting and confusing and difficult for everyone. I don't think any of us know quite how to proceed or how to handle any of it. I'm sure it has been just as hard for you as it has been for us." Sophia paused, pondering how to proceed. Beth seemed unpretentious and guileless. Sophia perceived no ill-intent in her demeanor. "You said some things that I wanted to hear more about, to try to understand. I'm hoping we can have that conversation, just the two of us. Can I ask you some questions?"

"Of course. I'll do my best to answer them."

"I'm not really sure where to even start. You said that your mom was involved with my father when she was a student of his. Do you know how long they saw each other?"

"My mother told me that it only lasted a few months and that it ended…" Beth trailed off, uncertain as to whether or not to continue.

"Ended…?" A puzzled frown creased Sophia's face. Her expression relaxed as realization dawned. "It ended when Addie died, didn't it? That's how she knew about her? They had been seeing each other before it happened?"

"Yes. It wasn't long after she died that they stopped their relationship. He stopped it. Mom said the day she found out she was pregnant with me was the day Addie died. It was a terrible day for both of them. She felt really awful about the whole thing. I know it's no excuse, but she said she was so young, and he was so handsome and smart and charismatic that she fell for him and was amazed that someone like him would even notice her. I think she carried that guilt until the day she died. That's why she didn't tell me much about him, or you and Marcus, until she was sick and dying. I think if she could have done things over, she would not have gotten involved with him, although she always told me that I was the one thing about the relationship that she didn't regret."

"But he knew about you? She told him about being pregnant before he ended it?"

"She told him the last time they were together, which was the day Addie died. He was upset and angry and said some hurtful things about her trying to trap him and then he left. The next day she heard on campus that Addie had died and he would be out for a while, someone else would cover his classes. They only spoke a couple more times after that, and it was all pretty nasty. He made it clear that he wanted nothing to do with me or her anymore. I guess he even questioned my mom about if he had been the only one, doubting if I was really his. She ended up dropping out of school, so she never spoke to him again. He never tried to find her or me, so she raised me by herself until she met someone else."

"Did my mother know about her?" Sophia's mind was whirling, trying to put all the pieces together. What she was hearing was consistent with the Russ she knew; mean, irresponsible, self-focused, the kind of man who would deny paternity and accuse the other person to shift the blame.

"I'm not sure. I don't think my mom was ever sure about that part. If your mother did know, he never said anything about it."

"So what was it like when you met him at the end? What did he have to say for himself?" Sophia had difficulty imagining what this had been like, for either Beth or Russ.

While this ordeal had been tough and dredged up ugly memories, she was beginning to like this soft-spoken woman and her directness.

Beth rearranged herself on the recliner, pulling her knees up close to her chest, enclosing them with her arms. "I sent him a letter to begin with, to give him time to think about it and decide if he was willing to meet me. I told him a little about what I'd heard from my mom and what my life had been like. Then I waited. About a month later he wrote me back and said he'd like to meet. Once we did, we had regular coffee dates until just before he died. He was very kind to me, always. Very apologetic, very willing to offer help with anything I needed. I could see why my mother had fallen for him. Even in his older age, he was still quite intelligent, well-spoken, and thoughtful. He told me that once he saw me there was no doubt in his mind that I was his daughter. Once I saw you, I understood why." She smiled shyly, acknowledging the resemblance.

Thoughtful? Apologetic? Helpful? Russ? A thought cacophony clattered as Sophia tried to reconcile Beth's description of Russ with her own experiences. Childhood resentment rippled, reminding her that vastly different perceptions could be formed of the same person. Were their standards so different? Was his treatment of each so diverse? It was a riddle she had never solved. Perhaps with more time Beth would have seen some of the same temper, irrational accusations, and hurtful comments that had caused others to back away or find other methods of shielding themselves. Hadn't he accused her mother of sleeping around? Hadn't he essentially disowned his own daughter all these years?

"Doesn't it bother you that he basically refused to accept you until just before he died?"

A long pause passed as the two women regarded each other, thinking over all that the question entailed, "Sure it does. It made things harder for my mom and probably for me too in ways I didn't even realize when I was younger. I was pretty upset and confused when my mom told me the truth about him and my stepfather. But the more I thought about it, the more it seemed to make things more clear. Things I hadn't understood, but had felt, I could now put a name to or have an explanation for. Things I thought were because of me I figured out had nothing to do with me, but with other people and the things that haunted them. It allowed me to let go. And I feel so sorry for your mom and what she went through that I wouldn't have wanted to add to that. So in a way, I'm glad he chose what he did and we lived our own life. At least I don't have that to deal with and neither did my mom. I think she felt pretty awful about Addie, too, and what you were going through. I'm just grateful I had a chance to know who he was before it was too late. I think he was, too. I guess that's what I try to focus on, what good can be found, not what's missing."

Begrudgingly, Sophia understood that. It was actually a pretty healthy way to look at it and she admired Beth's objective point of view.

"What did he tell you about us? What did you know about us once you were meeting, and why didn't he tell us about you?"

Beth shifted in her chair again, rubbing a foot as though it had gone to sleep. "I'm not sure why he didn't tell you about me. He might have with more time. We were just getting to know each other a little. Maybe he wasn't sure he wanted all of us to know each other yet, until he knew more about me. I'm really not sure. He did tell me a little about each of you, what you did for a living, where you lived, if you had family of your own, basic things like that. He always seemed to be proud of you and what you've accomplished. Even Dylan, who he said had struggled in the past, but was doing better more recently."

"Did he tell you that he and I hadn't spoken in years?" Sophia asked pointedly. "That we didn't get along well?"

"He said you didn't speak often, but didn't go into details about why. I assumed it was work schedules and other obligations that caused it," Beth responded guardedly, uncertain how to deal with what Sophia had shared.

"Your experience of our father was new and minimal. You appear to have seen him at his best. He wasn't always at his best, and when he wasn't, he could be quite hurtful. I made the decision to stay away from him and his unpredictable behavior. Part of me understands you have a limited view of him, so it would be easy to see him positively. But another part feels like you've been shown a lie or at best a partial truth, and now that he's gone you have nothing but our word on what he was like. That bothers me. It's like we don't really have the same father, even though we do."

Beth nodded silently then said, "I have never told myself I had the entire story. I don't usually feel I know anyone fully, even when I've known them for a long time. We can only know what people choose to show us, or tell us, and what we feel we learn based on our experiences with them. Remember, I was surprised to hear I had a father other than my stepfather, and that my mother kept this secret for most of my life. It was a surprise to find out the people I was closest to had basically lied. I know my limited experiences have only shown me part of him. I wouldn't mind hearing more about him from you or any of the others if you want to share it with me some day. As I said, I'm just happy to have had any information about him at all. I have to wonder if my mom didn't tell me about him because she knew he might not be a good person for me to know, based on what you just shared. And at this point, I'm really more interested in all of you. It would be wonderful if we could have more visits like this one, or like what I was doing with Russ, if you thought you wanted to."

Sophia found herself torn. She was intrigued by Beth, even liked aspects of her already. She wondered if talking about

Russ to someone with such a limited perception of him might be too difficult and upsetting. She had always avoided talking to anyone about him if she could. On the other hand, if they limited that part, maybe they could form a friendship based on other commonalities and shared interests. She had always wondered what kind of sister Addie would have been. Would they have been close? Would they have looked out for each other, spent time together, or fought competitive battles through the years? Would Addie have been more like her or Marcus? More like their mother or their father? The thoughts had been brief, triggered randomly when she saw two sisters enjoying each other, and quickly put away before popping the cork on memories she hid away. Beth's appearance had reshaped the cork, making it fit less tightly in the neck of repression. Perhaps getting to know Beth would help fill a hole she had always felt inside, a hole Annie had never filled.

But what if it doesn't? What if you learn things that just make that hole bigger by chomping away at the edges? What if you find out there's yet another person you can't relate to or who can't understand who you are? What if it causes things to surface that need to stay buried? What if?

An anxious foreboding dripped into her thoughts, creating puddles of doubt and anticipatory dread. A tug-of-war ensued between her desire to learn more and her fear of what she might learn, fear which seemed unfounded, but reeked of something unknown trying to be seen.

Having allowed her eyes to drift back to the safety of the wall photographs, she brought them back to focus on Beth. "I think I might be open to that, but I need some time to think through what we've already talked about. I can't speak for any of the others though. They may feel very differently about the idea. I can let them know you are interested. I'm guessing we'll have more contact to sort out this will distribution stuff, so I can let you know once I have some time to think. I do appreciate what you were willing to tell me today. It was a tough time for everyone back then, and I'm sorry our father caused hardship to you and your mom." Sophia stood as she spoke, signaling her intention to end the conversation.

Uncurling, Beth faced Sophia as she stood. She had questions she wanted to ask but held back. The meeting had gone smoothly, and she had no desire to undo the possible beginnings of friendship. With both parents dead and no siblings, she felt adrift and alone much of the time. Although Sophia's emotional outburst spooked her, she wondered if she may have found a kindred spirit. She was willing to hold back her own questions until she saw more solid ground.

"Thanks again for coming," she said, opening the door. Watching from the window as Sophia drove away, she felt anticipation as well as wonder at how things were unfolding.

BLOOD TIDE

Flip a coin, roll the dice
Born in peace or born in vice
Who's the man that makes that call?
Says who will rise and who will fall?
You live life fast and take what you want
Ain't your bling, but still you flaunt
Hard and tough you take the blow
I see deep where scars don't show
Fabric of life was early torn
Into this life you think you were born
No matter the others you cause to mourn
Don't listen to those who try to warn
Eye to eye meets soul to soul
Connect your spirit to make you whole
Dig the depths to find your hope
Fill you up to help you cope
See you return to ugly street
Holding cell, where sins repeat
Where unseen chains shackle feet
And reputations hard to beat
Took the wrong stand and followed the creed
Watch your friend fall, can't stop the bleed
Her soul may be freed
But the same life you lead
Won't water new seed

Just let the hate feed
Up on the fence, see the flip side
Made me believe, now fear that you lied
Looking ahead, what do you see?
Watching kids grow or cell block "D"?
Ride the tide or wash ashore?
Write your story or build street lore?
Think you'll fly high but it's just a bore
Instead of the ceiling, you'll be on the floor
Throw away life, disrespect love
Prisoner clothes will fit like a glove
Endless paths are there to choose
The one you're on force you to lose
Not too late to turn away
Redefine honor, refuse to play
Plant roots in the soil like you mean to stay
Believe in yourself so nothing can sway
Don't make you weak to avoid the fray
Just make you safe when the bullets spray

Think about it D'Vrae.....Sophia

Familiar words, familiar signature, familiar name. The poem wrote itself through Sophia's hand, as her mind wrestled to understand why some people seemed born into a cursed life while others barely knew hardship; as she struggled to continue the uphill battle to help young people survive the quicksand of neighborhoods they returned to. When repeated discussions about possibilities left her feeling impotent and wrung dry, she spilled her angst onto the page. Now, staring at the smudged, wrinkled page held before her, she tried to absorb what she had just heard.

"You found it where?" reaching for the paper tentatively, as though it might burn on contact.

"It was in his pocket. Everything on him was given to his grandmother. She knew who you were and passed it along to us, thinking you might want it back and to know what happened. So you wrote this? And gave it to him?" Gabe Norse, head administrator of Dalton stood before her, arms crossed now that Sophia had taken the page from him, looking literally down his nose at her from his six and a half foot height.

"Wait….yes…what did you say about D'Vrae?" Sophia was having difficulty processing what Gabe was telling her, the words scrabbling through her brain trying to find a solid place to clutch and come into focus.

"He was killed two days ago in a drive-by. From what we know probably an old score being settled. That kid had a long history and so did his relatives. Not really a surprise to anyone I should think. He'd been in here enough times to set his course. Kid like that, not much hope for them no matter what we do." Gabe had supervised the center a long time and had largely given up thinking rehabilitation took place. He focused on maintaining safety and discipline until the youth were released, avoiding hope that might raise expectations or bring him disappointment.

Sophia's mind swirled with questions. *Was he out to settle scores? Was he doing what he was supposed to be doing but old grudges and past choices nailed him? Did he ever have a chance out there?* She had so wanted D'Vrae to be one of those who found a way out, escaping the cycle and floating into a new life buoyed by things he had learned. He had so much potential, she had seen it in him. Fatigue swept through her, fatigue and crushing sadness. *D'Vrae…damn it D'Vrae!*

"…against policy to give personal things to the youth." Gabe's voice gradually penetrated her awareness.

What? Policy?

Sophia shook her head, struggling to comprehend. After looking several times from the paper to Gabe's face, his point finally dawned on her, and it was now clear why he had brought the poem and came personally to tell her of D'Vrae's death. He viewed the poem as a protocol violation, a break in the policy of no personal gifts, a rule to avoid the appearance of developing inappropriate relationships or doing personal favors.

"It's a tool I use to have conversations with some of my clients," she responded after a moment's pause, struggling to find reason and shift it into gear. "I try to find creative ways to get them to think and reconsider their points of view. Sometimes I use songs or other writings, sometimes we talk about things they've written, and in this case, I shared something I had written as a way to question his assumed values and where they were taking him. D'Vrae was not the only person who saw that poem or discussed it with me."

Sophia knew that the mental health support here would see this differently from safety and security staff. Art and role-playing were often used to create different points of view, and to bring out guarded emotions and thoughts. It could also create powerful connections, which was what safety and security guarded against.

"And how did he end up with a copy of it?" Gabe asked expectantly.

"I gave him a copy as he exited, as a reminder of our discussions, hoping it might encourage him to make positive choices." Sophia tried to keep the grief and irritation out of her voice.

These questions, and the focus of his concern, were salt in the wound of D'Vrae's death. At this moment, Sophia couldn't have cared less about "policy." A baby born into a cultural cesspool had been shaped by unkind forces until he had broken like a twig.

Could we have a moment of remembrance and appreciation for what might have been before we launch into policy that does nothing but expand the void between those who are desperate and those who want to help? Do you even CARE that he's dead?

"Well, the way I see that, it's a violation of our policy against giving gifts. I'm afraid I'm going to have to investigate this further. I'll keep you informed after I look into it. We may have to put you on leave until it's resolved. I'll be in touch."

Taking the paper back from her as he spoke, Gabe turned and left the office, leaving Sophia both stunned and deflated. Heart pounding in anger and disbelief, tears forming, Sophia crossed to the door of her office and closed it. Walking back to the window, she gazed through the glass with unfocused eyes. She pictured D'Vrae as she had known him, flamboyant hair and engaging smile, swaggering walk camouflaging a child-like nature, preferring to use charm over hard work to get what he wanted....dead, lifeless, gunned down. All of it wasted.

Her reason tried to protect her against events like this, shrugging it off as the luck of the draw, roll of the dice, a bad hand dealt, while her emotions rebelled against the reality that all the resources put into turning it around had failed. It was all a sick joke. Maybe Gabe had it right. Maybe she should see them all as destined to stay on the path created for them; all we can do is hunker down and try not to get injured in the process. Why bother writing poetry to open minds and hearts, why bother trying to connect, or trying to shake unhealthy beliefs from distorted thought trees?

The disappointment choked her so completely she couldn't bring herself to care a battle was brewing with administrators over her methods. Gabe hadn't provided any details regarding what had happened, but Sophia knew she would hear them from other clients, for the grapevine was quick and thorough, especially in lockup. Knowing details was not going to help, however. Whether D'Vrae had instigated the situation or been the innocent victim, it was all the same. He had never had much of a chance for anything to be different. The on-going unfairness she saw daily gnawed at the edges of her determination and hope, and today's news swallowed such a chunk she thought she might never be the same.

Glancing at the clock she saw it was almost the end of her shift. *Close enough.* Picking up her coat, she made her way through the empty hallways and out the front gate, scanning the rows of cottages as she walked. *Haven't got a chance* continued to echo as she drove away, feeling as if someone had laid a thousand pound cloak over her.

UNDERTOW

It had taken several weeks, but the four of them eventually agreed on a plan of action regarding Russ's house. Dylan began on the outside cleanup with occasional help from Sophia, who had extra time due to her temporary leave pending the outcome of the investigation at Dalton. Expecting to be exonerated of any wrong-doing, she focused on being patient until the process determined the poem was not a gift so much as a tool for change. In the meantime, she tried to stop thinking about the students who were going without her support, as she offered what help she could to Dylan and the process of getting the house ready for sale, a task that was daunting, as well as littered with hidden traps. Away from work, Sophia processed the news about D'Vrae without having to face the daily discouragement his death had aroused.

She concentrated on outside work first, as the weather allowed it, encountering fewer unwanted memories there. There were times she worked alone and times when she and Dylan were both present, accomplishing needed tasks with minimal conversation, each lost in their own thoughts. As the days passed, the overgrown shrubbery and mossy sidewalks gradually transformed into the clean, trimmed pathways they once were. Sophia and Dylan both gleaned satisfaction from work that offered tangible results.

Today all five had arrived at the farm to deep clean the house. Jane and Annie packed items from the kitchen while Marcus sorted through mountains of written correspondence their father had kept. Prolific writer that he was, Russ accumulated countless stacks of yellow notepads with daily musings and letters received from others. Russ had an opinion on everything, whether he sent his response or not, he always replied to what he heard from others, in writing, providing an incoherent stream of consciousness. If one read long enough, one might connect some common threads that initially appeared to be a badly frayed mental fringe.

Marcus was dimly aware of the background chatter coming from the kitchen as Annie and Jane made decisions about what to do with items found, as well as the distant whine of a leaf blower. Years of listening to Russ' diatribes left him apathetic about the writings he sorted, so most of the notepads were filling cardboard boxes with minimal scrutiny. *Been there, heard that* played in his head as he gave them a cursory glance, dropping them into the box next to him.

While Marcus had maintained a superficial relationship with his father, it was not one he (or anyone) would have called close. Circling each other from opposite sides of life, they spoke cautiously about mundane things from time to time, but never developed the depth of relationship that can be reached when distrust is replaced with understanding and acceptance. Having little use for the philosophical musings Russ preferred to focus on, Marcus leaned more towards the current and practical. "*Being related does not mean having a relationship,*" Sophia had told Marcus when she cut ties with Russ. Marcus accepted her choice but had not felt the same need, feeling that resisting the urge to withdraw allowed him to "win" in some unclear way, his pride not admitting defeat to Russ.

"Looks like a fun job," Sophia's voice interrupted Marcus' thoughts.

Marcus looked up from where he sat on the floor and watched her settle into an oversized chair as she picked up the top pad in the box next to her.

"Yeah, lots of fun. The old man never had a shortage of words, did he?" Marcus said as he tossed another pad into the box.

"No. Words were the one thing he never ran out of. Find anything interesting in any of it?" She flipped through the pages without really focusing.

"Not really. Not reading much of it. Annie said she wanted these things so I'm just getting them organized for her. I'm pretty sure I've heard most of it already. She probably has, too, so I'm not sure why she wants it, but it's her choice I guess."

"I'm done with the porch area and thought I'd work on the bathroom. The kitchen has enough going on already."

Sophia didn't particularly like the thought of being in a small space with Annie and Jane and the conversations they might have, or face the expectation to participate when she didn't feel like it. It was difficult enough to engage in social chatter when emotions weren't aroused, and to do so in this situation felt like more than she could take on. She had been very aware in the past several weeks of how tightly wound she was, and how easily she could crack with little provocation.

"I've been looking for his more recent things because I've wondered if I'd find anything about Beth or her mother. But so far the dates I've seen are all his older stuff." Marcus tossed another pad onto the pile forming in the box. "Not sure I want to read them, but they might shed some light on her and why he's done what he has with the will. I still can't believe what he did there at the end. It really pisses me off!" Resentment crossed Marcus' face as he glared up at Sophia.

"If you find anything, I'd like to read them, too. I think. I hope," hesitation and conflicting feelings evident in Sophia's voice. "I'd like to understand all of this better. I'm still trying to sort out what I think and how I want to approach the whole Beth thing."

Marcus snorted, "I don't want to approach this Beth thing at all! Like you say to me, being related doesn't mean having a relationship, and I don't even want to at this point. I don't need this complication in my life. I don't get why you have any interest in her at all!"

Reflecting briefly before responding, Sophia leaned forward in the chair, hands clasped around her knees, "I don't either really. Curiosity? I wonder if somehow she might have answers to some things that seem unanswerable."

The pull was inexplicable, like having to look when you pass a terrible wreck, a needing to know even if the knowing was going to wound, like having the hair on the back of your neck stiffen, pulling your glance behind you in dreaded anticipation of something awful lurking just beyond reach. How could she help Marcus understand something she did not understand herself?

"I don't see how she could help anyone with answers. She doesn't know anything about us or what happened in our lives. She couldn't have known much about Russ either. Really, Sophia, you can be so morbid and naïve sometimes! I don't see anything but trouble coming out of this and any contact you have with her. I think you should stay away from her and forget about her once this is all taken care of, for your own sake," Marcus barked with vehement certainty as he reached under the bed and hauled out a dusty, cobwebbed box, removing the lid.

"Guess that's not up to you to decide, is it, Marcus? You can do as you see fit, and I'll do the same," Sophia tried to keep her voice steady and swallow back a surge of irritation. *Does the older sibling EVER stop trying to tell the younger one what to do, what to think, and how to feel?* "I'm not saying that I'm going to become best friends or anything, but I do have questions and would like to find out if she is someone I'd want to have any kind of relationship with, rather than just ignoring the fact that we are related. How she came to be isn't her fault. Who knows, maybe I'll find out I actually like her and have things in common with her."

Sophia braced for the expected cynical retort, but Marcus was absorbed in the contents of the box he had just opened. Assuming she had lost his attention, Sophia stood and took several steps toward the door, resuming her intention to work on emptying the bathroom.

"Soph?" a hesitant, choked voice stopped her mid-step.

Turning, she saw a pained expression she'd never seen before on Marcus' face. "What is it?" she asked urgently.

Slowly lifting his head to look at her, Marcus responded in a quiet voice, "These are very old writings and letters, dating back to when we were kids. Judging from the dates on them, there seem to be some that are from Mom to him after they separated, and his journaling through that time."

Marcus had allowed the papers and envelopes in his hands to slide absently down onto his lap and the floor as he looked up at Sophia. He gripped his knees with his hands. Eyes locked, brother and sister each silently struggled to absorb this discovery and what it might mean…answers or more mysteries, bandages or new cuts, reality or fiction?

Sophia broke the trance first, approaching Marcus and dropping to the floor next to him. In a hushed voice she spoke first, "Wow. That could be really cool or really awful, huh?" She picked up an envelope and examined the handwriting. *That looks like Mom's writing all right.*

Marcus paused before answering. While he had no interest in most of what Russ wrote and talked about, this was more connected to his own history, his own life story. He felt interested, but also like somehow he was lifting the covers to look under forbidden sheets, into private quarters. "That pretty much sums it up, all right. Seems fascinating, and yet kind of creepy."

CRASH! Marcus and Sophia both jumped, startling at the sound of breaking glass.

"Sorry!" Jane's voice carried from the kitchen. "Too many breakables on the counter and we knocked one off! Don't worry, already cleaning it up. Be careful if you walk out here."

"Okay, don't worry about it," Marcus called to her and then looked again at Sophia, trying to read her expression. In a softer voice he said, "So I'm thinking this is not the time or place to take a look at these things, if we decide we want to at all. What are you thinking?"

Fingering the dirty, tattered box Sophia replied, "Definitely not here or now. How about if one of us takes it and we think about if we really want to do this. I do think if we decide we want to read them, we need to do it together."

As much as Sophia bristled at Marcus and how he treated her, there was something about this task that seemed unnerving and she wasn't sure she wanted to peer inside without company and backup. Having watched Marcus' expression and hesitation, she was pretty sure he might be feeling the same way.

Showing visible relief, Marcus agreed, and they decided Sophia would take the papers home until they decided what to do next. They searched under the bed to determine if there was more from those years, but only found more recent journals. Marcus carried the box to Sophia's car and returned to his sorting task while Sophia worked in the bathroom, each quietly contemplating what those pages might contain, and whether they wanted to unearth the buried.

Like having to look at a car accident….

FIGHT

Shuffling through the stack of papers on her desk, Sophia sorted those that needed immediate attention from those that could wait, noting with chagrin that the immediate attention pile was expanding faster than the other. As expected, after multiple meetings and explanations it was determined that Sophia had not violated any facility rules in using the poem as a counseling strategy, and she returned to work to dig out from under the unattended tasks. Unfortunately, hers was work no one could do in her absence so the stack of progress notes, intake files, incident reviews, and exit summaries all awaited her as she arrived for the first time in two weeks. Having completed the pile sorting, Sophia began making a list of which students remained in the facility and which would likely need attention first. Reading the incident reports was her first task, as those would identify who required extra intervention or isolation in her absence. Sighing, she recognized several familiar names on the MSU roster and put those names first on her list—Aiden, Derrick and Quinn. She was not surprised with Aiden and Quinn, but Derrick had been doing well on the unit, and in school, and Sophia was surprised to see he had received consequences for something.

"Good to have you back," Jerry grinned at her from the doorway.

"Good to be back, I think," Sophia answered somewhat hesitantly, returning his smile. "You hold down the fort for me while I was gone?"

Jerry shrugged and rolled his eyes, "About as well as anyone can. The place has been rockin' and rollin'. Got some new ones in, and being just off the streets they stirred the pot a bunch. Came in with all kinds of stories about what's going on out there and got everyone poppin'. You know how that goes, shifts the totem pole for a while."

Sophia nodded. With mixed feelings she asked, "Hear anything about what went down with D'Vrae in the new batch?"

Jerry crossed into the room and sat in the chair on the other side of her desk. He rubbed his bald head with both hands before answering, sad eyes meeting Sophia's.

"Yeah. Turns out he hooked up with some old homies almost as soon as he got out. Had some kind of falling out with his auntie, who had offered him a place to live, so he left and was hanging with the old gang. Wrong place and wrong time, and one of the rivals with a score to settle fired into a group of them. D'Vrae was the one they hit. May not have been aiming for him exactly, but he got capped for being guilty by association. Real shame. Likeable kid. Could have looked real different if he'd grown up in a different place and family." Jerry fingered the pen and pencil container on Sophia's desk absentmindedly, his eyes moving back and forth between that and Sophia. He had tried to dissuade D'Vrae from his impetuous embrace of fast, easy money and felt considerable disappointment and sadness at the recent outcome. Jerry, more than most, knew the battle it was to change, but also knew it could be done, having won it himself.

Sophia nodded in agreement, imagining the headstrong unwillingness to be parented that likely led to D'Vrae's return to the company of peers instead of accepting the relative safety of his aunt's house and rules. D'Vrae saw himself as a man, not a teenager, and that stubborn independence helped get him killed. Even if he hadn't actively returned to the gang life, he was hanging and associating so it was probably just a matter of time before he slipped back into the habits. All of the work that went into him, and that he had done, wasted.

Jerry continued, "I was going to go to his service, but they didn't have one, at least not a public one. I'm pretty sure the family had no money, and they were probably afraid of trouble at the service if they had one. D'Vrae was pretty well known in that community, and not in good ways. Whole family was. I called and talked to his Grandma and gave her my sympathies. Must be hard to lose so many family members that way, and outlive them all."

Sophia also wondered what that would be like to outlive your kids and grandkids and feel all alone in the world as you age. It was unnatural. It was beyond sad. "How did she seem?"

"Pretty resigned. Said she knew he wouldn't last long because of who he hung with. Sounded kind of beat up by it all, but not surprised. Said she'd tried to talk sense into him since he was little, but he was hell-bent on trying to get somewhere the easy way. She did thank us for trying to help him. Thinks he was doing better when he was in here but just couldn't hold onto it once he was back in the hood. Too much temptation around him."

"That's probably true. Didn't have strong enough roots to withstand the prevailing winds, no matter what we did. Grew up in arid soil," was Sophia's disheartened response. "Someday…"

"WHAT YOU SAY?"

The shout from the hallway startled Jerry and Sophia into jumping to their feet and sprinting across the room and out the door, Jerry leading.

"I said he was a DUMBASS and it was survival of the fittest! Hit bottom on the shallow end of the gene pool!"

Aiden's self-righteous voice was immediately followed by the sound of breaking glass, along with the shrill ring of the bell signaling class change.

Once in the hall, Sophia saw a stocky black boy she had never seen before with his hands around Aiden's neck as he smashed Aiden repeatedly against the wall half way down the hallway. Broken glass from a fire extinguisher compartment glittered around their feet and across the floor. Simultaneously, multiple classrooms spewed boys through open doorways. Jerry sprinted down the hall towards the combatants as Sophia ran in the opposite direction to the office.

"Call for extra security NOW! And get on the loudspeaker and tell the teachers to return their students to their classrooms!"

Without waiting for a reply she took off at a run towards the two boys, unable to see Aiden as milling students hid the two from view. Aiden would win any battle of wits and facts, but his wispy frame would snap like a twig in a fist-fight. Reaching the wall of jeans and gray sweatshirts as the overhead speakers barked directions to teachers and youth, Sophia tried to pull on those closest as she added her voice to the cacophony.

"Against the wall, NOW! MOVE! Code FOUR!" she bellowed, trying to be heard above the jubilant shouts feeding the energy of those fighting.

"Yeah!"

"Go for it!"

"Kick his know-it-all ASS!"

Code four was the emergency procedure indicating the situation was dire and in need of immediate compliance; line up facing the wall, hands clasped behind the back, voices off, eyes straight ahead until the adults gave the go-ahead to move. At the moment, despite clear consequences for not complying with a code four, the fight's centrifugal force was keeping many of the boys circling the arena. Sophia could see Jerry's determined face ahead of her, still trying to make it through the horde.

Panic increasing at the sound of punched flesh and skull cracking against cement, Sophia pulled harder on any fabric she could grasp and pushed the person wearing it towards the nearest wall, procedure and policy of not touching the youth out the window in her need to get to Aiden. Behind her she could hear the shouts of teachers as they tried to herd the agitated youth back into the classrooms or at least against the walls. The air was turbulent, as though all of the anxiety, rage, and desperation circulating in separate bodies had become instantly knit into a vengeful funnel. Every adult here feared this kind of moment, because they all knew they were outnumbered if the youth became united against them. Regaining control was a critical and immediate need, for everyone's sake.

"LET HIM GO PUNK-ASS!" A new voice pierced the fray.

Quinn…oh, please God…NO! Sophia began pushing furiously against the remaining boys to create a path for herself, no longer trying to get them against the wall. Her efforts finally allowed her to see those locked in combat.

Quinn, who was not afraid of a battle; Quinn, who carried a hidden soft spot for the underdog; Quinn, who regularly surprised you with how he reacted to a situation had jumped into the brawl. A determined expression on his face, his arm reaching around the aggressor creating a choke hold, he pulled him backwards and off balance. Almost unconscious, Aiden flobbled to the floor, his back resting against the wall. Blood trickled down the side of his head and past nearly closed eyes, one of which was already swelling. The unidentified student had grasped Quinn's arms and was trying to free himself from their grip as both boys shifted and swayed. Losing their battle with balance they crashed to the floor. Jerry was finally within reach.

"STOP! Both of you STOP! Quinn, back off, I've got this now!"

Jerry tried to get Quinn to drop his hold and allow him to take over as both boys continued to wrestle in a sweating, heaving heap. Unfortunately, he couldn't try to physically stop the fight until backup arrived, so he was armed only with ineffective pleas.

"I'll kill you, fucker! Get your hands off me!" Face contorted in rage, the unknown student rained blows on Quinn's oblivious arms and torso. This was nothing compared with what had calloused Quinn inside and out, and he barely felt it. The choke hold unrelenting, Quinn returned fire with his other fist. He showed no sign of hearing Jerry's order, much less any inclination to follow it.

The energy of those continuing to watch amplified. Quinn's reputation was well known, and his peers knew that his entrance into the battle would be an even more impressive show. Not only was this far more entertaining than school, or daily life on the unit, but it allowed a momentary purge of buried frustration, a long-distance release of futility. It was intoxicating; a dangerous moment, infused with emotional lightning, making one feel energetically alive. Sophia knew better than to attempt to physically control two feuding teenage boys, so she turned her attention to the throng of onlookers and Aiden.

"Back to class or line up on the wall!" she repeated in the loudest voice she could muster in her anxious state. "You know the procedure! Anyone not complying will face unit sanctions!"

It was a feeble attempt, she knew, but she couldn't just stand there and do nothing. As she shouted at the crowd, she knelt down next to Aiden to check on the damage.

"Aiden?" she probed, "How are you doing? What hurts and how badly does it hurt?" She gingerly touched his arm while inspecting his bleeding face at closer range.

Aiden opened the eye that was now swelling shut, rousing himself to see who was talking. "Number 301 on ways it would piss me off to die. Having a trained monkey with half my IQ manage to crack my head open so my impressive brain spills out. Just doesn't seem right, does it, Miss Sophia?" Vague hint of a wry smile moved his lips prior to a grimace of pain.

Slightly reassured that he could still speak and appeared mentally intact enough to conjure an insult, Sophia told Aiden to stay as he was while she turned her attention to the continuing conflict. Standing again, she renewed her attempt to guide students to the walls or classrooms. The first three boys scowled at the directions but complied, taking several steps away from where they had stood, turning to face the wall.

"Piss off!" was the response from the fourth boy, supplemented by a defiant look. Whistles and murmurs erupted from those facing the wall nearby.

Sophia paused for a moment, taking in the six foot frame, shaved head, and swastika tattoos on his neck and hands. She repeated her direction to go face the wall or return to his classroom, staring calmly back into insolent blue eyes. She knew the student only by name and reputation. Sean Landry had arrived shortly before her administrative leave. His file indicated criminal activity from the age of twelve, including involvement with a gang known for menacing, robbery, and assaults. His current charges involved a shooting that had left two dead. Sophia had not yet met him or had reason to interact with him, which left her no personal cards to play in enlisting his cooperation, and she knew it. Her gut constricted as she reminded herself to tread lightly.

"I need you against the wall," she repeated.

Ignoring her second direction, Sean took a step toward her, coming to within inches of where she stood. Sophia instinctively stepped backwards, poised to move further away if necessary, every muscle tense and on alert in response to his intimidating stance. She could still hear Jerry barking commands at Quinn, the scuffling sounds of the brawling boys behind her and the taunts of the those still on the perimeter of the fight, despite teacher efforts to contain them.

Sean took another step towards her, but before Sophia could react he staggered sideways and fell to the floor, choking. Derrick, coming from nowhere, had wrapped both arms around Sean's neck and legs around his torso, immobilizing Sean except for furious but ineffective writhing. Derrick's face was livid, while Sean was quickly turning a red-blue from lack of oxygen and blood flow.

"Derrick! Let him go! Please let him go!" Sophia pleaded as she squatted nearby, "This will only get you in trouble!"

"Not going to let him disrespect you," Derrick replied tersely, tightening his grip. "He ain't all that, like he thinks."

Sean's thrashing suddenly quieted, and Derrick relaxed his grip, realizing Sean was unconscious. Just then the hallway was awash with additional security shouting orders to adults and students alike, pushing youth against the wall and demanding silence. Two burly guards grabbed Derrick by each arm, yanking him to his feet, causing Sean's unresponsive head to slide onto the floor with a thud. They thrust Derrick backwards until he slammed against the wall, pinning his arms.

"Don't move!" one of them ordered. "You just earned yourself a nice long stay in MSU."

"I was just…" Derrick began.

"And don't talk either," the same guard spat, "You don't get to talk. You don't get to do anything but what we tell you to do." He spun Derrick around to face the wall, pushing his head into the concrete for emphasis. The dull thud of impact cracked open Derrick's self-preservation instinct and he began to struggle against the hold, pushing his head against the hand restraining it. As the adults' grips roughened, Derrick's frantic effort to free himself exploded, and the three of them were soon a tangle of thrashing limbs on the floor.

He was ten years old and choking as his father pulled him up the stairs by his neck, the backs of his legs thumping against the steps as his feet scrambled to find solid ground and failed. Unable to make a sound, explain, or resist, he was dragged into the room where the whips were kept. Terror formed a lump in his throat as his body braced and hardened, anticipating what was to come.

Sophia knew immediately the rough handling had triggered Derrick's past trauma, along with his sense of injustice at being punished for coming to her aid.

"Derrick, please stop. Just calm down and cooperate with them and it will all get straightened out!" begged Sophia as she assessed Sean's condition. The blood flow reestablished to his brain, Sean had begun twitching and moving arms and legs in a purposeless way, eyes open but unfocused.

Unable to process what he heard, Derrick bellowed in anger and began spitting and swearing at whichever guard he saw as his head whiplashed back and forth against the floor, arms and legs pinned by adults much larger than he. A third security guard appeared and pulled a vented hood over Derrick's head, securing it at the neck, protecting the staff from the fluid assault. As his eyes disappeared behind the hood, his one remaining weapon removed from his limited arsenal, Derrick let out an agonized roar and then went silent. His body collapsed into small, rhythmic jerks as he mutely sobbed.

Sean, rousing, sat up slowly, a confused look on his face as he tried to sort out what had happened. Certain Sean was going to recover but still cautious of his aggressive tendencies, Sophia stood and stepped backwards to put distance between them. She nodded towards him and spoke to the third security guard who had left Derrick, now that he was subdued.

"This gentleman might need an escort to comply with code four."

"No problem. He's all mine." He reached down and yanked Sean to his feet. Turning him around, he cuffed him and led him to a section of wall where there were no other youth. "Having a hard time following directions, are we?"

"I don't answer to you, or her," Sean sneered, nodding toward Sophia, "You're nothing without these cuffs, rent-a-cop."

Looking down the hallway at Derrick still lying on the floor, Sean's expression chilled Sophia as it telegraphed revenge plotting already under way. Despite his words, Sean stood as he was expected to and spoke no more. Like a predator, stalking, waiting for his opportunity, Sean was used to being patient.

Students were escorted back into classrooms by security staff, thinning the crowd enough to see what the outcome had been for the original combatants. Aiden still sat against the wall, tended by a nurse who had been summoned from the health clinic. A pile of blood soaked cloths lay in a heap as she applied bandages to a head wound needing a stitch or two. Sophia grimaced as she realized it could have been worse.

The student who attacked Aiden was handcuffed. Although he resisted minimally, the effort lacked conviction, as though he was simply trying to have the last non-spoken word. He was hoisted to his feet and placed against the wall near Sean, where two guards stood watch. His eye was turning color, and blood ran from his lip and nose. A check in the clinic later would show a broken rib from the fight, either from blows inflicted by Quinn or the fall to the ground with Quinn landing on top of him.

Quinn continued to struggle against those who held him, his limbs fueled by adrenaline, more than a match against multiple adults. Grunts and profanity spewed from his clenched jaw. Jerry knelt beside Quinn's head, attempting to talk him down. "Quinn, I need you to calm down. It's over. We have this now. Trust us and let us do our job. Settle down. Please relax."

Sophia closed the few steps between them, kneeling down next to Quinn, adding to Jerry's pleas, "Quinn, you need to calm yourself. Use what you know. Thank you for helping Aiden. He's going to be fine. We need you to follow directions now so this doesn't get any worse. You can do this Quinn. I know you can. Quiet yourself so we can help you sort this out." She put a calming hand on his shoulder, hoping to break through the physical whirlpool that continued to spin him.

Quinn's eyes came into focus, resting on Sophia's face, then her eyes. As their eyes met, Sophia concentrated on conveying her belief in Quinn, her own sense of "everything will be all right", her positive regard for the person he was despite his challenges. *Please trust me enough to do this* she thought as she held his eyes, continuing to caress his shoulder gently. She watched as the thrashing eased and the grunts quieted.

"That's it, Quinn. That's good," Jerry's quiet, soothing voice joined in the effort; his own hand on Quinn's other shoulder.

As Quinn quieted and his body relaxed, the adults holding him sat cautiously back on their heels and removed their hands, waiting to see if he would re-escalate. When he did not, they stood up, waiting for what Jerry needed from them next.

"Are you ready to get up, Quinn?" Jerry asked softly, still massaging Quinn's shoulder.

Still looking at Sophia, Quinn nodded. They all stood, Quinn surrounded by the adults.

"You know we have to cuff you, right?" Jerry checked. "You want me to do it?"

Quinn nodded again as he turned to look at Jerry and then turned away from him, putting his arms behind his back to allow it. Once he was restrained, a quick discussion among staff decided which direction to take him out, avoiding those lined up on the wall waiting for transport, particularly the one he had been fighting with. As two of the guards walked him out, holding him by the arms, Quinn gave a final silent nod to Sophia and Jerry.

"I'll get over there as soon as I can," parting words from Sophia, who knew he would need an advocate to receive fair treatment regarding the fight. She had questions to ask about the other student and why Aiden had been assaulted.

Jerry and Sophia helped the staff herd students into classrooms and then escort each class back to living units. Facility protocol required school to be cancelled when an event like this occurred, to calm everyone and prevent a rash of conflicts from breaking out. Those in handcuffs were taken by car to MSU and put into isolation cells. Aiden was taken to the clinic for further treatment. As they had room, others would be brought over to be assessed for damage as well, but for now the priority was to keep them apart. As they walked the empty halls back to her office, Sophia asked Jerry if he knew the student who had attacked Aiden.

"Yes. He was one of D'Vrae's homies. He came here recently on a weapons charge. If I had to take a guess, based on what we heard them say as we got there, Aiden was dissing on D'Vrae, and that would mean LaVonte would have to defend his honor. Aiden's lucky he didn't get hurt more seriously. He needs to learn not to poke a rattler." Jerry shook his head in disbelief. "I've heard enough about that one to know you don't want to mess with him."

Sighing, Sophia replied, "It's the one thing I haven't been able to get him to understand or change. He believes he is doing a public service to speak his truth and there is no tact in his DNA. The best I've done is teaching him not to speak if there is doubt about how it will be received. If someone asked a question or said something that tipped the scale for him, he'd be compelled to say what he thought without predicting the outcome from doing so, or without caring. And there was no love lost between him and D'Vrae. They come from different universes and were pretty incapable of understanding or accepting each other."

Changing subjects she looked away from the window she had been staring through and into Jerry's bright blue eyes. "Do you think you can help security understand that Quinn was trying to protect Aiden and not just looking for an easy fight? I'll do my best, too, but they often dismiss me for being too soft on them, and I've got to go explain Derrick's situation to them before someone sets him off again."

A snort followed by, "I'll try to explain, but they don't always see things the way I do either." Jerry shook his head, grimacing, as though already imagining the debate he was likely to encounter. "It's too bad the world is so black and white for them about these things. Motive doesn't matter, just the behavior. Aiden might well have had his head cracked open if Quinn hadn't stepped in when he did. Guess I'll go do the first round and see how far I get. I hope the rest of your day is calmer, Sophia."

Jerry tipped an imaginary hat to her as he exited the doorway, his heavy steps fading out of earshot.

AFTERMATH

Sophia quickly surveyed the piles on her desk to determine what might need attention before she went home for the day, reprioritizing to add damage control. Fortunately, with school cancelled for the day, she had some breathing room and some of today's tasks could now wait until tomorrow. After a couple phone calls to determine where to find administrators, she headed to MSU to check on Quinn and Derrick, and invite herself to a meeting administration was having regarding the fight. Quick response and containment were always necessary to avoid contagion and retaliation.

Fast-walking through an eerily quiet campus, Sophia reached MSU in several minutes. Letting herself through the two locked doors that opened into the administrative offices, she marched to the large conference room where she saw administrative staff from each unit represented, as well as MSU and overall facility administrators. Loud declarations by Eliza greeted her as she found an empty chair along the wall, a few feet behind the table where most of the others were seated. Those present included Gabe Norse, Dr. Blain, Jeff Colton, and several unit staff, including the outspoken Eliza.

"I don't see what difference an investigation would make! It won't matter what the answers are! They need to be taught they can't behave that way or the consequences will be severe. I don't care what the excuses might be; they simply have to follow the rules regardless of what is happening. WE are in charge, not them! The more they get away with these take-it-in-my-own-hands decisions the more at risk we are, not to mention their families and the community when they finally do make it out of here!"

"I think it's important to understand what led to their decisions and reactions in order to best support and teach them," countered Dr. Blain. All ten fingers touched their symmetrical counterpart, resting against his lips momentarily before he continued. "One cannot separate their actions from their histories, and change only happens when we understand what drives them so we can help them understand that as well. That is our mission, not simply to punish them for wrong actions. We can only gain that understanding through investigating all angles and hear what each person has to say." Fingers separated and became clasped behind his head. He fixed calm, contemplative eyes directly on Eliza.

Scott Duram, another unit manager, who tailgated Eliza's ideas in meetings due to underlying apprehension about the population he monitored, interjected, "I agree with Eliza. We have to be careful what message we send in a situation like this. I'd hate to see soft consequences give the idea they can do whatever they want and get away with it. We could easily have had a riot here today, and I think they all know it. I don't want any of my staff getting injured because we won't take a definite and hard stand against what they did."

Scott glanced at Eliza to see if his comment met with her approval and was rewarded by her nod of agreement. Most of the unit managers nodded and mumbled agreement. Fear and distrust were palpable.

"Well, we could apply the typical sanctions for fighting to all of them equally without even asking any questions," Colton offered. "Might not be fairest, but it will at least give a consistent message and won't require us to have to explain any differences in our response."

"Yes!" exclaimed Eliza, "That's what I'm saying. They all get the same treatment regardless of intent or choice, and maybe even an added punishment due to the very dangerous nature of what took place and the near riot we had."

Sophia could contain herself no longer, "I totally disagree with that approach. With all due respect, Eliza, you were not there. I was. I saw part of what happened and I know some of those involved. I think it is crucial that the entire picture is assessed before any of these decisions get made. You are talking about people who have been treated unfairly their entire lives. The last thing we need to do here is add to their distrust due to unfair treatment."

"Of course that is how you think!" snorted Eliza. "You always come to their rescue, trying to insulate them from well-deserved punishments. All that does is make our jobs harder, makes us have to work longer to get the message through to them that the world will not cater to their whims and will not forgive lawless behavior!"

A hot rush of adrenaline flooded Sophia, forcing her to work hard to conceal the anger she frequently felt in response to Eliza's viewpoints, "While I clearly understand the need to let them all know they cannot take matters into their own hands, there is a clear difference between those who engage in fighting to injure others and those who are trying to help or protect someone else, and end up involved in a fight. I know these kids and I know why they got involved. It was not just an opportunity for a brawl."

"What do you know of what took place?" asked Gabe.

"I haven't had a chance to talk to them all yet, but I can tell you that I believe Quinn was protecting Aiden from the boy who was beating him up pretty badly, and Derrick got involved because he thought Sean was threatening me. I don't think Quinn would have done anything if security had been able to get to Aiden, but when they couldn't, he could see

Aiden was no match for the guy who attacked him. In my opinion he stopped Aiden from being more seriously hurt."

Eliza emitted a contemptuous sound followed by, "We all know Quinn loves a good fight. He doesn't even like Aiden. He took the opportunity to nail someone, end of story. And if Derrick was defending you, why did he try to take on security when they showed up? You seriously expect us to believe that?"

Sophia looked coldly at Eliza, her patience ebbing by the second. "Derrick was triggered by being roughly handled by people assuming that he was out to do harm and disobey rules. That is exactly why I think a full investigation is essential before any consequences are given. I'm not saying they don't require consequences, I'm saying I believe there are extenuating circumstances needing to be factored in, so they can be dealt with in ways that move their treatment forward rather than backward. What none of them needs right now is to feel we will treat them with the disrespect and the same lack of fairness they have experienced all their lives."

"Why did Derrick feel you were being threatened?" Jeff asked.

"Landry had squared off with me, was not following directions, and had taken a couple steps towards me. I was concerned myself that he might come at me. He was certainly in an intimidating posture. Derrick is observant enough to have picked up on that. He used to see his father attack his mother, so I'm sure he was reading Sean's stance as threatening. He and I have had enough positive contact that I think he was concerned for me."

"Did you tell him to stop?" Eliza badgered.

"Of course I did. But he was intent at that point and told me he wasn't going to let Sean disrespect me. I think what he really meant was he wasn't going to let him harm me."

"Aha! I rest my case. He was just as noncompliant as the others, not following directions and acting like he was promoted to security. Not his job!" Eliza huffed backwards in her chair as though there was nothing further that needed to be said.

"I agree."

"Seems like it to me."

"Can't let them get away with that."

"Have to draw a firm line."

"Not their job to intervene."

Mutterings around the table indicated Eliza was not alone in her thinking and Sophia felt her hope sinking. She looked at Dr. Blain, eyes pleading for additional support.

Trying again, Dr. Blain explained, "If a couple of them got involved for more positive, pro-social reasons it would be important to factor that in to our response. We can actually use that information to acknowledge their empathy and increase their sense of connection to other people. That is a key building block to turning around antisocial behavior. It is a fundamental skill in forming healthy attachments. If those things are ignored in what we do, we can actually drive them further away from people and healthy behavior."

Yes! Sophia smiled gratefully at Dr. Blain and held her breath.

"Jeff, what do you think?" Gabe turned to him, thinking for the third time that the yellow and orange collage of colors in his shirt needed to be dialed down a notch. Preferring subtle solids to any kind of print, it had taken him a very long time to get used to Jeff's wild choices, but screaming shirts aside, he had learned to trust Jeff's instincts and broad point of view.

After a brief pause, Jeff began, "I hear what the doc and Sophia are saying, and I understand those concerns. But from a security point of view I think we have to be more concerned with the safety of the entire facility and everyone in it than the feelings of a few. This fight has the potential to blow this place apart. I guess I'm going to have to agree with the unit managers about sending a strong message to those who may be sitting on units right now thinking about what score they want to settle, or what name they want to make for themselves. It's just too important to take any chances. We'll have to rely on the mental health staff to help those who feel unfairly treated deal with it, and understand what had to take place. We'll just have to see it as collateral damage."

Heads nodded in agreement around the table.

Gabe gathered papers he had spread in front of him and addressed the group, "I think I concur. I was leaning that way from the beginning and this discussion has simply confirmed what I believe. In the interest of the overall facility and maintaining order, we will treat all participants equally, regardless of intent or extenuating circumstances and apply the appropriate sanctions. Sophia and Dr. Blain, we will rely on you and the rest of the mental health staff to help those involved tolerate and learn from those sanctions. Jeff and I will review the policies and determine the exact consequences and let you all know shortly. I will also prepare a statement for managers to read on each unit so everyone knows exactly how this will be viewed. Any further thoughts or questions?" he scanned the group, awaiting possible additions.

Glancing at Dr. Blain, who wore a look of resignation, Sophia recognized there was no use continuing her pleas, institutional safety and management politics having out-wrestled the needs of an individual. Pinned by a facility full nelson, she was forced to create ways to explain the disparities, to soften the blow of injustice, to encourage acceptance of what shouldn't have occurred, in her own mind as much as theirs.

Eliza, the only person having an additional thought, added, "I think you really need to throw the book at Quinn. As I've said for months, he is dangerous and should be in an adult facility. It's only a matter of time before he seriously hurts or kills someone. This is an opportunity to send him to one of those and get him out of here. I think we should press charges against him."

Several nearby heads nodded in agreement.

Incensed, Sophia exclaimed, "I totally disagree with that assessment, particularly since his motive was to protect a younger, weaker person from a vicious attack. He's still basically a kid, even younger than his years in many respects. He's still learning and developing. Sending him to be housed with more hardened men would be the absolute *worst* thing we could do! Here, he still has a chance. Don't you agree, Dr. Blain?"

Dr. Blain shifted uncomfortably in his seat, caught in the web of competing expectations. He had spent less time with Quinn, due to his and Sophia's different roles, and had wondered if Quinn was irreparably damaged. While he gave those he treated the benefit of the doubt whenever possible, he also knew from experience that some would not respond to the treatment offered.

Feeling pressure from the consensus in the room, he tilted his head to the side and answered hesitantly, "I know Quinn has not shown the progress we all hope for. There are many reasons for that and they go far back in his history. I'm impressed his reason in this case might have been to defend a less capable peer. If that's true, it's a good sign. I also know there will need to be much more progress before it would be safe for him to return to the community, so I understand the concerns Eliza expressed. I'm not sure I agree with charges at this time, given the circumstances, but we need to keep a careful eye on how he responds to the sanctions he is going to receive."

"All right. I've heard the concern and I'll give it some thought. As I said, I'll let you all know what we decide. This meeting is adjourned. Please make sure you keep me informed of the mood and behavior you are seeing on units as we sort this out. Thank you all for the continued good work you do in a tough job." With that, Gabe picked up his pile of papers and exited the room, followed by everyone but Sophia.

Hopelessness gripped Sophia as she stared out the only window in the room, struggling with outraged disagreement. They expected her to talk Quinn and Derrick into accepting something she didn't believe in; to spin unpleasant into palatable, to hide the injustice under moving cups in a shell game to maintain calm. Unable to shield them from the unfairness, she could only help them recognize it and their helplessness against it, even though each had experienced more than enough already. At what point would that twist them into something calloused and unreachable, molding them into exactly what Eliza already believed them to be? Working with them to accept the unacceptable felt unclean, like she had become one of the enemies, just as she had as a child, with her fear-based acceptance of the abuse Russ inflicted on those around him, or feeling forced into deceptive collusion in catering to his whims. Fighting guilt and disgust, she braced herself for what needed to be done.

Deciding a pre-consequence visit was better than trying to douse an emotional fire after it was lit; Sophia left the conference room and let herself into MSU to talk to them immediately. She looked for Quinn first and found him sitting cross legged and motionless in his isolation cell, his back to the window. He had the appearance of someone doing meditation, although Sophia knew he had neither the patience nor the inclination to partake in that practice.

Opening the door slot, she quietly called, "Quinn?"

A moment or two passed, and then he spun himself slowly around by planting his fists on the concrete, lifting himself up from the floor, and walking back and forth on his fists until he faced her. He bore no evidence of the fight he had just been involved in; his opponent apparently unable to land any significant blows during the scuffle. Quinn regarded her through partially shut eyes, face devoid of emotion. He put his hands into his lap, resuming his motionless posture.

"Are you okay?" she began.

"Yes."

"I'd like to ask you a few questions if that's all right. I think I know what happened, but I'd like to hear your perspective if that's okay?"

Quinn nodded.

"From what little I saw, it looked like a student I didn't know had attacked Aiden, who was no match for him. You grabbed him and were trying to keep him off Aiden. Is that right?"

Quinn nodded again.

"Did you know the student who attacked Aiden?"

"No. Seen him around. Heard of him. Heard his big ass mouth."

Quinn's mouth was the only body part which moved. He did not even appear to blink. Sophia had watched shows on predators and Quinn's posture was that of a mountain lion with some form of prey in its sights. If she hadn't known Quinn she might have shuddered at the concentrated energy that emanated from him.

"Have you had any previous issues with him? Fights? Threats? Arguments? Anything like that?" At Dalton, resentments occurred and percolated, waiting for an opportune moment to allow release of pressure. If that was the case, Sophia wanted to know about it.

"No. Talks big. Thinks he has to step up for homies and his hood. Aiden talks big, too, and doesn't know when to shut up. But he's weak. No need to give him ones just 'cause he talks too much. Kid ain't all there. Don't take much of a man to beat that one up. Ain't right."

"Can you tell me why you didn't stop when Jerry was asking you to?" Sophia asked this gently, thinking she knew the answer, trying to avoid causing the lion to spring.

Eyes opened an additional centimeter while Quinn paused, regarding Sophia mutely. When he spoke, his voice was softer with controlled tension. "I know how this place works. If I'd let go, he would have gone after him again or me, and Jerry couldn't do shit until someone else got there except try to talk to him. Kid was going to get hurt. I did what I had to do." The eyes lowered again.

"I do want to thank you for helping Aiden, Quinn. Whether you believe it or not, I understand what you were trying to do and why you got involved. I believe you kept Aiden from getting really badly hurt. I say that, even though I know it was against the rules for you to have done so. I say that because I believe it. If you were on the streets and this happened, you probably would have been thanked by others for stepping in and keeping someone from being beat up. I believe it says something good about you that you were willing to do that. I admire you for that. The problem is since it IS against the rules here it may well be seen as a violation regardless of the circumstances or intentions. I know that probably seems unfair and unreasonable to you. If it were up to me it would be handled differently, but it's not." Sophia watched Quinn intently, waiting to see what kind of response this would evoke. She knew it was risky to offer any words of support for his choice, but she couldn't bring herself to represent the facility response as her own or to support it; this was the least she could do.

Quinn finally moved. He stretched his arms above his head and then gradually brought them down, intertwining his fingers and pulling them backwards, making knuckles crack. Rubbing each knee with a hand he responded, "Miss Sophia, I stopped expecting fair in this joint a long time ago. They can do what they want. They can't hurt me. I did what I had to do."

Yes, I believe you did. Life has done so much harm already I'm guessing this will bounce right off those scars.

"I don't yet know what they will decide, but I want to help you get ready in any way I can. We both know much happens in life that doesn't seem fair or just. You have experienced that first hand. Sometimes the only choice left is to find a way to accept it without doing more harm to ourselves in the process. Can you think of a way to do that this time, regardless of what they decide or how they tell you about it?" she asked, acutely aware Quinn reacted more to the way a message was delivered, or who delivered it, than to the content.

Quinn was motionless again, as though already picturing the upcoming interaction. Eyes closed completely as he reflected for a moment. When they opened, all the way for the first time, they were almost black in color as he stared through her.

"They'll do what they do, and so will I. I'm ready to take what they give, as long as they don't mess with me. I won't disrespect them if they don't disrespect me. I know what you're telling me, but you aren't me, Miss Sophia. Sometimes they're just asking for a fight, and I'll give it to 'em if they do." His poised posture confirmed his words.

Disheartened to hear this response Sophia tried again, "Quinn, I totally understand that you feel disrespected at times, and are triggered by what they do and say. But when you let yourself be taken over by those emotional reactions, you play right into their hands. You give them exactly what they are after, which is control over you. And you make it much harder to get out of here, to have the freedom to go where you want and do what you want. Can you see it as momentarily swallowing your pride and anger for your own future's sake? Rather than believe you're being punked by them, can you see it as taking control of your own future?"

"What future is worth having if I get it by being punked? What does that say about me? Who wants to be that man?" raised volume and sharp tone telegraphed Quinn's tension. His sense of honor and need for respect trumped every other emotion, ignored all possible outcomes, worn like a shell, keeping the vulnerable underbelly safe.

Recognizing the limits of her influence, Sophia decided not to push him any farther. "Okay, Quinn, it sounds like you know you are probably going to have some kind of sanction, and you can accept that, which I'm relieved to hear. I do hope that when they talk to you about it the discussion is calm and you don't feel you have to prove anything to them. I know you have learned how to communicate with them and control your reactions, and I hope you remember to use it. Only you can decide what you are willing to live with. I'm sorry you are in this spot, and I know Aiden is probably grateful you stepped in on his behalf. I know I am."

Quinn surprised her with a mirthless laugh, "Maybe, maybe not. Not sure he even knows what that homie could have done to him. Like I said, he ain't right. Like to have kicked his ass a time or two myself for his mouth, but I know he can't help himself."

Quinn raised his head and looked Sophia squarely in the eyes. She noticed his were less black and ominous, which relieved her. Maybe he would be able to get through this after all. As long as no one put hands on him, he might absorb another injustice at the hands of authority.

Sophia wrapped up with Quinn and bid him good luck and goodbye, then moved to the other side of the MSU block to check on Derrick. Unlike the stillness she encountered in Quinn's room, Derrick was squirming with agitation, pacing circles on the other side of the door. He was startled at the sight of her in the window and the sound of her voice.

"How are you holding up, Derrick?" she began, noting the barely controlled frenzy in his face. Clearly the passage of time had not diminished the frustration he was feeling. If anything, it may have increased as he ruminated on it after being isolated.

"This is so messed up! I didn't do anything! I don't deserve this! No one will listen to me! I HATE this place!" Derrick slammed a wall with his fist for emphasis. His circles grew smaller, clomping back and forth in front of the opening so they could hear each other, unable to stop and stand still.

"Derrick, I know how frustrated you must feel, and I know it all seems very unfair. I know why you got involved, and it was for all the right reasons, reasons that are admirable. And I know it seems like that's all that should matter."

"That's all that SHOULD matter. He was threatening and disrespecting you. That guy's an asshole. I've seen what he does and who he messes with. He's just like guys back home who beat up their wives and kids. Trust me; I've seen them every day of my life. Thinks he's so big and tough but only proves that to those weaker than him. If rent-a-cops hadn't been so damn slow I would have stayed on the wall like I was. Wasn't going to wait and see if he came at you again. You KNOW that, you can TELL them for me!" Derrick paused long enough to stare intently into her eyes, hope sparking from his own.

"Please trust me, Derrick, I told them everything I knew about the situation and what I believed your reasons were. I did my best to help them understand, and to see you meant to help and not do harm."

"So when are they going to let me out of here?"

Sophia did not respond immediately, trying to think of the gentlest possible way of explaining. The momentary pause caused Derrick to rush to the door, intuition on high alert, radar for self-protection a siren in his head. He scanned her face through the window and then blew.

"They aren't going to, are they? Those assholes think I need to be sanctioned, don't they?" he began hitting the door repeatedly, each thud accompanied by a cry of protest.

"Derrick! Please stop and listen to me!" Sophia pleaded through the door, the sound of his pounding fists constricting her gut, reminding her of sounds and feelings in her own distant past. She fought to control her body's reactions and stay focused on him. "Please let me explain this." She knew if he didn't stop, security would appear to make him stop, escalating him further.

Derrick recoiled from the wall, taking several agitated laps around his room. This was such a familiar situation, one he despised. Growing up blamed for things he had not done, bearing the brunt of harsh consequences, smacked around just because an adult was in a bad mood or he had behaved like the child he was. Adults who did not listen to offered explanations and mocked his sensitivities, ignoring his needs and wishes. Tending his own needs from an early age, learning to distrust everyone around him, honing skills to notice changes in tone and mood for self-preservation; he had survived, but was emotionally threadbare from the lack of predictability in his life. Derrick felt himself unraveling, an impotent rage coursing through his blood, his hands clenching and unclenching as though grasping an invisible enemy by the throat.

Sophia tried again, "Derrick, you and I both know this isn't how things should be. If I could change this I would because I know you were looking out for me, and I appreciate that so much. Dr. Blain and I both tried to make them understand the entire picture. We both supported you. I don't know what they will decide for sure yet because they haven't said, but I wanted to prepare you for the possibility of sanctions and help you deal with whatever happens. I know how hard it will be but I also know you can do this if you put your mind to it. You are strong Derrick, stronger than you think."

Derrick rolled his eyes upwards and tilted his head back, releasing an anguished groan. He was tired of being strong. He was tired of being mistreated by people and systems. He was tired of walking the tightrope of what others thought he should do, only to lose his balance and find no net below.

Liars! All of them! There was no one he could count on. Not even Sophia. Did she really try? Did she really speak on his behalf? If she had, why was this happening? Wasn't she the shrink? Wouldn't they listen to her? Maybe she didn't try hard enough! An unstoppable tide of hate washed through him, slamming into every empty crevice formed inside where the absence of love had left a void. Hate, roiling into a frenzy, pushing him back to the door, fists once again slamming against the wall and glass, Sophia recoiling in alarm.

"PREPARE ME?!" he bellowed. "Prepare me for being SCREWED OVER AGAIN?"

In moments, security was at the door, insisting Sophia leave the area so they could get Derrick under control. Torn between wanting to help him and being frightened at his loss of control, she backed away from his room, but stood in the corner of the cell block without leaving. Security's arrival produced a chorus of profane shouts and insults as Derrick added feet to his assault on the walls. As the door was unlocked and opened, Derrick charged the three men there to intervene, a pinwheel of arms and legs spiraling into them, appearing impervious to pain in his single-minded focus to make someone pay for what he felt. Derrick managed to land a few blows before his arms and legs were pinned, leaving him with only his head and mouth as weapons.

"You BASTARDS! Get your hands off me! Let me GO! I didn't DO ANYTHNG!" Derrick head-butted Steve, the nearest guard trying to put cuffs on one arm so they could flip him and fasten the other one. Steve paused briefly, momentarily dazed by the impact. Grunting and panting mixed with body parts thumping the concrete floor as the four tangled. After several minutes of wrestling they managed to get Derrick flipped onto his stomach, cuffed and shackled.

They sat him up against the wall and Steve, squatting before him asked, "You want to calm down in your cell or have a turn on the table?"

Derrick responded by spitting in Steve's face. As a disgusted Steve wiped his face with a sleeve, the other two hoisted Derrick to his feet and turned him against the wall, holding his shoulders firmly against it to prevent any possibility of him repeating his liquid assault. Steve tried again, "Derrick, we can leave you like this for a while in your room or we can take you to the restraint room, your choice. If we leave you in your room, will you calm down?"

Derrick thrashed against the hold, throwing his head backwards; trying to connect with anyone he could to inflict more harm. "Screw you! I don't care what you do to me. You can't hurt me! If you want me to calm down, you get me out of this fucking place. I don't belong in here!"

Steve nodded silently to the others, and they each tightened their grip as they turned Derrick in the direction of the restraint room. Derrick's feet limited by ankle chains, his arms immobilized by the determined grip of the staff and handcuffs, his body reluctantly pushed forward by Steve's grip on the back of the waist belt, all generated a new level of frustration and fury that distorted his features as he was propelled past Sophia.

She tried once more, "Derrick, please try to calm down. Please think about what you are doing and try to do what you can to help yourself through this. You know..."

"SHUT UP! I don't want to hear what you think. You're just like all the rest of them. You're just like Andrew. He didn't care and YOU don't care. You get to walk out of here every night. You don't know what it's like here! It's all your fault. Just GO AWAY and LEAVE ME ALONE!" Derrick continued to flail against the vice grip holding him.

Sophia watched helplessly as Steve unlocked the door that Derrick was led through. She stayed behind, already visualizing the battle that would ensue as they strapped him down for his own safety. His words had stung. She reminded herself not to take it personally, that words spoken in anger are not always how one really feels, but is emotional chaff being culled to relieve pressure. Verbal debris flung from the explosion when intense emotional reactions cause us to lose faith in those around us; to fail to distinguish between those who support us and those who don't; to believe the worst about others in the black hole of distrust and pain.

But her own emotional reaction to what had occurred hijacked her reason, leaving doubt to question if she had failed him, failed to teach him enough, failed to instill enough hope, failed to counteract the destructive influences of early years, and worst of all, failed to be convincing enough with administrators to keep Derrick and Quinn from receiving unnecessary punishments. Derrick was right, she was just like Andrew. Andrew, the older cousin who had looked out for him, spent time with him, stepped between Derrick and the men his mother brought home as they went after him. Andrew, who took him fishing and camping and sheltered him when alcohol and drugs invaded his home, until life closed in on Andrew and he lost his way, shooting himself in the head, just as Derrick opened the door to look for him; leaving Derrick adrift, alone, unprotected in his violent world, and with a loss that thickened his distrust to impenetrable levels.

She didn't blame Derrick for being angry, she was angry with herself. If she were better at her job, if she were more assertive, if she could articulate more effectively, if she knew more so she could bring up better points, if, if, if. Some days she felt completely inadequate for the job and wondered how she ever got through graduate school.

"It's your fault!" echoed. He had stepped in to protect her, and now she had failed to protect him. *He's right. It is your fault and your failure. You should have argued more, convinced them somehow. You gave up too soon. Why are you in this job? You have nothing to offer.*

Sophia felt a familiar anxiety radiate outward until it reached her skin, creating drops of perspiration from head to toe. She wiped the dampness from her face with her sleeve, breathing as deeply as she could, attempting to control her reaction. *In, out, in, out…slowly, deeply.* She rocked gently back and forth as she shifted her weight between each foot, concentrating on relaxing her body, trying to control the flood of emotion so her logic could come back on line.

She was startled by Quinn's voice, coming from behind the door of his room. "He's wrong. It's not your fault."

Completely absorbed with Derrick, Sophia had forgotten that Quinn was able to see and hear all that had transpired. There was little privacy in this cell block, and Derrick had been loud enough for every room to hear. The sound of Quinn's voice pulled her back into the here and now, and out of the funnel that had spun through her head.

"Quinn, I'm sorry you had to see and hear that. Are you okay?" Sophia took several steps in the direction of his cell, searching the window for his face. She was still reeling from the interaction, but struggled to refocus.

"I'm fine. He's not fine. But he shouldn't have blamed you. Needs to man up."

Sophia smiled wanly despite her distress, grateful for the encouragement Quinn offered, even as he faced his own struggle. "He was just really upset. I'm not sure he even meant what he said. I'm sure he and I will have a chance to talk it out once he's calm again. But thank you, I appreciate hearing what you think. I'm still hoping you can handle whatever they decide and not get into the situation he just did."

One eye twinkled and squinted as Quinn regarded her through the glass, "I feel ya'. Can't say, Miss Sophia. Don't worry about me. It's all good."

"Okay, Quinn. Thanks again, and I'll check in with you tomorrow when we're back. Try to have a good night."

Sophia let herself through the locked doors and walked back to her office. The air was colder and the wind had picked up, swirling loose leaves and loudly flapping the flag on its pole. Although attempting to concentrate on the files she had organized earlier, she found herself replaying the events of the day, trying to find places she could have done things differently; trying to evaluate each step she had taken and if it was a misstep and to reassure herself she hadn't messed something up irreparably. Familiar feelings coursed through her, feelings of impotence, guilt, anger, mixed with compassion for those she sought to help and a yearning to feel she had alleviated historic wrongs.

Near the end of the day, after finding no clear answers to any of her internal questions, she received the email detailing the consequences for the fight. Both Quinn and Derrick would spend a week in MSU, with time being extended for any inappropriate behavior while there. Derrick was already looking at additional time.

Derrick was right. I get to walk out of here at the end of the day, while he pays a price for trying to look out for me. I don't know what it's like in here. I am pretty much just like the rest of them. How could he see it any differently?

The comparison to Andrew stung the most, knowing how abandoned Derrick had felt upon his death, the only person in his past he had trusted. She hoped she could eventually help him see that trust, as powerful as it was, could not assure any particular outcome, regardless of committed efforts.

Sophia returned the last file she had worked on to the cabinet and put on her coat. This was a day she was glad to see end.

FACELESS

July 10th 2017
2:30 pm

Walking among them but never with them, always apart, feeling the waters of humanity separate, drawing away as he enters. His boots to their sandals, his heavy jeans to their cotton shorts, his hooded sweatshirt to their tank tops, his face obscured beneath the hood, theirs open to the sun's rays, his frown to their smiles, his despair to their joy. Unseen. Unheard. Unknown. Walking among them but looked through or past, never noticed. Watching as they hug, and laugh, and dance. Watching as they talk and sing and play. Had he ever played or sang or danced? He couldn't remember. Wondering if behind closed doors their laughter died, as his had. If hugging turned to hitting and singing warbled into pleading, as his did. Can any of them feel the pain shrouding him like a smoky aura as he moves among them? Will the fire inside ignite them if he reaches out to graze them as he walks past? Feeling his body tighten as he draws closer to the music, each beat a ratchet wrench. Imagining…this woman, that boy, those men, he follows them with his eyes. Who first? How many before they stop him? Shrieks of amusement and fun becoming screams of terror and pain…what would that arouse? Will he drink it in as nourishing nectar, his final meal? Or will he feel regret and sadness for what he causes? Unanswerable. Imagining the moment when it was over, when he splatters himself against the wall of enough, when he finally embraces peace. He was almost ready. Turning from the crowd, he snakes back to his refuge in the bushes, to his calm before the storm.

DIVISION

"Ah, Beth, you're here. Welcome." Mr. Stanwick, the attorney, greeted Beth as she entered the room and took a seat at a corner of the rectangular table that filled most of the small space. Beth shrugged off her jacket and removed the white knit scarf from around her neck, letting it drop into her lap. Her face mirrored the apprehension felt by the five already seated at the table. She clasped her hands in her lap as she nodded a silent greeting to Marcus, Sophia, Jane, Dylan and Annie. There had been no contact between Beth and the others since the day she and Sophia had visited, and she was unsure what to expect from this meeting. While trying not to anticipate the worst, she had nonetheless tried to prepare herself for whatever might come.

"Hello, Beth," Sophia offered, the only one to speak. Dylan nodded, while the other three remained motionless. Beth managed a tentative smile.

"Well, now that we're all here, let's get down to it," Stanwick began.

He had been standing, shuffling papers lying on the table before him. As he spoke he unbuttoned his jacket, revealing his considerable girth, and then sat down in the chair at the head of the table. He was a short man with a semi-circle of closely cropped hair that orbited his otherwise bald head between one ear and the other.

Picking up several pages and glancing through them, he continued, "As you know, your father recently revised his will, making a significant change when he did. While his previous will had divided his estate four ways equally, this new one gives one third of the value to Elizabeth and divides the remaining two thirds between the four of you." Stanwick nodded towards the five sitting to his right. Ignoring the snort from Marcus, he continued, "The assets I'm aware of include his house, a life insurance policy, and his pension. He probably has at least something in checking and savings accounts, and there may also be miscellaneous household goods such as furnishings and vehicles that have some value. Marcus, you are still named as executor in this revision, so it will still fall to you to carry out his wishes if you are willing. There are certain tasks you will have to carry out as executor. I'm providing you a list of those tasks and an approximate timeline to follow. Given the size of the estate, it will have to go through probate, so the court will be watching what you do to make sure you follow the law and his wishes, and you will have to submit information to the court and get it signed off for things to close." Stanwick handed the paper to Marcus as he spoke. "Do you have any questions at this point?"

"Do I have to follow this revision or can I contest it?" Marcus asked sharply.

"There are several reasons people contest wills. First, if it was not signed and witnessed properly, second, if it has been revoked and another will is found, and third, you believe the will did not represent the person's true wishes. This new will was definitely signed and witnessed properly, and it appears to accurately represent what Russ wanted. So unless you have another one that revokes this one that I don't know about, I think your chances of contesting it successfully are slim." Stanwick rotated his glance from one to another as he spoke, noting the variable expressions on each face as he scanned.

"Isn't this supposed to be fair? How fair is it that a daughter he just met gets twice what any of us get? How fair is it that I get asked to do all the work just to hand the lions share over to her? How fair is it that we put up with his crap his entire life just to get knifed in the back in the end?" Marcus fumed.

Jane's hands covered her mouth, as though something were trying to escape. Sophia and Dylan stiffened but remained silent. Annie's downcast eyes stared into her lap as her hands picked apathetically at invisible lint. Beth stared at Stanwick, avoiding Marcus' eyes, her face frozen.

"Realistically, when it comes to leaving one's estate, fair is something people seem to see quite differently. Wills are individual, and all sorts of things go into what makes a person decide as they do. Sometimes they leave explanations as to their decisions, but often they do not. Russ did not, so we are left assuming or guessing what might have been behind this change. That is not something he discussed with me when we revised it so I can't shed any light on that for you. I do know that he was coherent and adamant about making the change, and it was important to him this be done." Stanwick glanced at Beth, offering a slight smile of encouragement to her.

"Well how about if she refuses it? Can she do that?" Marcus turned in his seat to look squarely at Beth. "Would you do that, out of decency?"

Beth returned his gaze, face inscrutable, but did not speak. Her silence threw logs on Marcus' fire.

"I have a family to support! I have kids that will be heading off to college before long! You, by your own account, are just you and don't have the kind of expenses I have. You don't need this money, and you don't even deserve it! How can you live with yourself? Why don't you do the decent thing and just step aside? I would in your shoes. The old man had to have been out of his mind, regardless of what Stanwick thinks," Marcus thumped the table for emphasis.

Sophia, having waited as long as she could, interjected saying, "Marcus, this isn't her fault. Stop blaming Beth for what Russ has done. It isn't right to ask her to step aside, and she doesn't have to. The law protects her rights just like it does ours, and just like it protects Russ' right to do this no matter how we feel about it. We just need to accept it as it is written and move forward."

Marcus wasn't finished yet. Turning to the others he demanded, "How about the rest of you? Do you want to just accept this or fight it? Maybe if you all supported me she'd give some thought to doing what's right."

Jane shifted uncomfortably in her seat, her hands dancing around the front of her shirt and pulling at her necklace, "I'll let you decide, Marcus. You usually know best about these things."

Nice punt from the cooked spaghetti spine, Sophia mused.

Annie, without ever looking up from where she had glued her downward glance, said, "I know I feel betrayed by his decision. This really sucks. I don't know what the right thing is. It's not her fault, and it sounds like it is what he wanted, but I'm having a hard time accepting it. I just always thought it would be different than this. I wish I could make this all go way." *It feels so mean to be angry with him now, but I AM angry! It's not even about the money or things, it just feels like he forgot us, forgot me, like I don't matter now.*

Dylan glanced sympathetically at his sister and cleared his throat, "I don't see what choice we have. Dad did what he wanted, just like he always has. What he told us never did match up to reality. Sure it's disappointing, but isn't that what we've come to expect?" *Just like my whole life, one disappointment after another, one letdown after another, don't count on anything he says, or what anyone says. The only person you can count on is yourself.*

"So no one's going to help me fight this? You're all going to take it lying down? What a mess," Marcus sat back heavily, crossing his arms.

Feeling the need for a little damage control, Sophia turned to Beth, "I hope you can try to understand that this is a really emotional thing for some of us. Russ had always told us what he intended but then he didn't follow through on it, and on the heels of finding out about you for the first time, it's just a lot to process and accept. I don't think anyone means it personally."

Beth returned her gaze and in a calm but cautious voice said, "I guess I can imagine why this is hard for all of you, in multiple ways. I wonder if any of you can understand that it is equally hard for me. I did not ask for any of this either. I simply wanted to meet my real father and know who he was. When he talked about doing this I didn't really think he would. But when he talked about it, he said he wanted to make up for his past decisions. I know that money can't fix any of that, but I also know that the intention was there to try to mend what he thought he had broken. For that, I am grateful. For that, I want to honor his wishes. If I didn't it would feel as though I betrayed him. You all got to know him, I didn't, for very long anyhow." *Do they see me as some greedy gold-digger? Do they think I looked him up just so I could get something from him? Why would they make such ugly assumptions about me when they don't even know me? And if that is how they see me without even knowing me, how will I ever convince them otherwise?*

"You haven't missed much! You'll probably enjoy his money more than him in the long run," Marcus countered, oblivious that this last round of remarks had led to Annie sobbing quietly. He turned to Stanwick and said, "Well, since I'm executor, it still falls to me to take care of what needs to be done. We have already started cleaning up the house, and there is more to do to get that ready to sell. I need to know how much I need to include her in the decision making or if I can just go about what I need to do."

"Ultimately she will need to accept and sign off on what goes through probate, as will the rest of you. You, as executor, are free to make decisions and take care of the required tasks, but if you think there would be any disagreements about how that is done, it would be prudent to check with all the named heirs to avoid last minute objections or complaints that bog down the process."

Marcus glared at Beth, "Are you going to micromanage me in this? Are you going to feel you have a say in it? Are you going to make me fill you in on every step I take?"

God forbid that someone have an opinion that differs from your own! The irony of his concern was not lost on Sophia, who remembered countless times she and others were overruled by him.

"No, I don't think it would be helpful to anyone for me to do that. If you want my opinion on something you can ask, or if there is something you think I need to know you can tell me. Otherwise, I'm going to let the rest of you decide how things get done," Beth offered.

A snide snicker preceded Marcus', "Just take the money and run, huh?"

Beth blushed a deep shade of red, "I was going to say that I'd be happy to help in any way that I can, but it seems pretty clear that my help is not welcome. I think staying out of the way is probably the best help I can give under the circumstances."

"I appreciate that, Beth," said Sophia, seeing her discomfort. "This is really awkward. I appreciate that you would be willing to help, and also see that helping might not look the same for everyone due to circumstances. I think between the five of us we can take care of what is needed, and hire out the things that might seem too big and time consuming."

"Then it looks like we are all clear on what needs to take place and how things need to progress. If you have any additional questions, you can call my office and ask either me or my associate. Marcus, you need to make an appointment for about a month from now to give me an update on your progress so I can make sure we are meeting court timelines. If no one has any questions for now, I have another appointment waiting." Receiving no further questions, Stanwick picked up his pile of papers and exited the room.

Beth quickly wrapped the scarf around her neck, stood to put on her coat and followed him out of the room, grateful the meeting had ended.

"Are you okay, Annie?" Sophia asked, seeing that Annie continued to sob.

Finally looking up from her lap, Annie shouted through tears, "I HATE him! Why did he DO this? All I ever did was love him and try to help him and keep him company. Why did he lie to me? Why has he betrayed me, betrayed all of us? It feels like he didn't even LOVE us!" Covering her face in her hands, she bent forward until the top of her head rested on the table, shoulders shaking in grief.

"I'm not sure that man was capable of true love," Marcus spat. "This feels like one more of his capricious "feel good" deeds. He gets to go out feeling like a hero by paying attention to one part of the picture."

Jane gave several quick pats to Annie's shoulder in an effort to comfort her, "Oh, Annie, I'm sure Russ loved you. I'm sure he loved all of us in his own way."

Random thoughts ricocheted as Sophia absorbed the reactions her siblings had to Russ' decision. *What does love mean, after all? Is the expression of love in the eye of the beholder or is there a common understanding and definition? If I do something out of a sense of love, but you feel hurt by my choice and not loved, has love really occurred? Does love only exist in the heart and intention of the one loving or does it require a landing spot, a resting zone outside oneself in order to be real and complete; like the wiring in a house that must be continuous, without breaks, for the electrical charge to actually travel to the intended destination? Can a different perception cause a break in the line between one individual and another that shorts out the connection? Is love an intellectual decision or an emotional feeling? Can one act with love without feeling it? Can one feel it and fail to act on it? How is it measured? How does one recognize it? How does one make sure that our expressions of love are recognized as such by those we are trying to love?*

Did she feel unloved by this decision? No more so than she had most of her life when it came to Russ. She felt more unloved when he failed to show interest in her life or failed to listen when she tried to express her feelings. She felt more unloved when he hurt her and failed to be accountable for it or make any efforts to mend it. And what if he did feel love towards them but was abominable at expressing it in any recognizable way? What if this was his way of expressing love? Why express the most to the child who just appeared, rather than those who had been there all along? To even the score of love, to balance the scale?

Maybe Annie was right. Regardless of what the decision was meant to convey, Sophia believed strongly in his right to make it, and she was determined to accept it. She was used to disappointment from Russ. While she had grown a protective crust to keep from expecting much from him, she was realizing that the others had not done so and were being injured more by their view of his final act. *I guess that is the silver lining in this….I've already grieved this loss and can't be hurt by it anymore.*

Marcus spoke again, "Whatever his reasons, it looks like we have no choice but to accept this since she won't step aside. We still have some things to do at the house so we need to get that scheduled so I can move this along. The sooner it's all said and done the better as far as I'm concerned."

Annie was sitting up again, dabbing at her face with a tissue, tears staunched and emotions contained, for the moment. They compared schedules and decided a date to tackle the rest of the house cleanup. Dylan committed to additional days on his own to do the remaining outside tasks. Driving home after they parted, Sophia wondered if all relationship turbulence resulted from the wind shear of conflicting expectations.

SHAME

Sophia stared at the unopened box on the floor, still covered in dust and tangled cobwebs, as she rocked in her recliner, attempting to calm her apprehension with a glass of wine. Gentle jazz played in the background. After the week she had just lived, she considered canceling the plan with Marcus but decided against it given the difficulty they had integrating their schedules. She recognized she was on edge and feeling vulnerable, and the uncertainty of what might lurk within the cardboard nibbled at the border of her resolve.

Her mother Grace had been gone for some time now and reading her words, meant for someone else, felt somewhat invasive, particularly because she had been such a stoic, private woman. On the other hand, being allowed a brief moment inside her mother's thought process could be both informative and comforting. Their relationship had been a close one even though there were noticeable differences between them. Sophia leaned towards frankness and was willing to discuss anything with those she was close to, perhaps to a fault. Her mother had been more likely to keep her thoughts to herself and her feelings even more tamped down. Grace always offered words of support, but showed her love rather than spoke it, perhaps the result of growing up in an era where that was the norm, as well as the outcome of living through hardships that scooped feelings into a sheltered place so one foot could continue to be put in front of another.

Sophia missed her mother, the meals they shared and phone calls just to see how she was or to tell her how the day had gone. Losing her after a sudden illness had been much more difficult than losing Russ.

The doorbell chime drew her from her reminiscence. She opened the door and Marcus strode through, taking off a wet coat and hanging it on a coat rack in the corner next to the entrance.

"Hello, Sophia," he said tensely, brow knit. "How are you?"

"Okay. It's been a rough week and I'm not sure I'm ready for this, but I didn't want to cancel on you," she replied honestly, wondering if the expression worn by Marcus indicated his own mixed feelings. "Would you like something to drink?"

"Sure. I'll take whatever you have."

Sophia was gone for a moment while Marcus found a place on the couch to sit. When she returned she handed him a full glass of red wine.

"That's it I assume?" Marcus nodded in the direction of the box as he took a sip.

"Yes. I haven't opened it yet. Not even to look inside," Sophia relaxed back into the recliner and pulled the box closer to her with one foot. "I'm not sure how to even begin this except to maybe check for dates and try to establish an order so we can go through it sequentially. What do you think?"

"That probably makes sense. Whatever is written might make more sense if it was in chronological order. How about we each take a stack and organize them and then compare our dates and integrate them?"

Sophia nodded agreement as she pulled the box open. She lifted out a stack of papers and then slid the box towards Marcus. Marcus retrieved his own stack, putting them on his lap. As he began to sort, he created piles on the coffee table in front of him, while Sophia used a side table next to her chair.

They each found an assortment of content as they sorted, letters from Grace, journal entries from Russ, miscellaneous news articles from the time period, and a few letters from other people. Once sorted, they combined the Russ and Grace items by any date they could find, assuming that if they read a letter from Grace it would likely be followed by a journal entry by Russ. Most of them were dated, and they commented on how that custom seemed to have faded in recent years with so much communication taking place by other means. Russ and Grace grew up in a time with more social rules, which in this case made the task that much easier.

By the time the piles were sorted, the wine glasses were empty, and both Marcus and Sophia needed a break. Marcus excused himself to use the bathroom, and Sophia replenished the wine, stretching kinked muscles. As they made their respective ways back to the stack of papers, they paused, looking tentatively at each other.

"Soooo….now what?" *Moment of truth, Sophia mused. Can we still decide not to?* Uncertainty still churned.

Marcus inhaled deeply, letting the air out slowly and deliberately before answering. "Well, I guess we start reading them. The question is do we read them aloud or silently taking turns or just try to read them at the same time looking at them together? Do you have a preference?"

Feeling conflicted and hesitant, Sophia found herself wishing for Marcus' usual bossy, take-charge self.

"How about we try reading them out loud and see how that goes. If it doesn't seem to work we can try a different approach. Will you read them?" Sophia put Marcus back in charge subtly through her choice.

"Okay, if that's what you want."

Marcus began reading from the first letter. Sophia, legs curled up beneath her, listened intently as she fingered her wine glass. The first letters detailed the pain of separation and betrayal, as well as the need to establish financial settlements.

"…unforgiveable….that woman….our baby is dead…need to move on…two other children…need to go back to work…your income…child support…medical expenses…funeral costs…how can you live with yourself…don't deserve this…visitation…don't want to see you…don't punish the children…humiliated…believed your lies…broken our family…"

Russ' journals revealed his processing in response. "*…not to blame…trapped by women…gender battles…enemies in every room…my savage intelligence…tricked me…Addison was the only one worth anything…I am unfairly punished…they just want my money…no time for these mundane worries…never wanted to be a father or a husband…meant to be a priest…led astray by women…the battles I have fought…*"

Marcus paused after reading several of the pages and whistled softly. "Sure do hope he got this out of his system before he actually wrote her back. I'd hate to think she had to read any of this crap," he said, glancing up at Sophia.

Overwhelmed with compassion for her mother, Sophia spat, "He is *such* an ass! I know they both lost a child but that is seriously narcissistic! He never takes responsibility for anything! Always the victim, never the victimizer! Unbelievable!"

She was surprised at the depth of feeling expressed by her mother in the letters. Grace apparently felt more comfortable expressing strong emotions in writing than she ever had in speaking. Sophia felt as though she had been transported back in time and was witnessing a heated exchange between her parents.

"Shall I continue, or did you want a turn to read?" Marcus checked.

"You keep going. This works okay." The thought of seeing her mother's handwriting as she read and saying the words out loud still felt like too much to Sophia, like being pulled too close to the edge where footing might give way.

Marcus continued as the content of the letters eased away from the pain of a child's death and the discovery of an affair to the ongoing issue of getting through a divorce, obtaining child support and seeing the two remaining children. As they read, Marcus and Sophia became increasingly aware of the battle Grace had endured on their behalf. It was clear Russ had been haphazard in carrying out his responsibility to his first two children. Grace's letters were full of bounced checks, pleas for consistency, and accusations of putting Annie and Dylan ahead of the first two. Russ's journals outlined excuses, justifications, and deflections, presenting Russ as the wretched casualty of wicked women. As children, they had been somewhat aware of the tension and occasional conflict between their parents, but were not told the details. Grace never made negative comments about Russ to Marcus or Sophia, nor did she share the struggles she had in obtaining child support.

Sophia marveled at her restraint as she listened. *Where did she keep all those feelings during those years? How did she keep bitterness from exposing all his faults and crappy decisions? How did she keep herself from trying to make us hate him, as she must have? How did she keep it from spilling out onto the two of them, as she navigated through single parenting and trained to be employable?*

Picking up the last letter from Grace, Marcus said, "Well, here is where this ends," and began to read.

"*Dear Russ. This will be the last time I will write you. It is clear that trying to communicate with you to resolve issues is pointless. You neither hear me nor accept my perspective. I am letting you know that I will be hiring a lawyer to pursue court ordered child support and monitoring, as you seem unable or unwilling to consistently send what you have agreed to. It is my intention to ask that you be responsible for the court costs, as it is your lack of consistency that has made this step necessary. I will also be asking to set up acceptable parameters around child visitation. All communication from now on will occur through lawyers. Do not write me or call me again. Your last letter was ugly and hurtful. How dare you tell me that if I'd been more attentive Addison would not be dead! How dare you suggest that Sophia might have had something to do with her fall through the crib! What kind of monster are you? Don't you ever say anything like that again, to anyone, but most certainly not to HER!"*

"Wow!" Marcus whispered as he looked up at his sister in disbelief.

Sophia had frozen, her throat constricting, cinched with invisible threads. The not quite empty wine glass dropped from her hands as she clawed at her throat, trying to release the contraction. Red wine bled into the fabric of her pants as the glass rolled from her lap onto the floor. Staccato squeaks hiccupped through parted lips, as bulging eyes strained to see through unexpected darkness. An ember licked into the edge of emotional dynamite, kindling memory ashes into flames.

Shame: a painful feeling of humiliation or distress caused by the consciousness of wrong or foolish behavior, the intensely painful feeling that we are unworthy of love and belonging. Of all human emotions, it is the most painful and destructive. One can attempt to camouflage with bold exotic colors, brash behavior, jeweled accessories, and ceaseless good deeds but still believe oneself to be the emperor in invisible new clothes, sure that others see and smell the rotten core beneath the façade.

Sophia choked with shame. Marcus bolted from the couch and over to his sister.

"Sophia!" he shouted. "Sophia, it's all right. Calm down!"

Kicking the wine glass aside, he knelt beside her, gripping her shoulders. The moment his hands touched her, heaving sobs erupted. The hands that had gripped her throat now clawed at the skin of her arms, creating deep gouges oozing red. Marcus struggled to wrap his arms around her from the side, trying to immobilize her so she couldn't continue to rip open her skin. Sophia struggled against his hold, slapping at his arms and head, rocking, writhing, and trying to break loose.

There it is…get it off! The image was there and then not there. Wiping, clawing, pinching, it shifted just as she had it, taunting her as it reappeared in a new spot, inviting more frantic exorcism. That mysterious shadow that burned, itched, terrified and changed shape and color just as she had it isolated. What was it? Why did it come back just as she thought it was gone for good? How would she ever get rid of it…that blemish that couldn't be covered up? That inner flaw that eroded anything she did on the outside, like a sink hole that swallows anything built on the edges; that THING that haunted her that had no face, no name, no substance but still enveloped her with strangling vines, whispering….worthless…pitiful….fatally flawed….waste of life.

"Sophia, please!" Marcus pleaded, wet with perspiration from the struggle to contain her. "Stop it!"

Sophia continued rubbing fiercely at the gashes she had dug into her flesh, as though trying to remove leeches. The blows directed at Marcus had left crimson streaks where they landed.

"Let me go! Get away! Don't look at me! Oh my God….oh my God….," Sophia moaned, and as though a switch had been thrown, went limp and silent, body curled up, her bloody arms covering her head.

Marcus relaxed his grip but continued to hold her, rocking gently, "It's okay Soph, it's okay. They're just words. It doesn't mean anything. You know the old man was always full of crap. And he was always looking to put blame on someone else. Mom didn't deserve that. I wish I'd known he'd said something like that to her, I'd have kicked his ass!"

Sophia stiffened and then shook with silent sobs, visions and sounds reeling randomly inside her head, a video fast-forwarding out of control.

Crib bars, slamming doors, baby feet, shouting voices, musical teddy bear. Angry faces, silence, hiding. Cooing, bottles, bath toys, smiling, scrubbing, scrubbing, scrubbing…can't get it off. Falling, hiding, hiding, hiding, boxes, scared, silence…

What the hell? Marcus puzzled. *I get that it's hard to hear about Addie, and it's harder to hear that the old man put undeserved blame on Mom, but what the hell is this? It was so long ago, how can it be this upsetting?*

Marcus had never understood these moments with Sophia. He had tried to help her through them, but she could never tell him why they happened so they just lived them and put them away and went on. He believed it must be the difference in how males and females felt and processed things. He had definitely noticed differences in how his own children dealt with things, and his daughter was much more emotionally reactive than his son. It was odd that Sophia, who was usually a very rational and controlled person would become so overwhelmed and lost. Marcus felt a little lost dealing with it when it occurred and found himself wishing it didn't because he hated not knowing what to do. He was as willing to forget about it as Sophia was, when all it did was cause him uncomfortable feelings.

"I'm so sorry. I'm so sorry…" Sophia whimpered, barely audible, head still buried under her arms and into the cushion of the chair. The pin-balling visions continued and expanded.

Gunfire, fences, graveyard, crows, restraint beds, clanking metal gates, red-rimmed eyes, fists on flesh, shaking chills, running, ice clinking, fear, debilitating fear. Make it stop-make it stop-make it stop!

Startled, Marcus asked, "Sorry for what? It's okay Soph. I know it's upsetting to think about, but you haven't done anything."

"You don't understand. You don't know. I can't tell you. I can't…" she shrank into herself even more. She had become one of them, one of her clients, cornered in the moment when the protective shield is threatening to crack as shame's poison balloons like an atomic mushroom cloud.

Beyond alarmed, Marcus reached under her and lifted her out of the chair. Moving to the couch he lowered her first and sank down next to her. Sophia curled over, arms wrapped around her legs, head resting on her knees, face turned away, trembling with tension. Marcus draped an arm over her back and stroked her shoulder.

"What's the matter, Sophia? Why are you so freaked out? There's nothing to be sorry for."

Breaking point: the moment of greatest strain at which someone or something gives way, perhaps a hillside heaves as gravity trumps tamped ground, or a dam bursts through a weakened point, or a fissure ruptures the crypt of closely guarded secrets, unearthing indistinct recollections and feelings in a memory quake.

"I can't say it. You'll hate me. I hate myself. I don't know how to live with it," she wailed between sobs, her entire body shaking.

Baffled, Marcus grabbed a wad of tissues from a nearby box, placing them into the hand closest to him. Whatever was eating at her, it seemed huge, and he wondered if he was prepared to hear it.

"I'm not going to hate you Sophia. Come on, what's going on?" *I HOPE I can take this. This is beyond crazy.*

Sophia took several deep breaths, trying to calm herself and quiet the trembling, torn between letting the determined beast out of the cage and wanting to put another lock on the door to prevent it. "I…I…I think I did something terrible….to Addie. I…" she trailed off, unable to finish.

Shock stiffened Marcus, "Don't be absurd! Of course you didn't! Why would you say such a thing? You *know* the old man was full of it! Don't listen to that letter. Now I wish we'd never read them!"

Sophia shook her head back and forth, wiping at her nose with the tissues. She had lifted her head slightly, and was staring straight ahead, not looking at Marcus.

"It wasn't the letter, Marcus, at least not just that. I can remember things. Not clearly, but flashes of things and feelings. Something always felt wrong to me after Addie died, but I couldn't figure out why. What Mom wrote in that letter, well, it's like it put all those parts together and turned a spotlight on it. I could see it all more clearly for the first time. Oh God...." She lowered her head again, not wanting to be seen, unable to look at Marcus. The realization, fully formed for the first time, flooded her with shame and self-loathing.

Puzzled, Marcus wasn't sure whether to ask more questions or just wait until she began again. He didn't want to unsettle her but couldn't grasp what she thought she had done. Pulling a few more tissues from the box, he dabbed at the cuts on her arm, "I wish you wouldn't do this to yourself, Soph. I don't understand why you want to hurt yourself like this."

"Because I deserve it!" she wailed. "Don't you see? It's my fault she died. I did something. I tried to get her or was trying to play with her, and because I was so young I did it wrong and she died! It's my fault, it's all my fault! Mom must have hated me. Russ must have hated me! I have hated myself my whole life because of it! I've tried to make up for it, but nothing I do is any good. Nothing I do takes it away. Nothing I do makes it feel right or clean. I wish it had been me to die, not her!"

Sophia hid her face in her hands and rocked back and forth, bracing for her brother's judgement and scorn. Once the words were out, once the memory exposed, terror twisted her into a tight knot. If she could will herself dead she would have in that moment to escape the unbearable feelings associated with naked vulnerability, and the certainty that there was nothing worth loving about her. Without meaning to, she had unearthed the oppressive shadow haunting her for as long as she could remember, the whisper molding her thought process into relentless doubt and dissatisfaction and causing her to hide her unworthiness in shadows and behind walls, the taunt that told her she wasn't like everyone else, bringing her to mutilate her skin as she tried to scrape away the ugliness stained into her.

Stunned, Marcus exclaimed, "Sophia that makes no sense. You didn't hurt Addie. You couldn't have! No one hated you. It was just an accident. It wasn't anyone's fault. Are you telling me you've always thought that? Why on earth would you think that?" He stared at her in disbelief, bloody tissue frozen above her arms.

Sophia moaned in anguish, and then spewed her answer, "The things I remember. Her room. The things in her room. Mom and Dad yelling. And Dad saying so to Mom and to me. He was so angry. I'm so sorry, Marcus. I think I've forgotten a lot, but sometimes I'd have these flashbacks about that time and other times all mixed together, and I didn't know how to make sense of it. I didn't know what was real or dreamt or imagined. But the feelings, the feelings were always the same. I was terrified and felt such shame, like I'd done something unforgiveable."

"Dad told you that you caused Addie's death? He actually said that to you? Are you sure?" Marcus demanded.

"I…think so. It's almost more a feeling than an actual memory. It's like I felt his blame but can't remember any words he actually said. I don't know how to explain it. It's just, when I heard Mom's words in that letter it was like I recognized something finally that's been in there all along, but I couldn't see clearly and didn't have words for." Sophia tried to draw solid lines around undulant thoughts and feelings to capture them in words and make Marcus understand. It was like trying on mental bifocals, the focus shifting between clear and distorted. She whispered, "Please don't hate me, Marcus."

Marcus shook his head, flooded with his own memories. A littered tide of feelings swept through him, disbelief, anger, sadness, confusion. All those times he had found her in an incoherent puddle, now he understood. He recognized the death of their sister had been the root from which a distorted, diseased tree had grown. Anger flooded him, at their father, at his mother, even at himself for not having seen or stopped it.

"Sophia, look at me," Marcus rotated more to face her.

"I can't," she whimpered, hiding behind her hands.

Marcus took both her hands in his own, pulling them away from her face. Sophia dropped her head, unable to meet his gaze.

"Sophia, you have this all wrong. You did not hurt Addie. I know this. You need to listen to me. Soph, I don't know what the old man said to you, or if he said anything at all, but this I do know. You were not even home when Addie died. You were next door playing with a neighbor all day. I remember because I had to keep checking on you to make sure you were still there and getting along. There is no way you could have done anything no matter what you think you remember or what anyone said. You were so little, you must be confusing memories. It's no wonder since we never really talked about any of it. Sophia, this was *not* your fault!" Marcus squeezed her hands for emphasis.

Sophia froze in stunned disbelief and confusion. Not her fault? How could that be? As awful as it had felt to vaguely believe she was responsible for Addie's death, she did not know what to feel in hearing she might not be. Or, that she definitely was not, according to Marcus. Was he just saying that to ease her guilt and shame? Would Marcus do that? Maybe Marcus wasn't remembering things accurately; he was pretty young too.

She kept repeating the words Marcus had spoken. "Not even home…not even home" as though they needed an extra push to make the journey from her ears to her brain. She felt mentally clogged, as if something needed to move and shift but was caught fast; like when she tried to buy something from a vending machine and the item started the path to the edge but got hung up just before dropping and stopped, hovering. She wanted to bang the side of her head to dislodge what was wedged. Relief fighting to get through the funnel and cram into her awareness but the space was too small, too blocked from years of believing half-formed memories.

"Marcus, are you sure? Are you positive? How can that be when I remember all these other things? It's such a powerful feeling."

"I don't know what you think you remember or how those memories got there, but I'm sure about where you were that day. And I know you didn't have anything to do with what happened. If I know the old man, and I think I do, you might have overheard some nasty comments he made to mom, or just him ranting, or maybe he even said something directly to you. I don't know. I know when he was angry he'd say anything to anyone. And then deny it. It's obvious he said something to Mom at least, which is why she wrote what she did. And she was trying to keep him from saying such a thing to you, although maybe he already had, or within earshot. You might be remembering bits and pieces of things about Addie when she was alive, and then mixing those things up with the day she died and things that happened afterwards. Being so young, I'm sure you didn't understand a lot of it and it would be easy for it to become a mixed up story in your head," Marcus explained.

"But I always felt something. Why did I always feel so, I don't know, flawed?" Sophia agonized.

"I don't know. You're the one who knows more about that stuff than I do. But if you felt on some level like you were responsible, well, I can see how that might influence how you feel about yourself. It really pisses me off that Dad put that in your head. What an asshole! Who does that to their kid?"

Staring at Marcus, Sophia withdrew her hands from his. Nothing felt real. She could see her hands and her couch and the room around her but it was as though they were all near replicas of what had been there before, like a piece of art that had been copied and although technically sound, lacked the heart and vision of the original artist. You could feel a difference that you couldn't explain.

A foundational brick in her self-view had been flawed. Years of experience wrapped around this inner core, tendrils of assumptions and beliefs, unraveled as the core foundered. How do you reframe a lifetime of feelings? How do you rewrite decades of misunderstanding? What gap do you find to insert an essential puzzle piece when the finished product has been shellacked by certainty and neglected for years? How do you recognize the pattern of who you are when the center portion falls away?

"I don't know what to say. Or do. Or feel anymore. I don't even know who I am anymore," Sophia whispered.

"You are still just you, Sophia. The same you who works with messed up kids no one else will touch. The same you who sees good in people even when no one else can. Sometimes you and I are pretty different, and I know you can make me crazy, just like I make you crazy. We disagree on a lot of things, but you have done good things in your life no matter what Dad said or didn't say or how he made you feel about things. You have to forget all that and just keep doing what you do. You didn't deserve to carry that around with you all these years. Maybe if we'd talked about some of these episodes you've had I would have realized what was causing them and been able to tell you sooner. It explains why you stopped having much to do with him. You just need to put this behind you and forget it was ever said." Marcus tried to reassure Sophia, uncertain what to say, as this was far outside his comfort zone. Seeing her through new eyes, the past incomprehensible moments were becoming less so.

Sophia continued to struggle. "But maybe I see good in other people because compared to me everyone seems good, or better, better than me. Maybe I work with messed up kids because deep down I knew how messed up I was and it helped to try to "fix" something since I couldn't "fix" what was messed up in me. What if I've been trying to find some way to feel less guilty or less horrible about myself all this time? I've even resented you and Jane and your kids because it seems like you are so perfect and have things so good, things I can't have. Even Zac…" she trailed off as her voice failed her.

"What about Zac?" Marcus prompted quietly.

"When I did get something wonderful and unexpected, I lost it. I felt like I was being punished for..." she dropped her head again, shame welling.

Marcus shook his head in disbelief, "Geez Sophia. You didn't deserve what happened to Zac. It was just an accident, like Addie. I can't believe you took it that way. Why didn't you say something?"

"I couldn't. I'm not sure I even understood why I felt like I was being punished, I just did. I knew it was crazy, but I couldn't help feeling it. It's impossible to explain to someone else something you don't understand yourself. It's impossible to share something when the very thought of it makes you feel like you are going to be sick. And I hated feeling like I did."

"Well, there's no need to be jealous of Jane and me and the kids either. It's no picnic to be married and raise kids. Hardest job in the world and some days I'm not sure it's worth it. You know, it's funny, I always thought you were the lucky one. Single, able to do anything you wanted without answering to anyone, able to come home and relax and not have any obligations to help with homework or transportation or personal crises. There were days I felt a little envious of you, too!" Marcus ended with a chuckle, trying to ease the tension, "I don't know much about what makes people do things, Soph, but even if you are right about what encouraged you into your line of work, is that a bad thing?"

Sophia rubbed her face with both hands, "Maybe not. I'm not sure. It feels a little fraudulent or something. Like I've been pretending to be someone I'm not. Like, who am I to help someone else live a better life when I can't fix my own, or myself."

"But if what you thought isn't the case, you don't have anything to fix other than your mistaken idea of what happened. You are who you are despite all that early crap, and you use it to help others. That's not fraudulent."

Sophia pondered this thought. The logjam in her thought process seemed to be slowly easing, creating tributaries of ideas and reflections that gently parted and ambled along new pathways. She found she could not follow them all, much as she wanted to, but had to grasp one at a time. *What if? An entire world of possibilities was opening.*

"Marcus, what do you know about the day it happened? What do you remember?"

Marcus inhaled deeply and rubbed his head quickly. These were old memories untouched for decades. "I don't remember a lot. I do know you were gone, like I said. I was watching TV, some sports program. I don't remember what exactly. Mom had put Addie down for a nap and was cleaning the house. She occasionally asked me to go check on you, which I did, and you were doing fine playing next door with your friend. I remember being annoyed I had to because it was making me miss the game, football I think it was. Anyhow, I had been gone to check on you and came back to the house and mom was on the phone, hysterical. She was holding Addie, but Addie didn't look right. As soon as I came in Mom told me to go to my room and wait until she came to get me. I could tell something was wrong so I went, but I tried to listen from the door. Pretty soon there were people there, police and paramedics. I couldn't hear all of it but I could tell something had happened to Addie. Mom was a mess." Marcus' face contorted as his memory churned long-forgotten sights and sounds.

"After a little while Mom brought you into my room. The neighbors had kept you there, out of the way, until the commotion was over, and then brought you home to see what Mom might need. Mom asked me to watch you and keep you busy for a while so she could find Dad. She said she would explain in a while. We played in my room, not sure how long. I'm guessing Mom was trying to get a grip as well as find the old man before dealing with us. It was really quiet until Dad got home, and then all hell broke loose, lots of shouting and crying. He was always good in a crisis as you know. I think Dad left the house because all I remember is Mom coming in to tell us that Addie was gone, and I don't remember seeing Dad that evening. I didn't ask any questions because Mom was so upset, so I don't know where he was. She was on the phone a lot to people, and a friend came by for a while and they talked in the bedroom. Maybe he was gone dealing with arrangements or something, or maybe he went back to the school. You didn't really even understand because you kept looking for Addie and asking for her."

Sophia rubbed the arm of the couch and bit her lower lip, "I don't think he was making arrangements or back to school."

Marcus raised a quizzical eyebrow, "Really? Why not?"

Sophia decided it was time to share what Beth had told her, "Don't freak out, but I had a meeting with Beth after we met her and found out some things from her."

Marcus' face morphed from curious to a mixture of scorn and apprehension. "Ohhh?"

"I had questions about what she knew and wanted to see if she could fill in some blanks for me. I also wanted to see more of what she was like."

"And what was she like and what did she know about what took place?" Marcus asked hesitantly, not sure he was going to like the answers.

Sophia nut-shelled the information Beth had shared, as well as the impression she had formed of the woman they both shared genetics with.

Marcus listened without interruption or comment, and then said, "So, the old man was with his student that day, hearing she was pregnant? And then got to come home to the news his youngest child had died. That might explain the yelling I heard. Even if Mom didn't know where he was, his own guilt must have been pretty unbearable, and I'm pretty sure his way of dealing would be to get mad at something or someone else. Best defense being a good offense, as they say. So, I wonder where he did go when he left."

"I don't know, but somehow I don't think he could face anyone at that point. I think he would have had a tough time dealing with any arrangements or doing something as routine as working. According to Beth he didn't teach classes for a little while after that."

Sophia and Marcus sat quietly for a few minutes, lost in their own thoughts, imagining how they might have reacted under the circumstances, certain their own reactions would have been nothing like that of their father; the compassion attached to losing a child churned away by the turbulence of betrayal and rejection of responsibility. For each of them, fragmented memories and beliefs shifted and reattached, transforming their view of the past.

Sophia was the first to speak, "I have a hard time resenting Beth because of all that happened. It's almost like she got punished because Russ couldn't deal with the guilt. She didn't deserve to be ignored, and it wasn't her fault how she came to be."

Marcus shifted uncomfortably in his seat, "I don't resent Beth as much as I resent the old man. I resent that he chose what he did, and I resent that he kept this entirely from us and just let us find out once he died. It's cowardly. He had plenty of time to let me know and he didn't. What's with that?"

"I don't know…guilt maybe. Ego?" Sophia ventured. "You know how much he needed to be admired. He could never handle it when he thought someone was unhappy with him or felt he had done something wrong. Telling us about Beth would mean telling us about her mother, too, which would generate questions about that time that I'm pretty sure he had no interest in answering. Too many skeletons to want to open that closet door. Letting us find out this way saves him from having to face it, while he can still atone for it to Beth. That's the only thing I can figure out."

"Maybe," Marcus offered begrudgingly, "Still feels pretty chicken-shit, if you ask me. Might have been a final opportunity to atone to us as well, especially you, given what you just told me about your own memories and struggles. Do you think he or Mom knew what you believed about Addie's death?"

Sophia shook her head vigorously, "I didn't even know it myself, fully, so I don't know how either of them would have, unless something was said when I was so young I don't remember. Like I said, I never talked about it or even really understood it all. It's just been in there, deep down, like a mirage that moves when I try to get near it. No one ever wanted to talk about it, remember?"

"Yeah, I remember," Marcus sighed, "It was a tough time, and to have the parents split shortly after made it even tougher. It seemed better for Mom to avoid bringing it up, and adjust to all the changes on our own."

"Were you aware of those financial stresses she talked about?" Sophia asked, thinking their difference in age might have resulted in Marcus knowing things she had not.

"A little; I remember her being pretty stressed about bills at times, and phone calls to Dad that always seemed to be angry ones. One of the times we moved and I was helping to pack up the kitchen, I came across a big bag of rice that had a label on it for needy families. I was surprised by it because I'd never seen us as needy. When I was older and started working, I had to use some of my own money for things I wanted or needed because she couldn't afford a lot of extras. I went into insurance because I knew I could make good money, and I wanted to give my kids things we didn't have. I know it wasn't Mom's fault and she did all she could, but I didn't want to live on a shoestring like she had to. I blamed Dad for a lot of that, and I learned early on that if I wanted something I had to earn it myself. One time when I did ask him for money to pay for something school related he threw the money at me, along with some choice words. I never asked him again. I think I've done pretty well, despite no help from him. That's why this irritates me so much. I thought I'd finally get something from him that evens the score a little or help me feel he was making up for all those years he did so little for us or mom."

Sophia considered Marcus' words for a moment, realizing her perception of an "I'm better than you because I have lots of money and cool things" attitude from her brother might have actually been Marcus creating a safety net against anxiety, and a shield against the pain he was worth less in the eyes of their father than their half-siblings. Beth's appearance in this had cracked that shield.

Maybe you're not the ass I've always thought you were. Maybe it wasn't love of money and status that drove you but seeking money as a substitute for love and self-worth. Maybe that's the damage at your own center that I knew nothing of. There are a hundred ways a psychological sink hole created early in life can swallow confidence and force you to dig tunnels out. Maybe you built a ladder of money to climb out on.

"I guess I can understand that on the one hand, Marcus. But on the other hand, imagine what Beth must be feeling about being rejected and ignored as though she had no importance to him at all, and then to connect in the end and have us all mad at her for existing. Maybe it's easier for me because I had cut ties with him and had no more expectations. I can see that it's been harder for you three, well, four now. You were all still in touch and expected something different because of that. And Russ let you expect those things, shame on him for that. "

"Yeah, shame on him for a lot of things. All those years growing up I tried to please him, but to this day I don't know what he thought about me. I don't know if he was proud of what I have accomplished or who I am or not. It's not really the money part that bothers me, but the fact that I might have finally felt like he *was* proud of me if he had left me an equal share. I know it's not even logical to think that way, but that's how I feel. This feels like a slap in the face after everything I've tried to do, and everything I've put up with from him my whole life."

Sophia nodded, "I get it, Marcus. It feels a little like a final statement from him somehow. But Russ often had conflicting desires and fulfilling one of those desires could interfere with the others. I think he had a final desire, based on a lot of guilt, and this was the way he tried to go out cleaner. By giving in to that desire, he dismissed some other things he probably also cared about. Beth told us he talked about us in a positive way. That's something."

"Too tough to tell us that himself though," Marcus shook his head, "I don't know how to feel about her. You have a point about it not being her fault, but it's like she's a physical reminder of everything that bothers me about all this. She's a reminder of what he did and didn't do, of all the choices that influenced us through the years. I don't know how to look past that to see who the person is. I don't know if I even want to. Mostly I just want to get this all done and move on."

Sophia understood and was grateful she had already buried those feelings. She had given up believing Russ could contribute anything positive to their relationship. She had stopped looking for affirmation or support and took steps to protect herself from further harm. She had grieved the loss of her father long ago, the actual man and the idealistic yearning for a positive paternal influence.

Listening to Marcus, she realized he had continued to seek what Russ seemed unable to give, and that reality was hitting hard now that he was gone. *I guess you never get too old to want to know your parent thinks well of you and loves you.*

Her stony view of Marcus began softening as she listened, new sides added to a flattened square creating a prism of vulnerable child, anxious teen and injured adult determined to survive. The familiar longings and struggles, hidden until now, eased some of the tension and resentment that had always stood between them. Grateful for his tender concern, and information which had freed her from the snare of false beliefs, Sophia wondered if their relationship could change, just as her understanding of the past had. Perhaps they could find a way to build a friendship.

"I get that too, Marcus. I think we all want to get through this and have it behind us. I think the best we can do is avoid taking our feelings about Russ out on Beth, as hard as that might be, and see how this plays out. No one has to become best friends with her; I just don't want to be unnecessarily unkind to her."

Sophia leaned back into the couch cushions, exhausted, looking down at arms and hands she didn't recognize, like someone had played Mr. Potato Head with her body parts, bloody tissues still wadded in one hand. "And, Marcus, thank you. Thank you for…" tearing up, she was unable to continue.

Marcus self-consciously patted her hand, also feeling overwhelmed, "You're welcome. I wish we could have cleared that up a long time ago."

"Me, too," Sophia concurred, "Marcus, do you have that same feeling about Dylan and Annie? I mean, do you resent them because they also remind you of what Russ did or didn't do for any of us?"

Marcus pondered the question briefly and then said, "At times. I don't think they are bad people and I can't blame them for us basically losing our father because he remarried and had more kids, but there have been times when he seemed to favor them or help them out while he didn't do the same for us. I've never understood that, but it always felt like he paid more attention to their needs and what they wanted while he just expected Mom to do that for us so he didn't have to."

Sophia nodded, "I have to wonder now if he was more distant from us because of that guilt, if we were reminders to him of things he didn't want to have to think about or remember. I have always wondered what happened to him that led to his being as he was. I really didn't know much about him, other than the things he wanted to say about himself. I know our grandfather died when Russ was pretty young. I wish I knew how that affected him."

"I don't know much about him either. He wasn't one to talk about his past. And he has no living siblings to ask so I guess we'll never know unless Dylan or Annie knows something. I hadn't really thought about it, but I suppose it's possible we reminded him of things he felt guilty about. It seems like he should have found a way to get past that for our sakes. I wish I could have been inside his head as he died. I really wonder what people think about as they get to the end and know it's coming. I wish he would have voiced any regrets he had. Somehow it would feel better to know he was at least aware of the things that bothered me or the ways he had hurt people at times. Now we will never know."

"Well, even if you did feel some resentment about the other two, you seemed to get along with them okay. You had more relationship with them than I did," Sophia shifted in her seat to face Marcus. Talking about things they had never before discussed was surprisingly reassuring, as though they had finally found the trail out after wandering lost in undergrowth.

"Yeah, I suppose so, although I wouldn't call it a strong one. We'd run into each other sometimes and I heard about what they were up to. But it's not like we did things together or called each other up to talk. At least not since we all grew up and went our separate ways. Dylan got lost for a while and wasn't in touch with anyone. He might have gotten the worst Dad had to offer. Dad seemed to target him most of all and was relentlessly mean. I think it really messed Dylan up for a while. He seems to be doing better now, although it's hard to get to know him, always quiet and standoffish."

Sophia nodded, "He's quiet. I have the feeling he's carrying around a lot of stuff that never gets talked about." She smiled sheepishly, "Kind of like me. Kind of like you. Maybe kind of like most of the people out there but we all try to hide it."

"Now don't go all psychobabble on me, Soph," Marcus teased, "I've had all I can take in one day! But, yeah, it's not much of a stretch to see Dylan's been damaged by the Russ influence."

"How were you able to continue to be in touch with Russ? How did you put up with him for so long?" Sophia asked the question she had puzzled over for years.

Marcus sighed loudly, "I think it was different with me. When I was a kid and he was a jackass to me, I chose not to go spend time with him. I got busy with sports and then my job which meant I really didn't see him all that often. When I visited, I was often outside doing something so we really didn't have a lot of personal contact. Once I was an adult and called him on his bull, he seemed to back off, almost like there was a part of him that was intimidated by me and my willingness to push back. He was a school yard bully who needed a weaker victim, not someone who would take him on. Once he didn't try to mess with me anymore we had what I would call a wary truce, and then I focused on checking in on him and making sure things were okay. It's not like it was a warm fuzzy relationship or anything like that. More me doing what I thought I "should" do as the oldest kid, looking out for their aging parent." A mixture of chagrin and resignation crossed Marcus' face, "And look where that's gotten me."

Sophia let that sink in for a moment before responding, "Well, I give you credit for doing that much because I couldn't bring myself to take it on. Maybe it was easier to stay away because I knew the rest of you were in touch with him and he was looked after, so I took care of myself and didn't guilt myself into thinking I needed to do it, too."

"Any regrets on that?"

"Not at this point. Maybe I'll feel some later, but the truth is our relationship died a long time before he did. I couldn't trust him, and I wasn't sure I even liked him very much. I needed to stay away to keep him from hurting me anymore. I've never told you this before, but one of the summers I was staying there with him he got mad about the dogs getting out of the property. They had gotten out under the fence somewhere. He brought out a rifle and was going to shoot them. Dylan and I were trying to protect them, and he threatened to shoot us if we didn't get out of the way. We both took off running in different directions, and I heard the rifle go off. I never knew if he was shooting at one of us or the dogs. I ran into the woods and hid until almost dark because I was afraid to go back until I was sure he was asleep or passed out. The dogs were both okay so I don't know where he was aiming when he fired that gun."

Sophia paused briefly, shaking her head, "He never even apologized the next day. It was like it just didn't happen at all. I think that bothered me as much as believing he might have been shooting at me. Those kinds of things happened all the time. Usually after he'd been drinking, but he wasn't even always drunk when something ticked him off and he took it out on someone. I could never relax when he was around because I never knew when something might set him off or who was going to get hurt when he did go off."

Marcus whistled, his eyes wide with astonishment, "Wow, I guess it's easy to understand why you chose to put some distance between the two of you. He could be an arrogant ass to me but he never pulled anything that outrageous. I can't believe he did with you. I don't have any regrets either, because I know I did what I could and I tried to look past his faults. But, my experience with him was different from yours, and if I'd been in your shoes, I probably would have done the same thing. Annie seems to dote on him, and I think Dylan was beginning to be around more than in the past, although he might have had the same reasons to stay away as you did."

"I do wonder what stories each of them would have to tell about growing up with him. I saw some awful things when I used to visit. Russ was always so mean to Dylan, tearing into him over the smallest things and then belittling him if he cried. I watched Russ kick him and throw him down a few times, too. I felt so sorry for him and how he was treated. He could be just as unpredictable and mean to Annie, although most of that was verbal rather than physical. Annie seemed really skilled at staying invisible or doing things that side-tracked him when he started to go off. I suppose it was a survival skill. She seemed to get the more positive things he had to offer, more than any of the rest of us. I've thought about asking them what things were like; part of me wants to ask, but most of me doesn't want that information in my head. I have more bad memories than I wish I had already. Even though I was there for some of the things that happened to them we just didn't talk about any of it. I think we all tried to pretend it didn't happen. I don't know how Annie can be so, I don't know, committed to him," Sophia shook her head with a puzzled look.

"Annie seems to accept everyone she meets. She lets things roll off and focuses on something else. Although she seems pretty thrown by this last minute change of will and the appearance of a sister she knew nothing of. I've wondered if she feels a little replaced by Beth's appearance. Annie was closest to Dad, and it must feel like a slap in the face to find out he kept this from her and was spending time with Beth when he could have been spending that time with her."

Sophia glanced sideways at Marcus, asking, "Do you remember him hitting mom?"

Marcus startled at the bluntness of such a difficult question and frowned slightly, "I'm not sure. I mean, I don't remember seeing that but sometimes when things got heated and they were in another room I wondered because of the things I heard. Mom always tried to make sure we were somewhere else when he got ticked off about something. Why? Do you remember that?"

Sophia chewed her bottom lip gently, "No…but I remember feeling really unsafe sometimes and hiding. Since I can't trust my memory I just wondered if that was why I felt like hiding when I was younger. I did see him abuse our stepmother at times and it was awful. He would say the most horrible things and call her the ugliest names. And then he would hit and kick her or throw her down. I was out walking one day on the farm and saw her lying on the ground as he was trying to run over her with the motorcycle. I felt so helpless and sick about it because I had no idea what to do and was too afraid to try to help her. My feelings then were similar to the feelings I had when I hid before the divorce, or when I would have those episodes, as you call them. So I just wondered if…" Sophia stopped as tears welled in her eyes, overflowing onto her cheeks, stomach clenching instinctively as unbidden memories reeled.

Marcus gazed at Sophia, understanding gently dawning. When he had been home during the conflicts, his mother had charged him with watching over Sophia and going somewhere else. But the difference in age meant there were times he was gone to school or with friends while she was home. What was seen and heard when he was not home to shield her, or during visits to Russ when Marcus decided to stay home or had other places to be? How many times had she felt helpless and blamed herself for the ugly things happening to people around her? Just like with Addie. Memory of Sophia's agitated episodes flooded through him, and he understood how, being overcome with helpless fear and self-blame, she would need to mentally check out, to slide into self-protective emotional shock. Reliving the moments when comforting her had been impossible, Marcus felt sick himself.

Why didn't it ever occur to me? If I'd realized I might have been able to do something different and sooner. Maybe I should have said something to Mom about it instead of just dealing with things on my own. How could I be so irritated about her decision to distance herself from our old man? Did I make it worse for her by giving her crap all those years? Even when I'm half teasing, I know it bothers her. I should have known better.

Not until now had Marcus wanted the opportunity to do something over, to choose differently, but there was no revising this. He made a mental note to be more aware in future interactions. That much he could do.

"I wish you hadn't had to see any of that crap, Soph. Why didn't you ever tell me?"

"I don't know, Marcus. You always seemed to handle everything so stoically and didn't seem bothered by it. I guess I figured talking about it would make everything worse so I tried to forget it. It bothered me that it bothered me," Sophia gave a mirthless laugh at the absurdity of that. "It made me feel so weak and vulnerable that I tried to hide it, even from myself. I tried to stuff it away and deal and be grown up about it. I tried to be stoic like you."

Sophia was feeling more vulnerable now than she had ever felt in her life as she shared these things with Marcus. While she had begun to see a softer, gentler side to him, discussing memories and insecurities was uncharted ground, creating some of the very feelings she was describing. *Can I really trust you not to use what I'm sharing as a way to hurt me?*

"Stoic, huh?" Marcus responded, "Maybe on the outside. Things bothered me, but what could you do? Being older I had to step up and help out once the folks split, so I concentrated on that and not adding to Mom's burden. I didn't have the luxury of feeling sorry for myself or being angry about any of it. Things had to be done, we had to move forward. And since I didn't want to be like the old man, I did everything I could to do something different. There were times it was damn hard, and I resented the hell out of him and what we all had to do because of him. I'm proud of my family. We may not be perfect, but I think my kids have it a lot easier than you and I did. I'm hoping I've never made my kids want to punch me like I wanted to do to Russ at times. And I'm hoping I've never made them feel like I didn't love them or wasn't proud of them. I took what I saw and used it to push myself in the opposite direction. Maybe that's what you see that you call 'stoic'. Sometimes I thought I was going to explode from the pressure of it all, but I knew I couldn't. I had to help Mom and I had to look out for you. I had to grow up fast. I had to make my own way in life and look out for other people along the way. I didn't have time to fall apart. If that's stoic, then I guess I'm guilty as charged."

Again, Sophia experienced a kaleidoscope turn of impressions; realizing stoic could mean anything from indifferent and apathetic to patient, tolerant and enduring. When the word left her mouth she had been thinking indifferent, but Marcus' reply shifted it towards enduring. The same events had impacted Marcus, funneling his reactions into a course away from repeating family patterns to find his own solid ground. Instead of allowing the pressure of the situation to break him down, he used it to sculpt himself into someone he could face in the mirror without shame. Sophia wondered how many of the words she had chosen in the past to describe Marcus would undergo a similar transformation in the coming days, as increased awareness and understanding added layers and softened edges in what she told herself about him. It was becoming clear that assumptions they had each made about the other were not only inaccurate, but had built unnecessary walls between them.

Sophia dabbed at her still damp eyes, "I guess we all have our own scars from it, Annie and Dylan more than anyone since they had to live it every day."

"I think he got worse as he got older. Maybe it was trying to live with all that guilt. I don't think things were as bad when he was with Mom, but they sure seemed to get worse as we got older. That's why I limited my time visiting him. I didn't want to be around it. I assumed he wasn't as hard on you girls as he was on Dylan and me. I thought he had more gentleman in him than he did. I wish I had known. I would have done something about it." Marcus was still angry with himself for not realizing what Sophia might have been exposed to.

"I'm not sure what you could have done, Marcus. You were a kid, too."

"If nothing else I could have let Mom know, and she could have kept you from going. I could have threatened him once I got older. No one should have to put up with that crap."

"No, no one should. It's a common story though. I can't tell you how often I hear it from the students I work with. They would be shocked if I could tell them that I totally 'get it', which of course I can't, even though I think it would really help them to know. Imagine, Marcus, one man who shaped the lives of four different kids, I mean five, by how he treated them, but each in a different direction. Even though we all have some shared genetics and some of us have been through the same experiences, we don't all have the same impressions and don't draw the same conclusions. It's really remarkable how different we all are."

"That's true. Do you think that's true of all families?"

"I don't know, but I suspect it is. I suppose it can be both a curse and a blessing."

Marcus glanced briefly at his watch as he shifted forward on the couch, "It's getting late. Do you want me to stay here tonight? I'm happy to, but I need to let Jane know if I'm going to." While Sophia seemed to have recovered, he was concerned about leaving her alone after the discussion they'd had.

"Thanks, Marcus, but I really think I'm okay. I'm exhausted and ready for bed, but I think I'm fine and would appreciate some time to process this more, which I do better alone," she responded, standing up. She scooped the papers covering the table into the box they came from and picked up her wine glass from the floor.

"You're sure?" Marcus double-checked.

"I'm sure, but I really appreciate your willingness to," Sophia managed a weak smile as she moved to the kitchen with the glass. She rinsed the scratches on her arms with water and patted them dry with a towel. A stinging sensation informed her that feeling was returning to her skin, which was beginning to look like her own again.

Marcus had followed her into the kitchen with his own glass and put it on the counter. Glancing at her arm he said, "You might want to put something on that."

Sophia nodded, embarrassed, "I probably will. Thanks again, Marcus, for being here and for telling me what you remember."

Marcus gave her a quick, awkward hug, "No problem. We should have probably talked about this a long time ago. Hope you sleep. Will you call or text me tomorrow so I know all is well?"

Sophia nodded, followed him to the door, and locked it once he was gone. She glanced around the room and decided against cleaning up further, choosing instead to change into pajamas and get ready for bed. Sliding under the covers she realized how truly wrung out she felt.

As she worked to relax, she replayed some of the evening's conversation in her head, trying to steady the seismic shift that had taken place upon hearing Marcus' version of events. She imagined herself at three, unable to make sense of Addie's sudden death and disappearance and the fracturing of her family. Years of impressions and feelings forming without a mirror, without a sounding board, without dispute, had solidified into sensitivities and baffling automatic reactions that had shadowed her ever since. Sophia knew this was going to take some work, some deep reflection to redraw the outline of who she was. She mentally tried on new self-views, like when she would change the clothing on paper dolls she used to play with as a child. Could she finally discard the ill-fitting flawed outfit she had believed permanently bonded to her? Could she at last see the stain evaporate, or would it leave a stubborn ghostly outline? Could she still recognize herself without it? It seemed as though a dense cloak had been lifted off but was still attached by microscopic threads, grasping her, reluctant to be left behind no matter how unnecessary.

Sophia eventually fell into a troubled sleep, uncertain who would be reflected in the bathroom mirror when she looked into it the next day.

SHOWDOWN

Oblivious to the chill that fogged her breath and nipped her fingers, Sophia strode fiercely past the residential units, hunkered like hibernating beasts, beelining for the one farthest from the school. She partly hoped the anger would shrink by the time she arrived so she could control what she said, but mostly she no longer cared.

She had eased through numbed days after the evening with Marcus and the letters, going through the routines of her life with the vague sense she was tethered to herself from the outside, pulled along against her will. Sophia allowed herself to drift without question, without deciding she needed to grab the wheel and correct her course. She had passed through a storm and trusted the current to determine where she floated next.

The days had passed unremarkably, meeting with new students, checking on those she already saw, and shuffling the required paperwork, until today, when she had gone to speak with Quinn and learned he was going to face additional charges and be moved to an adult facility.

"I'm sorry to hear this, Quinn. How are holding up with that change?"

Shrug, "Doesn't matter. It's all lock-up. I know how to do time."

But it did matter. Sophia could see the withdrawal already settling into his expression, the protective veil muting the life in his gaze. Adult facilities did not encourage completion of school or provide counseling or vocational training, diminishing future opportunities. In talking with Quinn and others in MSU it became apparent that Eliza had succeeded in her quest. Compelled to confront Eliza, Sophia was not at all sure what she might say once there.

Reaching the unit, she let herself in, marching to the back corner office where Eliza sat at her desk, coffee cup in hand, eyes on her computer screen. Sophia slammed the door behind her as she entered the office, crossing the room to stand on the other side of the desk, glaring down at Eliza.

Eliza put her cup down and rolled backward in her chair, "Let me guess. You are here to yell at me about Quinn." Her insolent expression and tone succeeded in ratcheting Sophia's outrage.

"How can you possibly think this is going to be good for him? How can you possibly think this will lead to him getting out of custody or getting a job? How can he turn his life around if you keep throwing him into deeper holes?" Sophia demanded.

Eliza leaned backward in her chair, interlocking fingertips and resting her arms against her stomach as she regarded Sophia icily, "I don't. That's the difference in how you and I see things. I'm not trying to make sure things are good for him or he has a wonderful life when he gets out. I don't think he ever will get out, or at least not for any length of time. I see him spending most of his life in prison because he continues to offend every time he gets out. My goal is to protect everyone else FROM him and the sooner the better!"

"How can you be so cold? Why doesn't it matter to you that he does what he does because of how he was treated? Where's your compassion for another human being? Why do you stay in this job if you have so much disdain for the people you are supposed to be helping?" Sophia clutched the edge of the desk to keep indignation from sweeping all the items covering it onto the floor.

Eliza's arms dropped to her side, and she used her hands to push herself upright. A new expression appeared on her face, a mixture of fury and pain, as she locked eyes with Sophia.

"You think I'm cold? You think I'm heartless? You don't know the first thing about me! You don't know what *I've* lived! You come in here with that going-to-save-the-world attitude, always excusing their behavior and trying to make their world into Disneyland. Well let me tell you something, Ms. Connelly. I'm not here to HELP them! I'm here because these kinds of kids TOOK something from me. They took my life! They took everything I cared about. And I'm not going to let it happen to someone else. Not if I can help it! They don't deserve Disneyland! They deserve jail! And I consider it my job to make sure they get what they deserve and don't hurt other people," Eliza countered with glassy-eyed anger and clenched fists, her mouth barely moving as she spoke.

"These kids haven't done anything to you, so why would you punish them? You're right, I don't know what you've lived or how someone might have hurt you, but why does that mean you spend the rest of your life punishing others for whatever happened, even if they weren't involved?" The unbidden nugget of explanation just offered was side-stepped as Sophia's anger and sense of justice insisted on expression.

"Whether it was these particular thugs or not, they are just like those who injured me. Maybe if someone like me had been in their lives before none of it would have happened. Maybe I'd be looking forward to taking trips with my husband in retirement or attending my child's college graduation. Maybe I'd look forward to holidays instead of dreading them. Maybe I'd see kids as future teachers and doctors and businessmen instead of insolent, disobedient, lawbreakers. Who knows? I won't let the same thing happen to other people, which is why that dangerous boy needs to be locked up."

As she spoke, Eliza's eyes glistened with captive emotion. These words were not allowed expression, these events never shared. Eliza had spent her adult life on a mission to right a wrong that could never be corrected, and the relentless trying had resulted in callouses where the failure rubbed, dead spots where there should have been joy and hope.

Husband? Child? What in the world is she talking about?

The pained expression on Eliza's face jolted Sophia into realizing the assumptions she had made were less than accurate or generous. Sophia always sought information about the past experiences of her clients in order to understand their current behaviors and attitudes, but she had not done that with Eliza. She knew very little about her but had assumed a lot, given their constant clashes and different perceptions. The anger began to ebb through a newly formed spillway.

"Eliza, obviously something happened in your life that was beyond difficult. And it sounds like the guys here remind you of that. I can't imagine how hard it must be to come in every day and do your job with constant reminders. But I also think it's important to separate what your own experience was from what is best for the youth. I'd really like to understand better what your thinking is around this. Are you willing…?"

"NO!" Eliza shouted, "No, I won't talk about it with you, and no, I won't change my mind about Quinn. I've said more than I wanted to say already. It's none of your business or anyone else's. I have my reasons for thinking as I do, and I will continue to advocate for what I believe in. You feel free to do the same. Now if you don't mind, I was in the middle of a quarterly report when you barged in here uninvited, so I'd like you to leave and let me get back to it."

Sophia paused briefly and then offered, "All right, Eliza. I'm going. It's clear we are not going to find a compromise here. For what it's worth, I am sorry that something really painful happened to you."

Eliza slumped into her chair without comment, pulling within reach of the desk. She did not look up again as Sophia let herself out of the office and then the unit. She stared at the computer monitor as Sophia passed the window on her walk back to the school, her hands hovering over the keyboard without moving. She exhaled loudly as a single salty drop splashed the edge of her desk and she began to type, re-capping the inner well that had blown open, as she had done for 24 years.

Sophia fumed as she dodged puddles and dripping trees. She felt torn between wanting to have compassion for Eliza and whatever had twisted her beliefs and desires, and still advocate for young people. As she neared the school she was joined by Jerry, just coming on shift.

"Good morning, Sophia. How are things today? Anything I should know? You look kind of pissed."

"Ha! You might say that. I found out they're throwing more charges at Quinn and are in the process of shipping him to an adult facility. I just tried to talk with Eliza about it to see if I could change her thinking and got nowhere. This feels so WRONG! And there's nothing I can do to stop it."

Jerry whistled softly, "I'm sorry to hear that, but I'm also not surprised. Once Eliza makes up her mind that someone is dangerous, this is what usually happens."

"And there's nothing to stop it? Even if it seems like she is punishing these boys for some past personal issue having nothing to do with them?" Sophia stopped, turning to face Jerry. They had reached the school, but she was reluctant to carry this conversation inside where it might be overheard. "Do you know what happened to make her so cynical and hateful?"

Jerry's gaze telegraphed his hesitation as he considered her question, debating how to respond. He was disinclined to engage in gossip, but also knew Sophia was careful with information and used what she knew for good rather than to tear down.

"I can't agree with Eliza's take on people or events a lot of the time. But I understand why she has the take she has. She's never told me the story, but when you work here long enough you hear things and put things together. The story is that a long time ago Eliza was married and was expecting. She already worked here and had different ideas about the boys, more like how you and I see them now. She worked hard to help them improve and get out. Word has it she had a nephew who had been getting into trouble. His parents were struggling with him and he was getting involved in minor offenses that led to probation. Then both parents were killed in a car accident. Eliza agreed to take the kid in rather than see him go into foster care. Thought she could help him, with her background and all. Had good intentions.

"Long story short, the loss of the parents on top of whatever else was going on with him put him over the edge and things got worse rather than better despite her efforts. Started hanging out with some really rough characters, using drugs, being gone days at a time. One evening when they came home from dinner they found him and two others in the house. There was an argument when Eliza and her husband tried to get the others to leave. Eliza ended up being pushed down the stairs, and her husband was beaten so badly he died. Because of the fall Eliza miscarried. The nephew went to prison where he remains to this day, but the others were never tried. Turns out he had just met them, didn't even know names, and couldn't or wouldn't help find them. They'd come to the home to find things that could be traded for drugs they had and the nephew wanted. They could be in another country for all we know.

"Eliza was never the same after that. She gets a lot of slack here from those that were here when it happened. And she's made it clear that she never wants to talk about it so it doesn't get brought up." Jerry offered a wistful smile, "I've often wondered what she would be like today if none of that had happened. I guess we don't get to know."

Sophia shuddered, as much from the rush of compassion she felt for Eliza as from the cold air penetrating. *Wow. How can people carry around so much without it showing?*

Realizing how easily she had dismissed Eliza as simply dogmatic and unkind, she began to wish that hardship and pain were visible on people, like freckles or tattoos. She regretted never having considered the possibility that Eliza's harsh stance on issues might have been influenced by past tragedy. While she easily gave that consideration to the students she worked with, she had expected more from adults. She had expected adults to have conquered those prior influences and developed skills allowing them to create a different perspective. *Right! Just like I did? Haven't I just realized how I have been held hostage by past events for most of my life?*

She felt the psychological choke-chain pulling her up short again, reminding her of those damaging expectations, expectations at the root of so many social confusions and conflicts, expectations that appear like weeds in a relationship or interaction, creating cracks in the foundations, forcing things apart that may have otherwise been cohesive.

"Man, Jerry. I had no idea, obviously. That explains a lot, doesn't it? I mean, I still can't agree with the way she sees things or what she wants to do based on that, but it does help me see why she is so negative about them. How could you not hold on to some anger about that? Especially if you know a couple of them never faced consequences for what they did."

The loss of Zach fed Sophia's empathy for Eliza. It was hard enough to accept the result of an accident, to know someone's deliberate actions had caused it might have led her to the same jaded outlook, especially when it included an unborn child. There might be no greater pain than that.

"Yeah, I think it was pretty tough for her. I know she's been rough on you all these years, but I always thought it was because you remind her of her old self, still believing in the boys and believing they can be helped. That's probably hard on her too." Jerry pulled his coat tighter and blew on his hands, "I'm sorry to hear about Quinn. She may be right about him, but I wasn't ready to give up trying yet."

"Me neither," Sophia mused, "I really fear for what he may learn or experience with adults. I'm afraid he will come out the other end worse and more damaged and become the very thing she thinks he already is. I feel so helpless. I feel like there's a tsunami coming and I can't warn people to get out of the way."

And a personal tsunami curled in; memories of her father shouting, hurting, shooting, disparaging, bringing with it the realization that she had been drawn to this work to finally speak up, to defend and repair in whatever ways she could. The abuse in her past pushing her to protect through mending, the abuse in Eliza's leading her to protect by locking up.

Jerry winked at Sophia, trying to lighten the mood, "We both tried. We both just keep on trying as they come in and out the doors. All you can do."

"I suppose. Doesn't feel like enough, but I know you are right," Sophia said, pulling open the door and walking through it.

Warmth greeted them as they headed toward the office, shrill bell signaling the class period's end. As the students filed out of the classrooms and down the hallway, Jerry and Sophia stood against the wall nodding to those who made eye contact as they passed.

Which of you will make it? Who will go on to learn a trade, go to college, find a job, get married, or have children? Which of you will offend again, go to prison, become homeless, or end up dead?

Watching them shuffle past, Sophia wondered fatalistically if the outcomes were as capricious as playing Russian roulette. Who got to control that trigger?

VENGEANCE

"I go back to the unit today." Aiden slid his glasses up a still discolored and swollen nose. He eyed Sophia's feet and said, "Those boots are kind of old school aren't they?"

Sophia smiled at him, amused at his lack of tact. "Yes, I suppose they are. Are you glad to be getting out of the clinic finally?"

"Not really. I prefer this environment. I'd rather talk to intelligent people."

Sophia wondered if the clinic staff had enjoyed Aiden as much as he had them, or if they would be relieved to see him returned to his unit.

"Are you concerned about what going back will be like?" During Aiden's absence there had been changes in who was assigned to his unit, most importantly transferring out the boy who attacked him.

"No, I'm used to whatever idiots are there. No matter how low I set the bar of expectation, they manage to limbo under it. I accept that it is what it is, until it's something different. I'm sure they've messed with all my stuff, stolen what they wanted and somehow ruined or disposed of the rest." He scratched absently at an exposed knee. The shorts he wore, despite the cold, revealed almost hairless, white legs, more bone than flesh.

Sophia noted he seemed to have lacked a comb for the entire recuperative stay. *I wonder if I could find an authoritative book detailing the four quadrants of hair combing.*

"If you go back and find that they have been into your personal items, I hope you will report it to staff rather than do anything about it yourself. That way staff can help you figure it out and possibly find who is responsible, and you don't get yourself into trouble over it," Sophia advised.

Aiden shrugged, "The so-called adults are rarely able to figure out who did it when this happens, and they are equally unlikely to help me since they all hate me." Brandishing the notebook containing his cherished notes, he added, "Besides, as long as they don't get this I can handle them messing with the state issue junk. They have more where that came from."

One of the unit staff had brought Aiden his notebook to keep him from imploding while he healed in the medical unit. At least one person understood the value of a little prevention.

"I'm glad you were able to have it here so you didn't have to worry…" Sophia trailed off, distracted by a sudden commotion in the main office outside the room in which she and Aiden were visiting. "Hang on, Aiden…I'm going to go see what's going on."

Hurrying out the door she was almost run over by several security people carrying a transport litter down the hallway and into the crisis response room. She followed them, trying to see which youth was injured. A bloodied towel hid the face from view. The nurse on duty, Susan, slid past them to lift the towel and take a look at the face beneath.

"Derrick? Can you hear me, Derrick?"

Sophia gasped. *Derrick? What on earth has happened?*

"Derrick, the doctor has been paged and should be here any minute. Try not to move. We're going to take good care of you. You're going to be okay. Can you talk? Can you tell me where it hurts?" Susan was cutting off his T-shirt as she questioned him to look for additional injuries. Another nurse appeared carrying a cervical collar. She handed the collar to Susan and then gently lifted Derrick's head as Susan slid the collar into place.

A muffled groan was the only response.

"Can you squeeze my hand?" Susan had placed her fingers within Derrick's closest hand. She nodded as she felt a slight pressure. "Good, that's good. We've put the collar on you to make sure you don't move your neck until we figure out what you need, so it's important that you try to stay as still as you can. Can you see my finger? Blink if you can see it." Susan slowly moved her finger back and forth over his eyes.

A door clanged and Dr. Field, the facility's medical doctor, arrived at a trot. Turning towards Sophia and those who had transported Derrick he said, "I think we can handle this now. Thank you, but it might be best if you give us room to work. I was filled in by the unit on my way here. Susan, what can you tell me about his condition since he arrived, and have you called for an ambulance?"

As Sophia and the other four moved into the main reception area, she heard Susan affirm the ambulance call and begin to convey the stats she had been taking.

"What happened?" she asked Aaron, the nearest of the security staff. The other three nodded their goodbyes and let themselves through the door that separated the clinic from the security area.

"Sean Landry happened, in the cafeteria. Sean attacked him from behind as he was moving past Derrick on his way out after lunch. Was able to slam his face and head on the ground several times and looked like he was trying to break his neck in a head twist. Not sure how much damage was done. Sure was glad to see he could squeeze her hand." Aaron shook his head, looking down at the ground, "Sucker attack. Derrick didn't have a chance to defend himself. Sure hope he's okay."

Sean. Sophia shuddered, remembering the look on his face after Derrick had come to her aid during the school brawl.

This was exactly what she had been worried about. Derrick would be no match even if he had seen it coming. There was a foot of difference in height, fifty pounds difference in muscle, and Derrick lacked the current of hate that flowed through Sean.

"What kind of damage do you think might have been done?" Sophia asked, afraid to hear the answer.

"I don't know. I think his nose is broken. Wouldn't be surprised if he has a concussion at least. And I just hope like hell his neck or spine isn't damaged. Landry is a killing machine. He has some practiced moves and he's quick. Scary dude. World might be better off if they put him away for good." Aaron had seen a lot of boys come through the facility, and this one had him watching his own back.

Sophia winced. The call for the ambulance made sense now, in the face of possible serious injuries. Derrick would need scans done and might need more extensive treatment than what was offered for the superficial injuries more typically seen.

"And Sean is in isolation, I assume?"

"Oh yeah. Hopefully for a long time. Wouldn't mind seeing that one sent to an adult facility. He doesn't belong here."

"Did he put up a fight?"

"No. That's what's so unnerving about him. It was like he was intent on doing this and was only after Derrick. Once he had done what he wanted he stood there and allowed us to cuff him. I don't know what his beef was with Derrick. Derrick is pretty harmless most of the time. He must have been planning it, as easily and quickly as he pulled it off."

Sophia knew what his beef was, but was reluctant to share it with Aaron. Guilt wracked her. Despite knowing she hadn't encouraged Derrick to come to her rescue, she felt responsible. He chose to protect her because of the trusting relationship they had formed, but still he was punished by administration and then brutally attacked by a peer, another maddening outcome to good intentions.

Is it better to keep distant? Is it better to encourage them to think only of themselves and self-preservation? Why connect them to community only to have that community fashion the connection into a rope that hangs them? Poor, poor Derrick.

The sound of the EMT's arriving interrupted Sophia's self-recriminations. She waited as they moved Derrick onto the gurney and rolled him down the narrow hallway towards the door.

Approaching him she said, "I'm so sorry Derrick. They will take care of you. You've got this. Just do what they say and I'm sure you'll be fine." She patted his shoulder gingerly, fearful of hurting something. Derrick was unable to answer but returned her gaze until they reached the door and exited the clinic.

Sophia leaned against the wall, feeling as weak and discouraged as an un-watered plant. She could see him in the hospital, handcuffed to a bed, alone with his thoughts and broken body, machine hiccups and efficient nurses his only company. *Am I doing everyone a disservice? Will encouraging relationship and responsibility to someone besides themselves always get reshaped into an explosive vest awaiting detonation by another's finger?*

Rousing from her contemplation to see Aiden's quizzical face peering through the window at her, Sophia was reminded of their unfinished conversation. She realized she was in no condition to continue the conversation now, but opened the door to wrap up and encourage him to do what he could to successfully transition back to his unit.

"That guy must have pissed someone off royally!" Aiden's voice was a mix of agitation and excitement at the crisis. "Of course it only takes a mustard seed of provocation to make a gorilla swing, and we do live in a zoo! I guess I'm not the only one people want to pulverize!"

Close to tears, Sophia resisted the urge to simply shut the door and retreat, instead saying, "No one should be getting pulverized, Aiden, not you and not him. This has been a distraction you don't need. Please try to put it out of your mind and focus on going back to the unit peacefully. You might try writing down three things you can do if you feel like someone is messing with you. Three *acceptable* things that is," she cautioned, "and the first one might be to resist referring to your peers as gorillas, if you're picking up what I'm putting down."

Aiden fingered his glasses to their precision spot and said with a sideways grin, "Okay, Miss Sophia. Even though you and I know that is exactly how they behave and have the IQ's to match, I feel you. I don't really want to have my head bashed into the wall again, at least not until this headache heals. Doc says I need to be careful not to have another head injury because I'm still healing from this one. Don't want to lose any brain cells."

Sophia nodded her agreement, "I'll try to check in with you tomorrow to see how it's going. I know you aren't thrilled to be going back with the masses, but I hope you can try to hide that and do your part to get along."

"I'll work on dumbing myself down to their level. Maybe I can pretend that moron gave me brain damage!" Aiden chortled at the prospect.

Sophia gave him a mildly disapproving look, bringing additional laughter.

"Just kidding!" Aiden added, "I wouldn't give them the satisfaction."

"Okay. I hope it goes well, and I'll check with you tomorrow. See ya."

"Later," Aiden flopped backwards onto the bed with a wave of his hand.

Sophia exited into a hammering downpour, droplets bouncing so hard against the pavement that it seemed to rain in both directions. She flipped her jacket hood up, tilting her head to shield her face, but the water slithered around the edges like a determined snake. D'Vrae, Aiden, Derrick, Jasper, and Quinn circled in her thoughts, buffeting her desire to see their lives improve against the possibility she was shoveling dirt into a hole being excavated from the other side.

The sight of MSU briefly tempted her to stop to confront Sean, as though looking into his eyes would offer some kind of answer, some way to understand, maybe even some way to forgive. She had never believed that people were born bad, only that they could be driven to act badly by life circumstances. But in the brief moments she had experienced with him, she was disturbed and chilled by the lifelessness in Sean's eyes, eyes full of contempt. This attack on Derrick seemed to demonstrate what he was capable of. Whether he was born capable of such things or became capable of them through damaging experiences, the outcome would be similar; demonstrating the chasm between instinctive reactions of someone in an emotional uproar and a calculated unprovoked attack intended to maximize damage. People were unsafe around Sean. Shuddering, Sophia realized how differently things might have gone had Derrick not stepped in that day. The raised hairs on her arms added to the chill she felt trudging through the rain, leaving MSU behind.

Sean Landry had messed with her mental order, shaken the certainty of her beliefs. Sean might have been capable of pushing a pregnant Eliza down a flight of stairs and beating her husband to death. Eliza may have looked into such eyes before losing everything that was important to her. The retribution Sophia found herself wanting on Derrick's behalf could only be a fraction of what Eliza must yearn for. *I think I get it Eliza, at least a little bit.*

Sophia could see, with greater clarity, how fear and pain could create a filtering lens through which all people were now viewed, blurring the reality. She didn't want to begin seeing everyone as Sean Landry because they weren't all like that. But after today, she felt slippage that created a new compartment in her thinking, one that allowed for the possibility that there are some people so different, so damaged, that an essential part of their humanity might be missing. And it didn't really matter if it was by birth or circumstances, what mattered was she needed to be able to recognize them and the world needed to be kept safe from them. Realizing that Eliza must see them all that way and worked to keep the world safe from them, Sophia felt residual animosity for Eliza soften. She could disagree with Eliza without despising her.

Depleted by recent events, door closed to discourage interruption, Sophia spent a short time doing paperwork in her office, then left early for the day, unable to concentrate.

Drenching clouds had faded to ashen mist, needing only an occasional wiper swipe on a windshield reflecting soggy trees giving way to sand dunes and seagulls as she made the short drive to a nearby beach, to her therapy. Though her body remained motionless, she felt gently rocked by the sound and sight of the rolling dirge of waves stretching to the horizon. Her thoughts circled and dipped like the outside gulls; Russ' death, Beth's appearance, Marcus' memory of Addie's death, the triumphs, traumas and disappointments in her work, the doubts and anxieties slowly eroding her, and the overwhelming wish to simply feel at peace.

A question whispered into her awareness. Was it time to do something else? Could she leave this facility behind and look for some other way of being in the world? Could she continue to swim against this current exerting so much counterforce she felt held in place? What else could she do, what direction should she go? *Something with younger kids, maybe preschoolers who still could be shaped? Something completely different, like selling shoes? Maybe I could teach something on line and never have to leave my apartment.* The introvert in her pondered that for a moment with a measure of excitement before dismissing it.

She had enjoyed this work, the challenges offered and the learning encouraged. She had never considered being done with it, but she was deflating from a slow leak of resolve, squeezed out by compassion fatigue. She knew she needed to consider a change, and with each passing day had felt increasingly unbound by the script written in her early years. The loosening vines urging her to move in new directions, to try new experiences, to see who else she might be within this rewritten play.

The ding of an arriving text interrupted her contemplation. It was Jerry. '*Derrick unconscious but stable. Head injury resulted in hematoma which they had to drain to relieve the pressure. Broken nose. Neck swollen but spine okay. Docs hoping for the best but have to wait and see once he wakes up. Thought you'd want to know. Try not to worry.*'

'*Thanks, Jerry. You too. I guess it could have been worse*', Sophia texted back. She was relieved to hear his spine was not damaged but was concerned about the brain bleed, knowing it could leave some residual issues for Derrick, and wondered how well he would be able to deal with any of this.

She looked up from her phone at the horizon, now spilling tangerine and watermelon through torn pewter clouds, the setting sun nudging awareness that it was time she headed home. Issuing a silent plea to God and the universe to show some mercy, she started her car and headed back to town.

GOODBYES

The work completed on the property was rewarded with a quick and easy sale that spring, and the estate proceeds were distributed. The increase in resources allowed Sophia to resign her position, although still undecided as to what to do next. Daffodils and tulips dotted yards like sprinkled spice, seasoning the air with the promise of sunshine and reasons to be outside.

Derrick had physically recovered from his injuries and returned to Dalton, the incident with Sean leaving him more guardedly subdued. He rarely interacted with others, preferring the corners of the unit near staff. He answered minimally when Sophia visited him, a living example of Jasper's bad day description of "Everything's so gray!", as though his new world was as devoid of pigment as the walls around him.

When she told him she was leaving, he looked briefly anxious, and then expressionless. She understood. He was trying not to feel. If he could master that, he could get out, get away, and be free of the daily struggle to manage his reactivity. He had refused to talk about Sean or the fight that preceded Sean's retaliation, forcing Sophia to let it go and allow him to process what he could from it on his own. Her only solace was in knowing he was scheduled for release shortly after her last day. At least she could leave with the hope he might manage the outside world better than before, and experience fewer triggers than he had here. She wondered if he would ever be able to trust another person again, or if he would ever find joy.

Jasper, on the other hand, would be staying a while longer. He continued to earn consequences for doing the bidding of more manipulative peers despite all efforts to help him become more discerning. Sophia had come to inform him and prepare for the transition.

"Shut down sequence activated!" he responded, dropping his head wearing a crushed expression, clearly unhappy with the news.

Sophia smiled, despite herself. She was going to miss his unique expressions. "Someone will take my place, and I expect you to work hard with whoever it is so you get out of here, Jasper. You need to start thinking for yourself and not doing what others talk you into. They don't have your back and they will happily watch you sabotage yourself."

"I know. I will." Still highly distracted by his environment, Jasper's attention was pulled sideways by a hand drawn poster on the wall near where they sat.

"Hey! See that. I found one of those when I was visiting my Gram!" Jasper pointed excitedly at a picture of an eagle flying over a canyon, a feather dropping from one wing. "I still have that…that….I can't quite put my tongue on it. Oh, yeah, that bird leaf at home!"

"That's called a feather," Sophia corrected. Though she was delighted by his more descriptive name, he was target enough for peers without such misstatements.

Jasper had a cold and was repeatedly wiping his nose across one sweatshirt sleeve or the other as they talked. The silvery track he was leaving on the dark grey fabric reminded Sophia of a glazed doughnut, and having made that unbidden connection, was fairly certain she would never be able to eat one again.

Sophia worked on a transitional plan with Jasper for as long as she could hold his attention, knowing most of it would be forgotten within fifteen minutes of ending their conversation. She created copious notes to pass along to her successor and to unit staff working with him, uncertain what would become of this enchanting boy who was such a misfit here at Dalton, as well as the bigger world. She knew she would wonder about him the rest of her life, as she would Quinn, already transferred out. How would he fare with more hardened peers and staff? Who would he be once released, and where would he go? Aiden would have follow-up care and resources, which she hoped would be enough to help him find a place to thrive, perhaps in a repetitive job requiring little interaction with people. She was less sure he would be able to create a circle of friends, although she hoped so, even if it were only two or three. He really was quite bright and amusing, if one did not feel sand-papered against his rough edges and brutal honesty.

Multiple coworkers stopped by to wish her well and ask about her plans. It was difficult for Sophia to explain what came next since she didn't know herself. Some time to reflect, to heal, to unwind, to process, and to be open to directions that might appear through the fog.

"You'll be missed here, but I hope your next adventures are fantastic," Jerry said with a wink. "Always appreciated working with you. The boys are gonna miss you, too. You had a way with them."

"Thanks, Jerry. That means a lot to me. Felt like I was always getting by pretty much by the seat of my pants and guesswork. I've enjoyed working with you, too. I've learned a ton in the time I've been here and much of that has been from watching you. We'll have to keep in touch," Sophia offered, knowing as she said it best intentions didn't guarantee that outcome.

Finished with trying to represent complex people through inadequate words, she put the paperwork for her successor into a filing cabinet and locked it, then walked to the office to turn in keys. This was it, the last time she would be making this journey out of the building and off campus. The ground was littered, as though pink and white popcorn had been pushed from trees as velvet leaves slipped over knotty sills to dangle in the wind, the scent of Daphne spritzing the air. Sophia paused briefly as she neared the gate, seeing Eliza in the distance, debating whether she should make one final contact, a last intersection to convey her reshaped perception and regret. She decided to leave it alone, leave it as Eliza preferred, unspoken and unviewed. Sophia had her own history to deal with; it wasn't up to her to change Eliza's for her. Finding her car, she eased out of the lot, swallowing back a lumpy internal stew of mixed emotions, excitement, sadness, anticipation, loss, apprehension, and wonder. What would the coming months bring? She had jumped off a cliff, and the exhilaration of the plunge tangled with the uncertainty of an unknown landing.

CONFLUENCE

July 10th 2017
3:30 pm

During the months following her resignation, Sophia missed the young people she had worked with and wondered how they were, but was gradually reminded of them less often as she found new opportunities to focus on. The tentative truce established with Marcus allowed for easier, more peaceful contact with him and his family. Sophia discovered Lexi's wickedly funny sense of humor and irreverent comments never failed to make her laugh through tears. She and Drew formed a bond sweating and hammering together on a Habitat for Humanity project, vowing to make it an annual tradition as they watched the twin boys of the new owners put dibs on their bedrooms. Jane remained politely aloof and unknown, like a porcelain doll enclosed in a glass cabinet, too breakable to take out for play, forcing Sophia to accept that theirs would remain a superficial relatedness.

After allowing the pool of emotions to settle, Sophia and Beth began tentative and awkward contact, having a meal or a cup of coffee together. As they discovered shared ideas and points of view, they both relaxed into the comfort of growing trust, discussing similarities in their work and what they saw when life events twisted fragile stalks, finding their similarities ran deeper than outside appearance. Despite this, Sophia was unable to convince Marcus to join them, for Beth was a painful reminder of things he preferred to avoid. Sophia had not seen or talked with Annie or Dylan since the sale of the house, but knew from Beth that they had not been in contact with her either. The brief stirring of family sediment at the junction of Russ' death had settled back into the status quo as they were pulled by routines and well-worn paths back to life as before, except for Sophia, who felt permanently altered.

As the months passed and seasons changed, Sophia felt more confident and eager, willing to try new things, like a barren tree removing winter pajamas, allowing luxurious potential to be slipped on. In addition to the house she helped build, she experimented with a variety of volunteer opportunities.

She organized activities at a nearby hospital for kids facing life-threatening illnesses, helped with school fund-raisers, served meals at the local Mission and boxed up food at the food banks, became board secretary for a nonprofit providing transitional housing to women leaving prison, held babies in the NICU, and spent a day a week at a local preschool, reading to a small group of kids, the activity she most enjoyed, their lively eyes and flung hugs a welcome antidote to the discouragement at Dalton. Each day with them showed her human clay waiting for sculpting, bodies vibrantly anticipating a new friend or celebrating a fresh skill, fizzing like pop rocks in their moist milieu, reminded to calm down and slow down, for safety's sake, unlike the adolescents she'd known, who had needed IV infusions of enthusiasm. It was good for her soul. It nourished her hope and sense of purpose, the sound of children's laughter becoming a salve to her sadness, and it was children's laughter which had drawn her off her usual path to the park.

Out for her daily walk, she had been unaware of a music festival at the riverside park until coming within earshot. Her love of music alone would have drawn her, but the park was also bubbling with children and their parents, lounging on blankets with coolers full of drinks and snacks. As she approached, Sophia saw young children twirling and jigging unselfconsciously near the band's stage. Captivated, she stopped to watch, reedy arms flapping, legs hopping, a palette rhythmically spinning to the lively music, flinging elation through the air.

There was a time she would have felt awkward standing at the center of it, certain she did not belong, as though the joy were not meant for her. Today she basked in it, appreciating the sun's massage and the crowd's cheer, thankful to feel connected, even if vicariously and from a distance. This was her hope when she left Dalton, to find delight, to find laughter, to find the part missing from her life. She was beginning to greet each day with anticipation instead of dread or dogged determination, and to relish unexpected moments of pleasure.

Stunned by an excruciating pain in her chest, Sophia froze, and then dropped to her knees, unable to breathe. She stared at her chest, trying to see what had hit her, spastically gulping inadequate amounts of air. Puzzled, she looked around for a baseball or a rock, something that might explain this throbbing, but saw nothing.

Am I having a heart attack?

Reflexively, she put a hand on the pain, watching as her fingers turned crimson.

Blood? Why am I bleeding?

Dizzy and weak, she sank down, trying to clear her head, trying to understand. Dazed, she looked around, realizing the music had stopped. Drum beats had turned to gunshots, squeals of laughter had become terrified screams. The carefree dancing was now panicked children and parents trying to find each other in the mayhem, and run from the danger.

What on earth is going on?

Believing she should run, she tried to get up, but as she tried, a hot blistering replaced the ache, as though molten coal flared inside her chest, the spark traveling through her insides like a lit fuse. Overcome with pain she fell back to lie prone on the ground, her hand sticky with blood as she clutched her chest.

Oh my God. I've been shot. Am I dying? This can't be happening.

Disbelieving awareness dawned as she watched feet fly past while shots continued to ring out. *Where is that coming from?* She tried to look around without moving, trying to see who was shooting, every breath a dagger in her chest.

Is it some kind of gang conflict? Was there a personal vendetta and she just happened to get in the way? Were the police after someone?

Taking only shallow breaths and fighting nausea, Sophia twisted her head around in the direction she thought the shots were coming from. As her vision ebbed and flowed from clear to a hazy white-out, she saw a figure dressed in black. His head concealed under a hood kept her from seeing his face. The weapon he carried pointed randomly as he walked, uncommitted to any particular direction or target, his slouched meandering gait conveying the same dispassionate effort as the weapon, as though he were only half interested in what he was doing, in jarring contrast to the horror of those running for their lives. Sophia could see multiple people lying on the ground, injured or dead, as others found trees or buildings to use as a shield. Screams, weeping and the thunder of gunfire assaulted the air, pierced, finally, by the shrillness of distant sirens approaching.

Oh thank God, someone's coming. Stop shooting them! Run, babies, run!

Desperately wishing she could do something to stop him, but realizing she could not move and was barely able to breathe, she remained still, trying to appear dead, her eyes open and trained on him. *Who are you? Why are you doing this? Please stop!*

Continuing to follow him with her eyes as his amble brought him closer to where she was lying, she tried to see his face, his eyes, as though they would provide an answer to this madness. Would she see Quinn's rage loading the bullets or Aiden's loneliness leak from his eyes as he took aim? Would she see D'Vrae's distorted honor pull the trigger, or Jasper's grin, hoping to gain favor on a torpedo mission? Would she see Derrick's disappointments distilled into self-loathing staring back at her? Or would she see the eyes of Sean Landry, impenitent and remote, murky with chilled disdain like the bitter sludge at the bottom of an unused well?

Quinn, D'Vrae, Derrick, Aiden, Jasper, Sean, the faces floated through, their stories, their influences, their outcomes. Although she resisted the thought, it would not have surprised her to see any of their faces under that black hood. *How can we know them so we can stop them, before it comes to this? How can we reshuffle their cards?*

She wanted to know his history, his reason. Was he young with no sense of future or was he middle-aged and beaten down one too many times? *Someone might have been able to help you if you'd only reached out. Why didn't you reach out? Someone might have thrown you back in the water if you'd only shown them where you were bleeding.*

Sophia was becoming increasingly faint. Her face ashen and damp with sweat, while her body trembled in shock, the fire in her chest billowing and snaking into new areas, around to her back, down her arms. Were the sirens getting closer? She thought so but didn't trust her senses. The whine seemed louder, but was she just getting more sensitive as her body reactions ramped up? Her eyelids seemed to have a life of their own, opening and closing capriciously, not driven by her own will. As they opened and she realized she was staring at the boots of the shooter, she froze, afraid to even blink.

Her thoughts scattered, like leaves thrown into the wind. She wondered if she was going to die, bleeding out before help arrived, or be shot again if he realized she was still alive. Believing the thought should upset her, she realized instead it came with a certain peace, as though she was already resigned to the outcome without knowing why. She didn't feel the same urgency about her own outcome as she had for others she had seen running for safety or lying on the ground. Maybe it was shock. Maybe her body had enough to worry about without facing how she felt about dying.

The strangest things drifted through her mind as those scattered leaves began to settle. Would she see Zach when she died, or her mom, or Addie? Where was her purse, had she brought it to the park? Who would read to her little ones at the preschool? The milk in the refrigerator was going to spoil. She forgot to mail Lexi her birthday card and now it was going to be late. She wasn't going to get to read the book she had ordered and would arrive tomorrow. How would Marcus deal with this, and would he tell Beth? It would really piss Aiden off to die this way. Sophia felt no certainty regarding what happened after death, but hoped the mysteries would be explained, that the webs in her life would finally connect in a logical way.

Ricocheting thoughts froze as the boot nudged her leg. The world had gone silent except for the siren screams which appeared to have reached the park. The boot nudged her again. She remained motionless. She sensed him squat down next to her, felt him run his finger along her bloody hand. Distant shouts began to echo through the park.

This face. Where had he seen it? Finger gummy with warm blood, blood no longer safely inside. Ears ringing from the percussion of his weapon. Head cocked, trying to recognize. Weren't they all the same, as though they'd stepped off an assembly line into lives of having, while he was culled and discarded like pith. Hard to tell them apart. Still, something was familiar. Something reminded. A teacher never learning his name, a neighbor looking past him, a grocery clerk following him with suspicious eyes, a random stranger passing through his ghostly edges day after day without feeling the touch? Somewhere. The blood oozing a portrait, an abstract of his life. She was one of them, she was all of them.

"There he is!"

"Drop the weapon! Put your hands in the air!"

"Don't move!"

"Put the gun down and move away from it. Put the gun down NOW!"

The percussion jolted Sophia as he fired the rifle one last time. The thumping sound of his body hitting the ground did not relieve her enough to move, so she waited as apprehensive voices approached, shouting directions to each other. A swarm of police officers surrounded the two of them, securing the rifle and checking on the condition of the shooter. When it was clear he was no longer a threat, she shifted her head. She was still unable to see under the hood, as he had landed facing away from her. Her movement captured the attention of the nearest officer.

"Can you talk?" he asked, kneeling to check on her wound.

Sophia opened her mouth but was unable to force out any sound. She shook her head weakly.

The officer yelled to a paramedic arriving, now that the threat was gone, "Over here! This one needs attention right now!" He turned to Sophia and said, "We've got you now. They'll take good care of you."

Increasingly disoriented from loss of blood and pain, Sophia was only minimally aware of the paramedics assessing her condition and tending her, or of the stink of an oxygen mask sliding over her mouth and nose and pierce of IV. She heard vague, disconnected words and phrases as she slipped in and out of awareness.

Significant loss of blood…

Internal damage from the bullet…

Treat the shock…

Don't know what organs…

Immediate surgery…

She wondered what dying would feel like; if she would see the welcoming light and feel the loving presence that some described, or if she would fade into black nothingness. Would she knowingly feel herself slipping away or would she go from aware to unaware without transition? What would her last thought be? What had Russ' last thought been; Russ who died a day at a time for years, consumed by guilt? If she slid into black emptiness, she would do so clean, unfettered by regret or disappointment, finally confident she had found herself.

Sophia was grateful the blowtorch in her chest had diminished, silently thanking the paramedics for interventions that seemed to be working. She opened her eyes to see if she could silently convey her gratitude since she had lost her voice.

…Blood pressure tanking….we are losing her….

Unable to focus well, she blinked several times, staring straight ahead. *What was that? What am I seeing? Are my eyes open or closed?*

The swirling slowed and began to form edges as sound grew faint and disappeared. *Is that….?*

EPiLOGUE

Jerry pulled the letter from the envelope that had come addressed to Sophia. It was from Quinn, and had been given to Jerry to pass along to her since they were sporadically in touch, after administration determined getting it to her did not violate any of their policies. He had received one as well and wondered if Quinn had shared the same news with Sophia.

Dear Miss Sophia,

> *I hope things are going good with you. It's been a minute since I've seen you. I wanted to tell you that I'm doing okay. Leaving Dalton was the best thing that happened to me. It was hard at first getting used to prison, but once I let people know I wasn't going to be punked they left me alone. I stayed to myself and kept my head down. I read a lot of books about animals and veterinary stuff. I kept learning new words too! One of my favorites was pellucid! Anyhow, no one tried to get me to talk about anything and no one was messing with me or runnin' their big ass mouth, so it was easier time to do. Guards there pretty much leave you alone if you leave them alone. Since I didn't get in no more trouble they let me out early. I hung out at the mission at first 'cause I had no place to go, but I met a guy downtown that was looking for someone to work on his farm. I told him I was the guy so that's what I'm doing. Got a little trailer to live in on his farm and help him with his animals. Don't pay much but I don't need much. He's got cows and*

horses and sheep. Been learning how to shear sheep! All that reading I did gives me some ideas about what they might need too. Boss seems to like that. Anyhow, things are good for me now. I spend my time with the animals and have all this land to live on and nobody messes with me. I just wanted you to know how things turned out because I could always tell you cared, even when no one else did. If it hadn't been for you I probably would have been in even worse trouble at Dalton. For reals. You made me think about things and learn things. I wanted to thank you for believing in me. I think I got a future now. I hope you are doing good too. Thanks for everything.

Quinn

Jerry refolded the letter, inserting it back into the envelope. It pleased him that Quinn was not only doing well, but had grown enough to reach out and thank those who had intersected his path along the way. He knew it would please Sophia, too. The letter reminded him of the others he and Sophia had worked with during the years; D'Vrae, who was dead; Jasper, who continued to be set up by others in increasingly antisocial ways, unable to resist the appeal of pleasing others; Aiden, who had been released recently into a group home where he was doing well with community supports, finding a niche at local establishments offering trivia contests, where his encyclopedic brain was admired rather than disdained; and Derrick, who had exited shortly after Sophia's resignation and was staying out of legal trouble. Derrick's probation officer came to Dalton to see other clients and let Jerry know that Derrick was working at a gas station and had a small apartment where he lived alone. Jerry knew Sophia would be pleased to hear that getting out of Dalton, where he was so often cornered and triggered, had been a good thing for him. Like Sophia, Jerry questioned Derrick's willingness to form close friendships, but being able to hold a job and have a stable place to live was great progress for him.

Jerry folded the envelope, inserting it into his jacket pocket. He hadn't seen Sophia for a while so this would be a good opportunity to get in touch and see how she was. He looked forward to sharing some good news with her for a change. Good news was important, especially on a day like today when another mass shooting was all over the news. This one was far too close to home in the city park. He considered it both incomprehensible and not so much, based on the clientele he worked with, but it was abhorrent and heartbreaking nonetheless.

Jerry called Sophia's number to schedule a time to connect. After several rings a man answered. Taken aback Jerry asked, "I was looking for Sophia, do I have the right number?"

"It's Sophia's phone. This is Marcus, her brother. Who's this?"

"This is Jerry Collins. I worked with Sophia at Dalton. Is she available?"

"Oh…No, she's not," Marcus' voice cracked with emotion. "She's in surgery. She was at the park today and was shot by that maniac. I've just gotten here. I have no idea how she's doing except that she crashed in the ambulance and they're doing their best to save her. She had her phone in her pants pocket, so it was given to me when I arrived after they called me."

Jerry paused in stunned silence. Sophia had been at the park and was shot by whoever went on that rampage? What was bad enough just got immeasurably worse.

"Damn, Marcus. That's just unbelievable. I don't even know what to say. Would you mind if I come down there to wait with you? I have something that came for her and would love to be able to give it to her when she's out of surgery and is awake. Or give it to you to pass along if that's not possible right now. I think she could really use it after this. I'd also like to know how she's doing."

A stifled sob, followed by, "You mean IF she wakes up?" conveyed Marcus' concern for the gravity of the situation. Knowing that Sophia would have been the first to reach out to this unknown gunman if he had given her the chance, Marcus' anger and disbelief curdled within the ugly irony of this day.

"I'm going to believe she will until someone makes me believe otherwise," Jerry replied hopefully. He had already heard there were four others dead and several more critically wounded, but could not accept that Sophia would not make it.

"I hope you're right," Marcus responded, "It would be great to have you here. She always spoke highly of you."

Jerry turned the office lights off, making his way to the parking lot, passing units mutely motionless like napping grizzlies, those inside sheltered from today's news to ensure controlled calm. Like Sophia, Jerry wondered if any of the young men inside were capable of such an action; if one of them could fall into such unbearable despair the only rope they could grasp was one that released a hail of bullets as they plummeted to their own death. And like Sophia, he knew he had to live without understanding it, grateful he could not, for to understand might make him vulnerable to the same forces, should the perfect storm attack his own world. He headed to the hospital, the optimism of the letter in his pocket arguing with the heaviness in his heart.

ABOUT THE AUTHOR

CARMEL HANES is retired after working thirty-plus years with young people. She is a native Oregonian with a fascination for understanding what shapes human development, attitudes and behavior. This is her debut novel, inspired by the many enjoyable and unique misfits who have crossed her path and influenced who she became.